C000124887

SOULS TO HEAL

HIGHLAND WOLVES - BOOK 4

Version 16.02.21

To be the first to hear about new releases, sign up at:

www.tillywallace.com/newsletter

AUTHOR'S NOTE

This book is written using British English

Alice's terrier is called *Eilidh*.
In Scottish Gaelic it means "light", and is pronounced
AY-LEE

PROLOGUE

Ewan
Vitoria, Spain. June 1813

MOST HORSES WOULD FLEE if a predator landed on their backs, but not the equines ridden by the Highland Wolves. Their horses stood patiently beneath their lycanthrope riders while the mounts of other troops whinnied and jigged, unable to settle with the Unnatural creatures so close.

Captain Ewan Shaw held his reins in loose fingers, hands crossed over the pommel of his saddle as he watched a horse farther down the line rear and unseat its rider. Ewan experienced a moment of envy as the rider stood and brushed dirt from his uniform. He ached to shift position and relieve tired muscles, but he resisted the urge. Fellow soldiers admired his *sang-froid*, and he wasn't going to put his reputation in jeopardy by squirming like a new recruit. He would endure numb buttocks while the same bored look graced his features.

In 1812, after two years of keeping the Highland Wolves a military secret, the army finally decided to let their hounds off the tight leash. For more than a year they had struck fear into the enemy. They rode hard towards the French as men, then stood on the saddle and shifted mid-jump so that enormous wolves flew over their horses' ears.

Covert missions under the blanket of darkness were replaced with frontal assaults in full daylight. The Highland Wolves were dotted among the regular cavalry so the French had no way of knowing where the Unnatural assailants would appear.

While the French had their own monsters, their counter efforts were hampered by the sunlight aversion of their vampyres. The older ones were only weakened by bright light, but the youngsters smoked like wet, green wood on a fire.

Some days Ewan though he might die of boredom waiting for something to happen. Their secret missions were quick and decisive. Regular battles with the other troops involved an inordinate amount of sitting around and staring at your fingernails. At times, battles required more orchestration than the most lavish of balls. Just as matrons spent hours pondering seating layouts, the generals undertook a similar exercise in their tents, except markers denoted troops rather than bachelors and debutantes.

Ewan had been in the saddle since before dawn, watching the sun flicker over the horizon as they mustered. Distant cannon droned constantly like fat bees in summer. It was past noon, and the generals still hadn't emerged from their tents. Dare he look at his pocket watch, or would that betray his boredom? It was hard work maintaining an air of ennui and indifference.

They were arranged in neat parade rows, but the fellow cavalrymen around him shifted, wriggled, and muttered. Whispers of *wolf* swirled around him. The wolves were dubbed savage beasts by the rest of the army, much to Ewan's chagrin. His wolf was lethal and efficient; there was nothing savage about it. He also bathed on a regular basis which, judging by the smell wafting off the other soldiers, could not be said of them.

It was difficult to maintain a civilised reputation when your unit contained rough brutes like Alick Ferguson, who sat his horse virtually naked. Only the strip of plaid around his waist and tossed over his shoulder provided scant modesty. It was pointless trying to force him into a uniform that would be torn apart and scattered on the battlefield. But the generals wanted the dramatic impact of riders transforming, and that came with a hefty cost—a new uniform for each man every time they had to shift mid-gallop without the opportunity to remove their clothing first.

The bloody reputation of the Highland Wolves had other benefits. Their captain rose to major and behind him, Ewan stepped from lieutenant to captain. More unexpected was the sheer number of men wanting to join their ranks.

Bloody fools, Ewan thought. To be a wolf was to be reviled by most of society who thought you would shed on their furnishings. To spend your existence chained to a beast that would enact your deepest and darkest fears should it ever break loose.

The major instituted a probationary period for any soldier wishing to become one of the Highland Wolves. New recruits were assessed for their suitability to life as an Unnatural creature. While parliament gave them the same rights as any other Englishman, it could not make men treat them as equals. Better that new prospects see the naked underbelly of their lives and turn tail than change men who would daily regret their choice.

It took a special type of man to survive the bite. He had to hold himself still while the lycanthrope took his throat in its massive jaws. The wolf would bite down, tearing through skin and tendon and ripping open veins. The beast worried at the wound until blood poured forth. Then the creature would bite its own tongue and drool blood and saliva into the open wound, transferring the lycanthrope sickness to a new body.

And that was only the beginning of the excruciating pain awaiting the new recruit.

Some never survived their first transformation. The process of bones breaking and reforming, and skin tearing itself inside out turned a few into insane beasts. They had to be put out of their misery lest they go on unstoppable rampages. Major Logan hoped the probation period would weed out those unsuitable to be lycanthropes. The major took responsibility for turning the recruits himself. No longer did they use the wild beast from the Highlands that had been captured by a mage, and who had made the foundation members of the wolves' regiment.

Ewan's fingers curled on the reins, the only outward sign of his inner restlessness. He glanced around him, spotting the wolves interspersed with the regular cavalry. They didn't need the distinctive tartan strip on their trousers—the stillness of their mounts showed the horses were used to carrying unusual riders.

Major Hamish Logan was to his left with the newest recruit, a tough lad from Glasgow who took the bite with the ease of someone with lycanthropy in their family history. Some of them switched between man and beast as fluidly as a diver who never rippled the surface of a pool. The older wolves had spent weeks drilling the newest member in how to change forms while jumping from his horse, but this was his first battle and he had yet to be blooded.

Down the line to Ewan's right were sergeants Alick Ferguson and Quinn Muir. At least Quinn wore a uniform, unlike the rough Highlander with his scarred face. The two sergeants, along with Hamish and Ewan, composed a small band that undertook suicidal and secret missions. They were usually successful and to date only had one failure that haunted Ewan.

In his mind, he saw the British vampyre who had his neck torn out by Alick and a hole in his chest you could stick your fist through, courtesy of Alick's wildcat mate. The traitor had disappeared behind a wall of flames, and yet they found no sign of him in the smouldering rubble of the fire. At odd moments, Ewan found himself wondering what happened to the turncoat.

Bad pennies always turn up. Eventually.

Ewan's horse snorted and shook its head, and he scratched its wither.

"Soon, boy, soon," he murmured to the eager mount. Both horse and rider needed to stretch cramped muscles.

In answer to Ewan's quiet words, a change fell over the battlefield. The enemy's cannon fell silent. Men looked from one to another, and then the earth rumbled as a new sound washed over them—the steady march of thousands of boots as troops were mobilised.

Ewan's pulse quickened. His hand tightened on the reins. He waited, poised for a command to charge that was only moments away. Down the line, Alick tipped back his head and roared, causing the horses around him to startle sideways.

"Is he really married to a fine lady, sir?" the soldier next to Ewan asked.

"Sergeant Ferguson is wed to the daughter of a duke no less, as difficult as it is to believe." Despite his fine-born wife, Alick had kept his rough edges. Or perhaps he maintained them by rubbing on her sharp tongue.

Even the brute whose beast shimmered close to the surface had managed to find a mate. Both halves of man and beast were given peace and shelter by the woman who loved him. Yet Ewan, for all his supposed gifts and graces, remained unwed.

Finally, the order to advance was relayed along the line. The air became charged like during a storm when lightning built in the sky. The excitement of hundreds of men relayed to their mounts, and they danced and jogged on the spot, pulling reins, munching on their bits and eager for their heads.

Urging their horses forward at a walk, the cavalry advanced to the brow of a hill. Ewan nudged his horse into a trot and those around him followed, holding their line steady as they rode the gentle slope. As they hit the wide field, Ewan spurred his horse into a gallop. He had no sabre to draw like those around him because such a weapon was useless in his other form.

The French foot soldiers were packed tight, shoulder-to-shoulder. Ewan grinned as their men had trouble firing. The closed ranks didn't give them sufficient room to raise their rifles.

As he advanced, Ewan kicked his feet free of the stirrups and rose up in his saddle. He dropped the reins as he stood, the horse well trained to hold its line. Ewan touched the beast inside him and drew a deep breath. He jumped and at the same time allowed the beast to rise up through him.

Clothes and skin fell to the ground to be trod into the dirt by the following horses and men. He shifted form and continued over his horse's head. The French soldiers before him faltered as the beast launched at them.

Rifles and sabres were useless when men were packed so tight. The wolf with midnight fur and blue eyes lashed out with massive jaws. He snapped bones—

arms, legs . . . whatever he could reach, as he ploughed through the enemy.

While the large auburn wolf that contained Alick howled with blood lust, Ewan's wolf remained detached. He downed a man and moved on to the next one. Alick would waste valuable time smearing the enemy's blood over his muzzle as the berserker rage took hold of him.

An enemy officer stood at the rear, a pistol in his outstretched hand. Ewan snarled. Something about this one was different. He wrinkled his nose as he caught a faint whiff unlike smells of blood, excrement, and gunpowder that threatened to overwhelm. The officer had the taint of rotten meat about him.

Ewan shifted his weight and then sprang from his powerful hind muscles. The French officer fired his pistol as Ewan soared through the air. At first he thought the bullet had missed him, then fire bloomed over his right flank. He cried out and dropped awkwardly. The leg dragged behind him as pain crept along the bone and towards his spine.

He snarled and lashed out, the wolf unable to understand why this bullet hurt more than others it had shaken off over the last year. He shook his head, trying to clear the mist that descended. His body no longer obeyed his commands, and his legs collapsed under him.

At that moment, a riderless horse barrelled through the soldiers. A man struck out with a sabre, severing the artery in the horse's neck. It buckled and went down, the animal tumbling to one side and over the top of the injured wolf.

The air escaped from wolf-Ewan's lungs with a whoosh as he hit the ground with half a ton of horse weighing him down. He tried to draw gasps of air through his compressed torso. Pain rippled through his body, spreading through his veins until he burned from the inside.

The wolf howled. It could no longer hold its form. Fur and claws vanished to be replaced by a naked man, trapped under the dying horse. Broken ribs pressed into Ewan's lungs, and no matter how hard he tried, he couldn't draw enough breath. The horse expired and rolled to one side, crushing Ewan's outstretched arm.

The French officer advanced, his pistol extended. Whatever the weapon contained, it was capable of downing a wolf. Ewan needed to warn his brothers. The French mages had created a weapon to target them.

As Ewan struggled to breathe and the fire ate at his body, a strange thing happened. The world stopped turning on its axis and time suspended itself. The rest of the battle faded into darkness, leaving only Ewan and the Frenchman. They became starring players on a stage, acting under the spotlight while the rest of the audience watched in the shadows.

In those few seconds, Ewan experienced relief that he would be the one to die and not one of the other wolves who were his blood brothers. That mattered to him, for they were well loved. At least he wouldn't take a woman's heart with him to his grave.

When he lost his mother as a lad, winter had descended on his soul. His heart froze and he had never loved again. Now, as he waited for the final shot to pierce his chest, he wondered what it would be like, to love and be loved in return. But no woman could ever love a broken monster like him; he had held them all at arm's length for years.

Imminent death is a strange thing. In those long seconds while he waited, he swore he heard his mother whispering in his ear.

"But what of a woman who is made of shattered pieces?" she asked. "What if tiny shards from a broken woman could pierce the cracks in your soul?"

There was a puzzle. Did it take a broken woman to love a broken man? But if a woman were as broken as he, surely she would likewise be incapable of love? These were questions he could ponder for all of eternity, since he was about to greet his mother in Heaven. He wondered if he would be a man when he saw her, a wolf, or perhaps God might return him to the body of the ten-year-old boy who had cried for his mother.

Pain seared through his body, blood thrummed in his ears louder than a trumpet, and the world resumed its spinning. The French officer's finger tightened on the trigger, and Ewan's vision went black.

1

Alice
Northamptonshire, December 1813

NIGHTMARES DWELT IN THE SHADOWS. If Alice stepped too close or turned her back, they crept over her and pulled her under a wave of desolation. Yet at the same time, the dense foliage lured her near with its promise of encompassing embrace. The rustling of dead leaves on naked branches whispered of secrets to be told, and ancient trees contained magic carved in their trunks.

Four generations before, a powerful mage had been born in Alice's family. A trace of that power flowed through the blood of the generations following a mage and emerged as different talents. Alice's main gift was finding the lost and its inverse, hiding things.

Two years before, she had torn apart and hidden something immeasurably valuable—her soul. A soul eater had wanted to consume her, and she used her aftermage gift to foil him, but at a huge price. Now she was a broken thing, searching for her lost pieces.

She walked a delicate path hiding among the trees like a woodland sprite, dancing free of the darkness that tried to capture her. Eilidh barked at her heels. The little grey terrier was her constant guardian. Always alert to danger, she chased her mistress from the denser forest back into the watery winter sunshine.

Free of the shadowy foliage, Alice closed her eyes and spread her arms, letting the pale sun caress her face. Her once-alabaster skin was now tinted a shade of honey from her time spent roaming outside. Women in London, whether aristocratic or from the demimonde, would be scandalised; her lack of care for her appearance was so working class. In a world where status meant everything, milky white skin spoke of a life of ease and luxury.

Alice revelled in darkening her face. It placed another brick in the wall she built between her former life and the one she now led. No one would compare the ethereal young courtesan who had been the toast of London to the otherworldly creature who ran barefoot through the fields of rural England and Scotland. Although she currently wore boots in deference to winter's frosty bite.

The little terrier barked again for attention, and Alice opened her eyes and smiled on her heart's companion. Eilidh's fur was the colour of moonlight, a soft silver that carried an iridescent sheen. Perhaps the colour of her coat was what allowed her to guard Alice from the demons hiding in the shadows. The dog blended into the night and protected Alice's slumber.

Alice bent down and ruffled silken ears. "Come on, Eilidh, let's head back to the farmhouse. It will darken soon."

Awareness of time was still difficult for Alice to grasp. Light to dark was easy as she learned to read the position of the sun to know how much daylight was left. But longer periods caused her to frown; days and months ran together and became indistinguishable.

She knew she had a life *before*, and this one *after*, but her mind skittered around what happened during the period in-between. At times, she imagined before was simply a dream, for it seemed like a fairy tale of champagne and parties that dissolved into a nightmare. Then the dark claimed her and she tore herself apart to survive. The next thing she remembered was Eilidh pressed in her arms and then a carriage took them to Scotland.

For the last six months, Alice had lived on her friend Ianthe's secluded Northamptonshire farm. The dense forest surrounding the farm was her domain. Here, no one could gaze at her with pity filled eyes. No one would whisper, "Has there been any improvement?" No one would mutter that her broken mind would never heal after her stay in Bedlam.

But Bedlam didn't break her.

That happened long before, at the hands of a viscount whose idea of pleasure was tearing slivers from the soul of a powerless courtesan. The soul eater nibbled on the pieces as though they were caviar on toast, while the young woman writhed and screamed in pain at the excruciating agony of her essence being consumed.

But Alice defeated him. She scattered her soul far and wide where he couldn't reach it. Frustrated, he discarded the broken woman in the mental asylum. Now, Eilidh was her light, her warmth, the one creature who could reach her in the cold cave where her mind hid. She had torn herself into so many pieces that they didn't seem to fit back together right, no matter how many times she tried to complete the puzzle.

Alice and the dog skirted the edge of the forest, close enough to dart under the protective branches if necessary, but near the open expanse of the country-side. The ground undulated with gentle slopes and hills. The fields were full of waving, tall grasses with nodding, fat seed heads. There were also plenty of rabbits.

Once Eilidh was satisfied her mistress was a safe distance from the wood and following, the terrier shot off after a pair of ears just visible amid a patch of tuft-headed cocksfoot. Beast and prey bounded through the grass as they hurtled down the incline towards the flat pasture.

Small things made Alice happy. The babble of the water in the river, the feel of Eilidh pressed up next to her at night, the brush of a warm summer breeze against her face, or the crunch of frost under her boots. Perhaps the true madness was that she had once valued jewellery, dresses, and pretty things. None of that mattered at the end.

No dress saved her. No necklace had reached out and pulled her from the abyss.

Only a small dog with a warm, wet nose had touched her in the unrelenting dark and led her towards the light.

Once free of Bedlam, Alice ran wild in Scotland. That rugged countryside had embraced and shielded her. The ancient magic in the mist-shrouded Highlands tugged at the shackles around Alice's mind and awoke her aftermage power. Hidden in the fragrant heather, she began to find her missing parts and piece her soul back together.

This farm was nice, too, but in a more subdued way. Ianthe wanted to civilise Alice. To return her to what she had once been. To coax the skittish animal back into the embrace of society. But her friend didn't understand that girl was gone. She shattered into a million pieces and the wind blew her all away.

Dog and owner crested the last hill, and Alice paused for a moment. A warm sense of home washed over her as she stared down into the valley. Nestled at the foot of the hill sat the squat farmhouse. Two storeys high and made of solid grey stone, it withstood any storm the rough weather threw at it. A drift of smoke curled from the kitchen fire at one end of the house.

A large potager garden occupied the south side of the house, edged by rows of fruit trees. Now the trees stood naked, winter had stripped them of their leaves and they slept until spring. Only the hardy winter vegetables like leeks and cabbage survived the harsh cold in the well-maintained vegetable beds.

Next to the farmhouse stood a barn, as well constructed as the house. Ianthe wanted her prized horses as protected as those in the solid house. Behind both farmhouse and barn hid a smaller cottage, home to Ianthe's staff, Sarah and Perkins.

Spread out before the farmhouse were paddocks with dry stone walls keeping the stock safe. Despite the season, the paddocks had lush green grass as the playground for young horses, although they turned a favourite spot to mud that they could roll in and splash through. Yearlings chased each other while mothers dozed in the late afternoon light, their backsides turned to the cold northerly wind. There were only three youngsters in the paddock, but Ianthe had plans to slowly expand her horse breeding enterprise. But quality broodmares were expensive.

Eilidh barked and Alice turned to see if the terrier had spotted the rabbit again. The little dog quivered as she faced the road, her ears pricked and body tense. No rabbit, but riders. *Men.*

Alice's heart skipped a beat as a bubble of panic welled up in her chest and escaped as a sob. Why were men coming here, to this secluded corner of Northamptonshire? Men, whether natural or Unnatural, were not to be trusted. Alice had vowed no man would ever touch her, or have power over her, again.

She shielded her eyes against the descending sun as she watched the riders. Their horses had coats that gleamed with good health. One rider wore a distinctive grey and tartan jacket. Memories and snippets of conversation pushed through her mind.

Highland Wolves. Ianthe was also an aftermage, with the gift of second sight. For weeks she had seen a wolf with mistletoe stuck in its fur and was convinced the vision meant Quinn would be home for Christmas, even though the war with France continued abroad.

That identified one rider, but who was the other dressed in dark blue? As she stared at him, he turned and met her gaze across the fields. Despite the thickness of her wool coat, a chill ran over her skin.

Nothing good came from men. Or Wolves.

"Come on, Eilidh, Ianthe will want to know that Quinn is home." Alice tapped her leg and the pair of them ran down the hill towards the house.

"Ianthe!" Alice called as she flung open the kitchen door.

Her friend sat at the enormous kitchen table, an open ledger before her as she laboured over their expenses. Her head shot up on being summoned. A frown marred her delicate face. Ianthe always had something to shield her face when outside, and her skin remained an alabaster so pale one could see fine blue veins in her temple.

"Two riders approach. One in uniform." Alice pointed back through the open door.

"Quinn! I told you he would be home for Christmas." Ianthe squealed and leapt to her feet. Her outflung hand caught the ink pot and knocked it over.

Alice lunged and grabbed the pot before the dark liquid ruined Ianthe's work. She placed the pot down well away from the book and turned back to the door.

Alice walked but Ianthe ran, for once without a

bonnet or parasol. Ianthe picked up her skirts and hurtled down the beaten earth track towards the riders. The rider in uniform kicked his horse into a canter, and the two met at the edge of the paddock. Quinn hauled Ianthe up in front of his saddle and she threw her arms around his neck. They kissed while the horse kept walking.

Alice steeled herself for the masculine invasion. Eilidh crept closer, the terrier's body acting as an anchor for Alice and stopping her from turning tail and running away. She would control the fear. Ianthe loved Quinn and for her friend, Alice would try so hard to hold her position.

The horses stopped near the house. Ianthe slipped from the mount and dragged Quinn with her, the lovers still locked in each other's embrace. The other rider dropped awkwardly from the saddle. For a moment, his right leg seemed to buckle and he grabbed the saddle with his left hand to stay upright.

Alice watched him from under her eyelashes. He was slightly taller than Quinn but of a leaner build. Black hair glinted with blue in the sunlight, and a square jaw showed just the hint of afternoon shadow. His eyes, when he turned to regard Alice, were a piercing blue like a cloudless summer sky.

He arched a black eyebrow and shook his head at the lovers, who were still kissing one another. "It would appear if one has love, one does not need air. Shall we leave them to their reunion and see to the horses, Alice?"

Her heart stuttered. How did he know her name

when she had no recollection of him? Her feet stayed rooted to the spot and Eilidh pressed a little closer.

His gaze locked with hers and glided over her body as the river flows over rocks. "I'll not harm you, Alice. You have my word. These two could do with a little privacy after such a long time apart. It is rather cold out here, and the horses have had a long ride."

She wasn't so sure that Ianthe and Quinn needed privacy; they seemed oblivious to anyone else. When the other man stared at her, Alice was the rabbit pinned by a predator. She dug her nails into the palms of her hands and commanded the pounding in her chest to still. In that instant, she made a decision. She would no longer live in fear of men or allow them to force her to run and hide. She would turn her suffering upon them.

She would become the instrument of destruction for men who preyed on the vulnerable.

With that decision a measure of resolve crept through her body and she stood a little straighter. She pointed to the barn. "This way."

Reaching out, she took the reins to Quinn's mare from his slack fingers and led her to the stables. The other man followed, somewhat slower. From the corner of her eye, she saw the awkwardness to his gait and adjusted hers. She bent down and petted Eilidh until he caught up.

Two stalls were empty at one end of the barn, and Alice led the horse into one while the man took the other next to it. She unsaddled the mare and hung the saddle and bridle on racks at the end of the barn. Then she picked up handfuls of hay and brushed the mare's coat, dislodging sweat and loose hair. Once satisfied that the horse was well-tended, she checked that the water bucket and hay rack were full.

All the while, she gave the man time to complete the same tasks in his awkward manner. She didn't offer to help but busied herself with other jobs, making it look entirely coincidental that they both finished, at length, at the same time.

Despite the cold temperature, sweat dampened his brow as though the mere act of grooming caused him difficulty and great physical exertion.

"Shall we see if the other two are ready for company?" he asked, a gleam in his eyes.

2

Ewan

EWAN SWALLOWED the pain and plastered a bored smile on his face. God, it was exhausting to pretend that nothing bothered him. To disguise that his body turned traitor upon him, stole his feline grace and left him stumbling like a fat, three-legged house cat. He hated being injured, but more than that, he loathed the feeling of inadequacy. At least he managed to get off the horse without making a fool of himself. Although his busted leg nearly gave out on him, and only grabbing the saddle kept him upright.

The French mages had discovered that silver could incapacitate a lycanthrope, as evidenced by what happened to Ewan on the battlefield. The bullet that shot him had lodged deep in his femur and leached poison into his body. With the silver in his bone, he couldn't sustain his wolf form and was forced to return to his human skin. Nor could he shift back to heal faster as a wolf. For a man who only shifted when absolutely necessary, he now found he couldn't do it at all.

The surgeons hadn't been able to remove the bullet and wanted to take the leg off. The shot was so close to the head of his femur, they had planned to amputate at the hip. Only Ewan's brothers-in-arms had stopped them from dismembering him. Major Logan sent him home to seek the help of an English mage to remove the ensorcelled bullet.

Did anyone notice the extent of his disability?

Ianthe and Quinn were so wrapped up in each other they wouldn't have noticed if elephants had charged past them. What of Alice? He tried to remember the frail and broken creature they had rescued from Bedlam the previous year. This woman looked equally wild, but in a different way. When they rescued her, her hair had been closely cropped. Her blonde locks had regrown, but in an unrestrained manner. Her white gold strands rivalled the sun, and the ends curled around her face and tickled her jawline. Her skin was flushed with warmth and a healthy glow, and her body was lean but muscled, rather than starved.

She seemed so much more alive.

When he met her gaze, fear rampaged behind those forest green eyes. He cursed Viscount Hoth for what he had done to the woman and to others who did not survive his patronage. The soul eater had met a gratifyingly lingering and agonising death thanks to Quinn and the highly inventive mage, Lady Seraphina Miles.

"I'll not harm you, Alice. You have my word." It was all he could offer, if only she would believe him. He could well understand if she decided never to trust another man again, especially an Unnatural one. Not all monsters were the same, but how could one tell a damaged woman that?

Then as he watched, the fear drained from her eyes, a glint of steel crept in, and she stood a little taller. What thought had wrought such a change? He wanted to ask, to know what made her extend a fraction of trust towards him, but then she took charge of Quinn's horse and headed to the stone and wood barn.

Unsaddling his horse made him swear under his breath. His right hand refused to co-operate and his fingers curled uselessly around the girth. After he had been shot, a dead horse had toppled on him and smashed his right hand and forearm. The silver taint in his blood slowed his healing. A break that would have once knitted back together easily refused to mesh. He drew in his frustration and took each step slowly, teaching his left hand to take the lead where once it had always followed.

Grooming was somewhat easier, but took longer since he couldn't swap hands as he worked. He expected Alice to offer to help the cripple or to ask how much longer he would be. Instead, she seemed busy with the other horses. By some coincidence, she finished just as he did.

He needed to sit down, but even more, he needed a

drink to stave off the pain and let him continue to mask his true state. He hoped Ianthe and Quinn had taken the edge off their need for each other by the time he and Alice made it to the house.

He stared up at the solid stone walls as they crossed from the barn. The house looked as though it had stood for at least two hundred years. The stone was battered by wind, rain, and snow. Thick glass in the mullioned windows reflected the late afternoon light. Not quite the elegant town house he was used to, but then, he hadn't returned with Quinn to take up his former life in London.

He came to Northamptonshire to hide and lick his wounds before he presented himself to the mages tower at the Royal Arsenal in Woolwich. There he would be poked and prodded as the mages worked to counteract the silver's effects. He would no longer be the darling of society, but a pathetic laboratory subject.

Alice pushed open the oak door to a warm and charming kitchen. An enormous coal range set into a deep fireplace occupied one entire end of the kitchen. A fire behind the grate emitted a soft glow and a kettle sat on top of the cast iron box. Polished copper pots and pans hung on either side, neatly arranged by size.

Slate tiles underfoot showed wear from two hundred years of feet walking the same routes as meals were prepared and served. A pine table dominated the central space, with mismatched chairs arrayed along each side. A dark dresser against another wall held a colourful collection of plates, bowls, and delicate teacups. The north-facing wall had a long, narrow window that caught the descending sun and lit the kitchen. Underneath ran a worn bench, with open shelves below housing more pots, plates, and mugs.

They shrugged off their thick wool overcoats and hung them on hooks by the back door. Then Ewan let out a deep breath as he sank into a chair closest to the range. The heat felt good on his misaligned bones. The chill wind outside made him ache as though he were a hundred years old. He longed to pull off his boots, but he clung to some remnants of civilised behaviour and would save that until he retired to his room.

Quinn took the chair adjacent to him and winked.

"Feeling better?" Ewan murmured.

"I'm home with the woman I love in time for Christmas. Life doesn't get any better," the younger man replied.

Ianthe opened a cupboard and reached in. The soft chime of crystal heralded her return with a bottle and four glasses. "I knew you would be home. The sight has been showing me a wolf with mistletoe in its fur for weeks. A celebration is in order. This is the most marvellous present that I could have imagined."

Ianthe sat on Quinn's lap as she poured the drinks and handed around the glasses. "A toast to the Highland Wolves. May the war end soon, so that the others may all find their way home safely."

"To the Wolves," Ewan murmured. Three glasses clinked and then a timid fourth joined them before disappearing.

"What news of the others? Is Isabel still camped with the army?" Ianthe asked. She kissed Quinn's cheek and then slipped from his lap to help Alice lay out the evening meal.

Quinn laughed. "Oh yes. I wouldn't be surprised if she is running everything by now. Alick's mate is rather formidable, and she has proven herself to be a resourceful and competent aide-de-camp. I don't think anyone has dared point out women aren't supposed to hold military positions."

As the men related events and the war's progress, the women took gold-edged plates from the dresser and laid out the table. Bread and cheese were fetched from the larder and a delicious smelling stew hauled from the range's oven.

Ianthe continued a barrage of questions as she worked to feed everyone. "And Aster and Hamish? I have not had a letter since she had young Rab three months ago."

Ewan smiled as he thought of their leader's wife. "Incredibly busy, our dear Aster. Quite apart from helping Scoville decipher encrypted French communiqués and documenting Unnatural creatures, she also found time to present Hamish with an heir. Extraordinary woman. A man would have had his hands full undertaking just one of those tasks, but she juggles them all."

Ewan raised his glass to the absent member of their party, the woman who had set events in motion when she had entered their lives and changed them all.

"To Aster," Ianthe and Quinn said in unison.

As conversation flowed, Ewan remained aware of Alice. The woman flitted around the room like a butterfly trying to find somewhere to land. Eventually, once the table was laid and the meal prepared, she could avoid them no longer. She pulled out a chair and sat a distance from the other three.

Or was she simply staying out of arm's reach? How sad that a woman knew to stay beyond the distance a man could lunge across a table. A pang stabbed through his chest as he remembered another woman, long ago, who had learned the same lesson.

They ate in silence for a minute or two. The two men had ridden hard all day to reach the farm. Quinn had been determined to spend the night in his new home—or, more likely, determined to spend the night with a beautiful former courtesan rather than with Ewan. He tried not to take that personally. Once, men and women had clamoured to share his bed, but now he was a distinct second choice.

"What happened, Ewan?" Ianthe asked in a quiet tone.

He stared at his plate. He held his fork in his left hand. His traitorous right sat in his lap. Limp, the fingers curled into his palm. What he would give to be able to stretch out his fingers and relieve the constant ache in the tendons. Hard to believe that barely six months ago he had been fit and able bodied, charging full gallop into battle and shifting form effortlessly.

Now, he was a cripple, trapped in one form with no future except living off the charity of others.

"The Highland Wolves were deployed in Vitoria. We would gallop towards the French and stand in the saddle, shifting mid-jump to land amongst the enemy as wolves." His gaze drifted to his wineglass, but he found no solution to the pain that haunted his every move within the contents. He found only his distorted reflection.

"There was a French officer who smelt dead and who was, I believe, another type of Unnatural creature. He shot me with an ensorcelled silver bullet. Damn thing dropped me mid-leap. The silver tainted my blood and set me on fire from the inside. I was forced back into my human form just as a horse with its throat slit rolled over the top of me. The animal's weight crushed my arm and torso."

"Oh." Ianthe dropped her knife as her hand went to her chest, her gaze going from Ewan to Quinn. She was a woman passionate about horses, and the death of an equine would cut her as deeply as hearing of Ewan's injuries.

"There I was, naked and trapped under the dead horse, waiting for the French officer to finish the job." He took another drink. Even relating the story made the pain flare anew through his bones as though his blood were alcohol and someone set a match to it.

"Then what happened?" Ianthe leaned forward, her eyes wide.

He toyed with leaving her in suspense, although the ending to his story was spoiled somewhat by the fact that he was narrating it. If he had died a valiant death, another would have told the tale.

"Alick happened," Quinn said. Laughter shone in his brown eyes.

Ewan's comrades were woven into the fabric of this

story, his brothers by bonds stronger than mere blood. Through thick and thin, these men had remained fast at his side.

"Alick." Ewan raised his glass to the missing Scot and toasted his saviour. "The great brute is an ugly mix of Highlander, wolf, and Viking berserker. He has the fighting rage, and it is terrifying when it comes upon him in his wolf form. The Frenchie was about to fire a silver bullet into my head when a huge, insane, red wolf ploughed into him. The man who had been about to end my life suddenly found himself missing a vital piece of his anatomy and so failed in his task. For which I am forever grateful to Sergeant Ferguson."

"Alick tore the man's head off," Quinn whispered to a horrified Ianthe.

Ewan stabbed a piece of meat and popped it into his mouth. There was a debt Alick would never let him forget. His life was bound to the formidable Highlander. "I'm told Alick mowed down the enemy around me and kept them away until our soldiers could lift the dead horse off me and pull me out. I am ashamed to admit that I remember none of it. I had already lost my battle with consciousness and surrendered to nothingness. I woke up three days later in the field hospital to find Major Logan arguing with a surgeon who wanted to take my leg off."

"The field surgeons don't understand Unnaturals or how we heal. I think the man wanted to cut Ewan up to see if he contained a wolf on the inside." Quinn topped up their glasses.

Alice ate like a bird and then scraped her plate into

a bowl for the dog. She rested by the range, her shoulder leaning on the wall. Her gaze was on the dancing reds and oranges in the grate, but her head listed towards Ewan. She listened, even if she feigned disinterest.

Quinn pushed his plate away and then grabbed a slice of fresh bread. "Silver is poison to the wolves. With the bullet lodged in his bone, Ewan is unable to heal properly. It didn't help that the field hospitals are full of butchers. Idiots didn't even understand the bones should be straight before they're bound. Ewan's arm should have been re-broken and reset straight."

Ianthe winced. Even Ewan found it hard to hear. The injuries hurt enough, but to discuss how he was incapacitated humiliated him. Wolves were strong and fierce, and now he was useless dog who would be a burden on his pack.

The bored smile that concealed so much dropped over his face. "Well, if wishes were horses, beggars would ride."

Quinn gestured with his buttered bread. "Major Logan sent us back for the mages to study the damage to Ewan. We are to report to the Royal Arsenal after Christmas to see if they can discover a way to reverse the damage done by the silver and whatever spell the French wrote on the bullet."

"What of Lady Seraphina Miles? Could she not do anything to help?" Ianthe asked.

Lady Miles was the most powerful mage in England, and along her with husband Sir Warren

Miles, the eminent physician, they followed the army to be on hand to wield their particular skills.

"Lady Miles and two other women have been struck down by a most curious malady themselves." Ewan took another sip of wine. The French fought British magic with spells and weapons created by their mages. War created monstrosities that men could not imagine in times of peace.

"She is ill?" Alice whispered.

"They are dead," Quinn said.

Ianthe gasped. "No. Lady Miles fashioned the bullet that delivered justice to Hoth. Her husband must be bereft, and she will be a great loss to our mages."

Ewan ran a fingertip around the top of his glass. "Sir Warren is seeking a cure. It is rather taking all his time and energy as he consults with his wife."

"A cure for death?" Ianthe frowned and glanced to her lover.

Quinn nodded. "That is the curious part. The hearts of all three women have stilled and yet they continue to talk and go about their day. However, decay eats at their bodies and they have developed a craving that is not to be mentioned in polite company. That is the reason the major gave for me to accompany Ewan. I am to go to Lady Miles' London home and retrieve certain books she wants to consult."

Ianthe shuddered. "Well I have you until then, so let us talk of more pleasant topics than a walking death. I assume you will travel to London together?"

Ewan pushed his glass away. "Yes. Hamish generously allowed me time before I must face the London set and parade my disability for all to see, and the books Lady Miles wants are not overly urgent. I hoped to winter here if that was acceptable to you?"

"Of course." Ianthe reached across the table and gripped his left forearm. "You are always welcome here. What a grand Christmas we shall have with you both under this roof!"

The wraith slipped out the door and disappeared, the silver terrier hard on her heels. Ianthe sighed at the other woman's retreat.

"How does she fare?" he asked, curious as to what time had done for the unfortunate creature.

"She is healthier, but her mind . . ." Her voice trailed away as her gaze fixed on the closed door. "I cannot even imagine tearing my soul apart, and I wonder if the damage she did to escape Hoth is irreparable. She is protected here and she seems content, if a little wild."

Irreparable. Ewan knew what that was like.

He, too, was irreparable.

3

_____

Alice

ALICE STROKED Eilidh's ears as she lay in bed and listened to birds roosting in the eave. It was one thing to decide upon a plan, but quite another to put it into effect. In one moment when a quizzical blue gaze had swept over her, she decided to turn her world upside down. The prey would become the predator.

But how did one find the strength to stand up to one's greatest fear? She needed to change from the pitiful victim of a monster to being a woman in command of her own destiny.

The terrier had no answer to the questions swirling in Alice's mind. The dog's head lay on Alice's stomach, a furry body flush against her hip. A soft sigh wheezed from between Eilidh's jaws and Alice smiled. At least someone slept undisturbed by troubled thoughts. The arrival of the men created turmoil in her mind, as though someone had cracked the timbers holding back a dam, and the water swirled and rushed to escape.

She turned her head to watch clouds glide over the surface of the moon outside her window. She always kept her curtains open. Some said that if the moonlight caressed you while you slumbered, it drove you mad. The word *lunatic* meant those touched by the moon. But Alice was already mad, and the silvery light held no fear for her. Nothing could be worse than the nightmare she had already endured. The moon seemed inviting by comparison, and she welcomed its subtle caress.

The trace of mage power that flowed through her veins whispered that the presence of the men was a catalyst. No, not men. One particular man who hid his pain behind a bland smile. How did the others not see that his wounds were deeper than a silver bullet poisoning his blood? A man whose searing gaze stirred up a wind of change that would sweep over her and bring about a transformation.

She didn't have the sight like Ianthe. There was no clue to be found in her dreams as to what the wolves among them meant. She only had the tug, like the pull of a magnet to the compass needle. Her finding gift urged her that the wolf possessed something she sought.

It didn't seem possible that a wolf trapped in a man's skin possessed something that would help her transform. She would need to trust her power and let it guide her. After all, the caterpillar had no inkling it would turn into a butterfly when it spun its cocoon. The little insect undertook its work on faith, trusting in the instinct that urged it on. Layer by layer, it encased its body in silken strands with no idea of the path that lay ahead.

Alice wrapped her hand around the necklace at her throat—a wolf's head made of silver and given to her by an ancient mage in Scotland. She had wondered what the trinket meant at the time, but the wise woman had only cackled about protection. To Alice it meant the spirit of Eilidh, who protected her slumber. But could the necklace be a token of a more literal wolf?

She let out a sigh. Events would unfold in their own time. Alice would have to trust unseen forces and wait to see what magic wrapped around her.

WHATEVER THE SEASON, life on the farm followed a routine. Alice rose early and padded barefoot down to the kitchen. First, she opened the door for Eilidh to dart outside, and then she fed the range to revive the fire. While the range heated, she started the bread. Once yeast and flour were combined, she pounded and kneaded in the quiet of the slumbering house. The supple dough was shaped and dropped into two tins, covered with a towel, and left to rise in front of the fire.

Alice slipped on a pair of clogs and threw a shawl around her shoulders, tying the long ends around her waist to keep her warm against the cold blast outside. She walked across the yard to the barn, and Eilidh bounded from the taller grass to join her. Gentle snuffles and nickering came from within the barn as she pulled the doors open. She checked the horses, carted water to refill their buckets, and forked more hay into racks. As she finished, dawn crept over the horizon and painted the sky in soft oranges and gentle pinks.

Time to place the bread in the oven and boil the kettle. Normally Ianthe would appear, and after breakfast they would walk out to the paddock with the yearlings and broodmares. Today, she suspected the other woman might be sleeping late—or possibly not sleeping at all, given the giggling and cries that had punctuated the night.

Alice made breakfast and then finished the rest of her morning chores while the farmhouse lay silent. The porridge had just thickened when the door opened behind her.

"I thought you would sleep late today, or are you in search of sustenance?" she called.

"Sustenance. I am not one to lie abed without a compelling reason," a deep voice answered.

Alice dropped the spoon and turned to find Ewan Shaw staring at her. He leaned against the doorjamb, the epitome of morning elegance. Or was he resting against it because his leg pained him after descending the stairs? He wore pale breeches and polished Hessian boots. His cravat was already tied despite the early hour and tucked into a finely tailored waistcoat of navy blue. All trace of shadow had been removed from his freshly shaven face, and his black hair was damp and slicked back from his forehead.

"Captain Shaw." Her voice wavered and for a moment, her mind considered fleeing. Then she remembered her new resolve. No more fear. A transformation didn't happen instantaneously; she needed to make tiny steps to bring it about. Facing this man was one such small step.

She picked up the heavy spoon in case he came too close. "Breakfast is plain here, I am afraid. I can offer you porridge."

"Porridge is fine. Thank you." He limped across the room and took a seat. The terrier sat at his heel, and lupine murmured to canine as Alice dished out a large bowl of steaming porridge.

She pushed the pitcher of cream and a spoon towards him. He reached for it with his right hand, then it paused and dropped away. His left hand grabbed the handle instead and poured cream over the meal.

"I don't think we will see Ianthe and Quinn before noon. It has been a year and a half since they last saw each other." He added a dollop of honey before picking up his spoon.

Noon? What would she do with this man until then? The kitchen was large, and yet the mere act of him breathing seemed to wrap around her and sprout an intimacy as though they were squashed in a closet together playing sardines. She hoped after he had eaten his meal he would go sit in the parlour and perhaps read a book.

Quite apart from his breathing, his gaze unsettled her. It reminded her that once she had been a woman that men had fought to possess. Now she was a broken thing, a shattered dish that should have been swept into the rubbish.

With nothing else to do, she decided to dish up her own breakfast and fight her first battle—breakfast with a man without running from the room. She wished she had been born a powerful mage. She would whisper secret words and build a wall between them.

She set her bowl on the table, down and across from the captain. Then she poured two cups of tea and slid one towards him. He murmured his thanks but kept his thoughts to himself. They ate in silence and she avoided looking at him. She hurriedly finished eating and then rose and placed her dishes on the bench.

"I could help wash up?" He gathered up his bowl and brought it over. The teacup rattled and listed to one side as he missed a step.

"Leave them," Alice said. Ianthe loved that dinner service. It wouldn't do if he dropped one and smashed a plate on the unforgiving, hard floor. "Ianthe and Sarah will do them after they have eaten. I usually muck out the stalls now. You'll find a few books in the parlour to keep you entertained." She gestured across the hall.

He leaned his hip on the bench and crossed his arms over his chest. "If you could tolerate my company, I would like to assist. I have been idle for too long."

She wanted to scoff, to dismiss his help—but there was something in his eyes. A pang of need he couldn't disguise. Alice knew what it was to be broken and pitied. She understood the need to do something, even if you did it badly.

So instead of laughing, she nodded. *No more fear*, she whispered inside her head. "That would be appreciated. Thank you. Galahad can be something of a handful."

A heart-stopping smile graced Ewan's handsome face. This was a man used to charming any woman with a quirk of his full lips and that piercing blue stare. It took no difficulty to imagine him as the predatory wolf, stalking the salons and ballrooms in London. Women probably bared their throats to his jaws.

He took a woollen coat from the hooks by the door. "I don't have Quinn's touch with problematic stallions, I'm afraid. But I'm sure we'll manage between the two of us."

They did manage, despite her reservations and the way her heart hammered against her chest as though it were building a barn inside her. His presence near her raised goose bumps along her flesh. What was it about him that unnerved her?

Predator.

The silver might inhibit his ability to shift form, but the lethal creature lurked under his skin. He appraised her, as though assessing his chances of running her down.

She repeated her litany in her mind: *no more fear*. Those three little words kept her from bolting for freedom across the fields. A smidge of curiosity also held her in place. Her mage blood whispered that he possessed something that belonged to her.

With the horses in the barn seen to, they walked out to the paddock with the foals and broodmares. They leaned on the stone wall and watched the youngsters play. Constance, with her jet-black coat and long silken mane, walked over to have her ears scratched.

"She's a beauty," Ewan said as the mare leaned into Alice's touch.

"Isn't she? Her foal is the black colt. Although Ianthe says he will go grey like Galahad as he ages." Alice didn't have Ianthe's ability with horses, but she could appreciate the elegance and beauty of an equine, and there was something about being around a horse that soothed her fractured soul. The very aroma of warm horse seemed to bring peace with each inhale.

Eilidh barked and Alice turned to see what had attracted the dog's attention. A group of riders appeared around the bend in the road, their breaths frosting on the chill air. Three men trotted along, one out front and the other two each leading another horse behind. Hooves rang out on the frozen earth.

Alice's heart sank. More men. Her mind was drowning just dealing with the one beside her. She narrowed her gaze at the group, but none seemed familiar. A cold lump settled in her stomach.

The farm saw infrequent visitors. Ianthe had put the word around she was in the market for quality broodmares, and occasionally an opportunistic farmer or passing traveller would ride up with a mare for her to inspect. Alice thought the approaching harsh weather would have kept all casual visitors away until spring.

"It will be horses for Ianthe to view." She glanced backwards, but the farmhouse was silent, with no sign of movement through the thick mullioned windows. Why did Ianthe not appear? Panic clawed its way up Alice's body and her feet itched to run. Something about the approaching riders fed her panic.

Ewan made a sound in his throat that bordered on a growl and his nostrils flared. "Smells like trouble. Go wake Quinn."

Ewan's words echoed through her body in time with a beat that rippled through her veins. Her mage blood gave a familiar warning. Alice didn't just find people and missing objects, the magic in her veins also warned of approaching danger. She had ignored its warning once, drowning it out with champagne, and she had walked unseeing into a trap.

"I'll go fetch them." Alice would heed both the spoken warning and the internal one. Once she roused Ianthe and Quinn, she could bolt across the countryside and leave them to deal with the strangers.

Ewan arched one black eyebrow, an amused look in his eyes, as though he suspected she would run in the opposite direction to both men and farmhouse. "I shall greet the visitors while you wake the happy couple."

Relief washed through Alice. Ewan would deal with them. Now she only had wake Ianthe, and she could slip away until there were less people around. Picking up her skirts, she ran through the grass back to the house. Eilidh thought it a great game, and she barked and bounded next to her.

Alice pulled the door open, sure she would have to

rouse the couple from their bed, only to find them sitting at the table.

"Oh, you're up." Surprise stole her words for a moment.

Ianthe at least had dressed. Quinn, compared to Ewan, was undressed and dishevelled. His linen shirt gaped open at the neck, he wore no waistcoat, and his hair looked like Ianthe had her hands tangled in it all night long. A large, wolfish grin dominated his face.

Ianthe smiled and had a luminous glow. The woman looked entirely content with her life, or entirely physically satisfied. "Quinn has quite an appetite, and he needed feeding."

The young man did bear a remarkable resemblance to a starving wolfhound. It also explained the shaggy hair. He was eating the porridge straight from the pot with the serving spoon, and a pile of toast sat at his elbow.

Alice pointed back out the door. "Riders are approaching with mares. Ewan says they smell like trouble and for you to come, Quinn."

Quinn froze. Then he nodded and dropped the pot to the table with a mournful gaze, as though he had intended to lick it out and would now be unable. He rose and pulled a tweed waistcoat off the back of his chair. "I will join Ewan to greet your guests. Ewan can growl, but I can bite if needed."

Ianthe waved a hand. "I'm sure he is overreacting. It is not uncommon for men to show up with brood-mares, and we do need to find a few more mares for Galahad this spring."

Ianthe rose, brushed out her skirts, and tucked a stray curl of hair behind her ear. "Would you be a dear, Alice, and heat some ale for them? They will be thirsty and cold if they have ridden from the village, and if the mares are any good, it might make negotiations smoother."

Serving drinks wasn't in her plans; she had hoped to bolt like a startled rabbit. The ripple still ran through her blood, warning her the men were not to be trusted. She rubbed her arm, trying to dispel the whispers from under her skin.

A trickle of new resolve ran down her spine. She could do this. To overcome a fear, one must face it. First breakfast with one man, now serving drinks to several more. Today was the start of her trial by fire. She was the blade that would be strengthened by the flames.

"Of course," she said as the others left the cosy kitchen.

Alice filled a pot from the large barrel of ale in the pantry and set it to heat on the range. Then she stared at the dresser. Best to stay away from the finely painted porcelain she thought, and selected a plain, sturdy pottery pitcher. The jug went on the tray and she added half a dozen tin mugs, the ones they used for outside. Once steam began to rise from the pot, Alice wrapped a towel around the handle and poured hot ale into the pottery jug.

With slow, careful steps, she carried the tray outside to the men, who were now standing on the dirt yard in front of the barn. The yard was protected from the winter gusts blowing off the fields by the lee of the building and the hill behind. Quinn ran a hand over a piebald mare while Ianthe stood at its head. Ewan stared at the interlopers, his gaze flicking from one to the other.

"Would you care for a hot drink, gentlemen?" Ianthe asked as Alice stopped next to her.

"Aye, a drink to wet my whistle would be grand. Then perhaps we can run our hands over your fillies," one man said.

Alice set the tray down on the stump used for splitting wood and began pouring drinks.

Ianthe frowned. "I'm afraid you are mistaken. We don't have any fillies for sale."

The three rough visitors laughed and exchanged looks. "No need to play coy with us, we know what you're about out here."

Alice froze with a mug in her hand as the warning that pulsed through her blood turned from a slight tickle to the full-on gush of a river in flood. She met Ianthe's startled grey gaze.

Quinn dropped the mare's leg and straightened. "Perhaps it's time you gentlemen left. You seem to be here under a false understanding."

"Not without a bit of fun first to warm us all up for the ride back." The man closest to Alice lunged, grabbing her around the waist. Alice dropped the mug, and beer drained into the soil with a puff of steam. His hand stole up her body and squeezed her breast. Her mind screamed, but only a whimper broke free of her throat.

"You're a leggy thing. I'd like to take you for a ride." He ground his hips against her bottom.

Eilidh growled and launched herself at the man, sinking her teeth into the fabric of his trousers. The little dog tried to haul the man backwards, her little legs scrabbling in the dirt.

"Bloody dog is gonna bite me!" The man kicked out, and his arm bit deeper into Alice's stomach.

"That's not the dog you should be worried about," Quinn said.

Alice closed her eyes and a single tear rolled down her face. She would be a good girl and endure. Time would pass quicker if she were still.

But this time it was different. She was no longer alone. Now someone fought for her, or a number of someones. The terrier refused to let go until the fiend released her mistress. But there was another presence who reached out a hand to save her from the nightmare.

"Let her go, or you'll be picking your entrails out of the dirt." The words, softly spoken, carried the chill of winter frost. Alice opened her eyes to find a blue gaze locked on her face. "Stay with me, Alice. This is not your fault."

The world blurred around the edges as the nightmare pulled her down, but those eyes held in place. She wanted to run, to hide, to drown in his endless ocean. From one side came a low growl. Not from Eilidh, but from a creature much larger. One of the men swore and the other gasped.

"I'll be quiet," Alice sobbed. She would do what he

wanted. It was over quicker that way. If she fought or struggled, his breathing would quicken and he would take longer, drawing out her fear and pain as he tore a slither from her soul.

The man wrapped one hand around her throat, and his fingers bit into her skin. "Call the dog off or I might squeeze this one a little too hard."

As Alice's vision turned black at the outer edges, Ewan lunged. Unable to shift form, he instead struck out, his arm a cobra, and fastened on his prey.

The man holding Alice made a startled gasp and his grip loosened. Alice sobbed as she dropped to the ground. Her hands broke her fall and Eilidh was there, licking her face. She barely registered the enormous wolf standing on one of the men.

She just ran.

4

———

Ewan

EWAN KEPT his left hand wrapped around the man's throat until his eyes started to bulge. Desperate fingers clawed at his fist that controlled the man's airflow, but he wasn't going to relent. This man's short nails were nothing compared to the hot poker of fire that burned his other hand. The one he kept in his pocket, as though the encounter were something casual, rather than let his opponent see his weakness.

To one side of him, Quinn growled as he sat atop a man and flattened him into the dirt. Saliva fell from the wolf's exposed fangs onto the prone man, who whimpered with each drip. The third stranger was occupied hanging onto the lead rope of a terrified mare.

The man wheezed under Ewan's grip, and the red

veins in the unfortunate's eyes flooded with blood that seemed unable to flow down his neck. Ewan only let him go with a push once Alice's retreating figure disappeared in the shadow of the tree-covered hill.

The man gasped a few breaths and then stood straight and tried to appear undisturbed by the man who transformed into a wolf before their eyes. He shuffled to one side, putting the third man trying to wrangle the frightened horse between him and the Unnatural beast.

With slow, deliberate moves, he straightened the edges of his overcoat and then wiped his nose against his sleeve, marking the tweed with a silvery trail. "We were told the two women living here are whores, and we thought they'd like some business. We were going to do them a favour—let them earn some extra coin and spread some holiday cheer."

"The only thing the likes of you would spread is the pox." Ianthe's finger stabbed in the air.

Ewan stayed immobile lest his damaged leg belie his cool demeanour. Only his glacial stare turned on the man. "I don't know what stories you have heard about these ladies, but whoever told the tale omitted one vital detail. They are under the protection of an Unnatural wolf."

Quinn lowered his large head and snarled at the man under his paws, who emitted a high-pitched squeak like a compressed mouse. The horse nearby snorted and rolled its eyes until only the whites showed.

Ewan nodded in Quinn's direction. "That messy

brute is very protective and rather impulsive. Yours wouldn't be the first throats he's removed."

Ewan doubted he needed to defend Ianthe. Even without Quinn beside her, she always struck him as perfectly capable of fighting her own battles. But Alice —well, there was a woman who desperately needed someone to stand up for her. If Ewan had been capable, he would have happily changed form and taught the buffoon how wolves protected their own.

"Let him up, Quinn. They will be leaving now." Ewan spoke to his pack brother, but he kept the man before him pinned with a steely regard.

The wolf snorted and let out a short yap as though it disagreed. He leaned more of his weight on his front paws and the man's squeak was cut off.

"He can't leave if you're squashing him, and I don't want him fouling up the yard." Ianthe reached out and laid a hand on the wolf's massive head. She tried in vain to stroke the fur in one way, but it obeyed no order but its own and stuck out in several different directions.

The wolf sighed and took two steps back, freeing the man from its weight.

The squealer scrabbled backwards until he hit his friend's leg and then rose, his wide eyes never drifting from the creature. The three of them appeared braver once they all stood back to back, surrounded by a woman, a cripple and an overgrown dog.

"Say it ain't true, then, that you were never a whore." One puffed out his chest and threw a challenge to Ianthe.

"It is most definitely false, for I was never a whore. I

was a courtesan to the finest nobles of *my* selection. I wouldn't have let your sort empty my chamber pot."

Ianthe wasn't backing down. Quinn's wolf might have to sit on her to hold her back if she had a temper to match her fiery curls.

Ewan coughed politely into his hand to draw their attention back to him. "Don't get distracted, gentlemen. You were about to leave. I do believe you interrupted the wolf's breakfast, and he'd like to return to it, unless you have something else he can chew on?"

Quinn's long pink tongue licked his lips and rolled down a fang as he stared at the man, who gave another squawk.

The men grumbled but made their way to their horses as a pack, as though they feared walking singly in case they were picked off.

"Good riddance to you. Your mares have horrible conformation, and I wouldn't breed to them if I were drunk and desperate. That one is not only pigeon-toed but knock-kneed." Ianthe pointed to the piebald mare.

The creature had a sweet eye but legs that made even Ewan shudder. But then, he preferred much finer ankles. Like those revealed when a woman picked up her skirts and ran.

"You're too old anyway," one shouted, feeling braver now they had climbed into their saddles.

"Old? Old!" Ianthe lunged but something held her back as her hands swiped at the air. "Your dried up pizzle wouldn't satisfy a pig!"

The wolf had grabbed a mouthful of skirt and sat down, using its bulk as a counterweight to the swinging

Ianthe and stopping his mate from getting deeper into trouble.

Ewan swallowed a laugh as the beast rolled his eyes. Courtesans, even if retired, possessed rather colourful vocabularies.

Only as the riders took up the lead reins for the following mares and pointed their mounts down the driveway did Quinn let go of Ianthe's dress. Then he let out a loud howl that startled the horses. The interlopers bounced in the saddles as the panicked horses bolted away from the noise.

Ewan and Ianthe watched until they disappeared around the curve in the road. When Ewan turned around, a naked Quinn was putting his trousers back on.

Ianthe handed him his shirt and then scanned the countryside for her friend, a hand to her eyes as she searched the distant hills. "Blast those oafs. Alice could be gone for hours, and the nights are so cold that she will freeze out there if we don't find her before dark."

"I will go search for her." Ewan offered, although the way the woman bolted, she could be in the next county by now.

"It will be rather like trying to flush out a rabbit, and I'm afraid to say she may not let you anywhere near her after that." Ianthe bit her lip, worry for her friend written all over her face.

"I can be rather patient with frightened animals, and I doubt I will be much use around here." Ewan waved his useless hand.

Ianthe screwed up her face as she thought. "Very

well, if you don't mind. She was doing so well coping with you and Quinn, and now those horrid men have given her a scare."

"It might not be as bad as you think." Ewan remembered the way she had straightened and faced him the previous day, as though she found an ounce of courage. He hoped this was a temporary setback.

Ianthe squeezed his arm. "I pray you are right. I would give anything to hear her laugh again."

Ewan would search for the missing woman and coax her out of her hidey-hole. That seemed a far easier task than leading the frisky stallion out to the paddock with the mares. Or watching the openly affectionate couple who made loneliness bounce around his hollow interior. "Just point me in the best direction."

Ianthe gestured towards one of the hills, and Ewan fixed his sight on the right dip in the landscape. "Over that hill, the river cuts through the valley. Follow the river up to the small waterfall. Alice normally hides there. But if she is holed up, we might have to leave her a blanket."

Ewan walked over to the barn and picked up the bridle for his horse. He slipped the bit into the horse's mouth and slid the leather over its ears before struggling to do up the buckles with one good hand. With the help of a nearby barrel, he was able to climb on bareback. It felt good to let his left leg stretch down without worrying about a stirrup.

If his body were free of silver, he would shift to his wolf and follow Alice's scent. At times he didn't even know if the creature remained inside him or if the French mage's spell had burned all trace of the lycanthrope away. He had to reach deep inside his psyche to hear the beast whimper and find its injured body wrapped tight in silver chains. The bullet in its leg was an open wound that seeped poison and refused to heal.

His fellow Highland Wolves knew only that the bullet stopped him changing form. He had told no one that the creature was dying of its wounds. When he finally met with the mages at the Royal Arsenal, he would have to reveal the extent of the damage, but showing his weakness didn't come easily.

Ewan took a leisurely ride over the hills, assuming that Alice would need time to settle. A horse that bolted needed to run itself out before it could be turned. Through the rolling paddocks, man and horse wandered. He gave the gelding its head, and it snatched at tufts of grass as they walked. This part of Northamptonshire was quite picturesque if one was fond of rural life, being landlocked, and the complete lack of civilisation. Ewan suspected there wasn't a decent tailor for nearly a hundred miles. Or however far it was to London.

He forded the water at a shallow point and then followed its course back towards the hills. As the water turned a corner, a bark signalled that he neared his quarry. Halting the horse, he slid from its back, balancing on its neck as he let his feet touch the ground and waited to see if his damaged leg would take his weight.

Then he tied the horse's reins to a low hanging branch and approached the waterfall. Ewan walked carefully on the uneven ground and untrustworthy right leg. He didn't want to fall over and end up in the river. He found Alice by a large pool formed by the river tumbling down a rock face. The water gushed and gurgled as it hit the rocks below and then flowed out through the valley.

She turned her head as he approached, a wary expression in her sad green eyes. He halted a few paces from her. She was such a wild and flighty animal, and he didn't want to startle her further. Yet he saw no fear in her gaze, just an aching emptiness that echoed through his own chest.

"Would you hold me, please?" Her voice was so hesitant, lost, as though she expected him to laugh and say no.

In truth, he didn't know what to say. Her request was the last thing he had expected to hear. He assumed she would berate him for being a man and then banish him from her sight forever.

He was somewhat confused by the request for physical contact. "Are you sure that is what you want?"

"Yes." Her eyes shimmered with unshed tears, and if Ewan had possessed a heart, it would have broken at the sight. The beast within him roused from its lethargy and strained against its bonds, urging him to comfort the woman.

He eased himself down on the damp grass next to her and tried not to think of the damage the lush green surface would do to his pale breeches. Was there even a laundress out here who could remove stains? Another week and his cravats would desperately need a wash and fresh starch. He slipped his damaged right arm around Alice, still sure he must have misheard and he was taking a terrible liberty with the fragile woman.

As he embraced her, Alice sighed and wrapped her arms around his waist. Her head settled on his chest. For a long time, they sat like that. The shudder in Alice's body abated and her breathing became deeper.

Without meaning to, Ewan lowered his head until his cheek rested against her silken hair. He inhaled the fresh scent with the faint richness of lavender. The wolf inside him breathed her in and laid its head on the ground. A shudder ran through its broken body, and for the first time in six months, a moment of peace washed over it.

With nothing else to do to pass the time, Ewan ventured a quiet question. "Explain this to me. I would have thought the last thing you would want would be for a man to touch you."

"You know my history?" With a fingertip, she traced a silver button on his jacket.

"Yes." It still troubled him that no one in society had batted an eyelid as the young courtesan was abused.

It kept him awake at night that he and his fellow wolves were too late to save the other women Hoth had killed by devouring their souls. Only Alice's mage blood had kept her alive; otherwise she too would have been a sad pile of bones tied with ribbon in Hoth's basement.

"When he wasn't whittling at my soul or parading

me at soirees, he kept me isolated. He had a small dark room, like a closet, that he called 'the box.' I spent my time in there, alone. The whole time with Hoth and then in Bedlam, all I wanted was someone to hold me. He starved me of touch, but I desperately craved the feel of another person."

It was such a small thing, to hold a woman. If only it were enough to heal her.

After a while, she unwound her arms and wiped her face with the heel of her palms. "Thank you."

Strangely, Ewan was the one who now felt bereft as she moved away a fraction, his arms empty and the spot on his chest cooled. The wolf whimpered then fell back into its unconscious state. It disappeared beneath his surface like a rock thrown into water vanishes from view.

Odd—as though in the process of giving Alice comfort, a tiny piece of her had seeped into his soul and comforted him.

Alice stretched out her legs and watched the water. Eilidh sat at her mistress's ankles and snuffled at the grass. "Ianthe thinks I can be fixed, but she doesn't understand. I have found most of my pieces, but no matter how hard I try, I cannot make them fit back together. I can never be fixed."

"No," Ewan agreed with her, "you can't be fixed."

Only someone who had experienced their world exploding into hot shards understood how impossible it was to simply pick up the pieces and rebuild. You must mourn what died, bury it deep, and then emerge reborn. That's what he had done long ago, and it was what Alice needed to do if she had any hope of moving forward and rebuilding her life.

She angled her head to the side, and a worn smile flitted over her lips. "At least you are honest."

He shrugged. What was obvious to him was often a mystery to others. People who had seen the worst in others understood human nature better than those who lived blessed lives. The damaged ones learned to recognise warning signs in others. It was a sad statement about both their lives. "You can't be fixed, but you can be made anew."

She mulled over his words. "How?"

"You take all your broken pieces, you melt them down, and you forge something new." He trod a dangerous path with this woman. None of them understood how she had used her aftermage gift in a moment of terror to rend her soul into pieces and hide them from the soul eater.

While he didn't want to give her false hope, some gut instinct told him she needed a different approach than the one Ianthe had applied. Alice certainly looked much healthier for her time running wild, but her gaze was haunted.

Yesterday he had witnessed a sliver of steel working its way down her spine. He suspected all she needed was a direction. If she had something to navigate by, she might find the way to escape her nightmare.

She nodded as though he had triggered a deeper thought. "Create something new like the caterpillar does. He spins his chrysalis and transforms his body into the butterfly."

"Yes. The choice is yours. You hold all your shattered pieces, and they have the potential to become whatever you desire. What would you become, Alice?" He was curious what this young woman would pick as her path.

She laid a land on the small dog at her side. Her elegant fingers stroked tufts of silken hair as she considered what she was and what she could be.

"A blade," she whispered.

Yes, she understood. She didn't need to heal and return to exactly who she used to be; she needed to become something fiercer.

"Excellent choice," Ewan said. "A weapon forged in fire. You will be stronger than before."

Green eyes turned to him, and the glint of resolve crept into her gaze. "No man or Unnatural will ever hurt me again. I will become the blade, and you will teach me how."

The wild creature had claws and she sought his help to use them. This was the sort of challenge he needed to forget his maimed body and lack of a future. He would enjoy seeing Alice stretch and grow.

Her fingers stilled on Eilidh's fur. "You will teach me how to use a knife, and in return, I will work on your damaged arm."

"That is not necessary. My fate is in the hands of the mages and whatever solution they can conjure. Tell me Alice, how do you find things?"

Her hand brushed through the grass until she

found a pebble, then she tossed it into the pond. "How would you find where the pebble hit the water?"

He stared at the concentric circles that broke the surface of the water. "I would follow the ripples. They are narrower, or closer together, at the point of origin."

"That is how I find things. When I concentrate on an object, it is as though the air has ripples and I can follow them back to where the item resides. The ripples are tighter when I am closer but further apart if I stray off course."

"Could use your gift to find the bullet?" He dared not hope it could be so easy. Could this broken creature remove the silver from his bone?

She tilted her head, as though considering the idea. "No. I find the lost. The bullet in your leg is not lost. You know exactly where it is. You want to know whether I could retrieve it, which is a different gift to mine."

His face remained impassive while disappointment plunged through him.

"But there is still much that can be done. Massage and exercise will help stretch the tendons and regain the movement and strength in your hand. There are also herbal infusions which would reduce the pain." She met his gaze and, for once, didn't hide or duck her head.

As if on cue, an ache ran over his palm and up his arm. If the lass knew some remedy to ease the pain, then what harm was there? Perhaps she wasn't the only one who craved touch. What would it be like to have her hands on his body? He was as unused to comfort as Alice.

"A trade then. We shall help each other piece together our broken lives," he said.

She held out her hand and he took it. Their fates were now bound together.

5

Alice

THE NEXT MORNING, Alice followed her usual routine. She rose early, put the bread on to rise, and completed her rounds of the horses in the barn. Then she made quite different preparations in the kitchen while Ewan silently ate his porridge. He tracked her movements in the warm space, but he didn't speak.

Alice had learned that magic was not the answer to every question. Millions of souls managed to live without spells or enchantments to solve their daily problems. Her family had supplemented their after-mage gifts with herbal lore, and today she drew upon the knowledge she learned as a girl.

She found oil and poured some off into a pot before setting the kettle to boil for tea. From her small store of herbs she added peppermint, camomile, and thyme and placed the pot on the range. She made tea while the oil infused, then wrapped a towel around the handle of the copper pot and carried it to the table. Carefully, she poured the fragrant mix into a pottery bowl with a moulded spout. Returning the pot to the range, she at last took a seat next to Ewan.

"You will need to roll up your shirt please, Captain Shaw." She tried to ignore how close they sat, despite her skin prickling at the proximity. She had to touch him after all, but a fraction closer and their knees would rub.

"Will you call me Ewan?" He undid the button at his wrist and then rolled the linen shirt up past his elbow. He laid the arm flat, or as flat as it would lie, on the table between them. Angry red lines criss-crossed his forearm where the bones had protruded from his flesh. His fingers curled inward, as though they no longer obeyed his command to straighten.

In wolf form he would limp quite badly. She doubted the forearm would carry the animal's weight, especially when coupled with a damaged hind leg. In nature, a creature with such injuries wouldn't last long.

"Using your Christian name would be improper, Captain." She poured a little oil into her palm, rubbed her hands together, and then she began. With long strokes, she ran her thumbs from wrist to elbow, distributing the oil and feeling his muscles and tendons under the skin.

"I think creatures like you and I are excused from matters of propriety." He sucked in the last syllable.

She glanced up at his tight jaw and eased back the

pressure. But not much. To be effective, she had to convince the tight tendons to release their burden so they could stretch back into their former position and relinquish the grip that curled his fingers closed.

Alice was a country girl from a small village who had ventured into London to seek out excitement. The captain was from a noble family who moved among the upper classes. His Christian name shouldn't pass her lips in ordinary circumstances.

But then neither of them was ordinary. He was a lycanthrope and she was an aftermage. The same pairing as Ianthe and Quinn, who had found an extraordinary type of love with each other. Was that why Alice's blood tugged her towards Ewan? Thinking of what might connect them made up Alice's mind to break the etiquette rule.

"Very well, Ewan." She liked the sound of his name in her mouth, the way it gathered on her tongue before escaping as a whisper over her lips. How many women had gasped his name in pleasure?

She was aware of the captain's reputation. He was a far more successful courtesan than she had ever been. When she had been one of the demimonde, she heard of husbands who paid him handsomely to ensure their wives were kept satisfied and therefore less likely to question their own dalliances.

His breathing evened out as she worked and she glanced up, assessing his reactions to her massage.

"Pain is good," she murmured.

"How so?" he asked. "Surely it's better not to feel pain?"

In many ways he seemed so like her—broken. But in other ways he was so different. He presented such a façade of indifference, as though he felt nothing at all. Could someone be broken in body and spirit, but push it aside and not let it affect them? Questions swirled deep in her mind as she wondered what had broken him and how had he found the strength to survive it.

"If it hurts, it means you feel something," she said.

He was silent for a long moment. "There are things I would rather not feel. I keep such things locked away so as not to disturb my peace. Life is easier that way."

He made it sound so simple; as if all she had to do was a shut a door and her mind would settle. She lived a life constantly bombarded by pain, fear, and anguish. What would it be like to experience peace again? Having dwelt so long in a nightmare land, she couldn't even imagine that peace was possible. "Is that how you manage, by shutting everything away?"

They conversed in hushed whispers. With their heads bowed together, there was no need to speak loudly. The quietest word was heard, passed between them with each breath.

"Do you feel everything, Alice?"

Those blue eyes saw into her fractured soul. She didn't need to answer; he plucked the response straight from her mind. She could never hide her pain because there was so much of it. Some days she drowned in agony. As though Ewan were her confessor, she unburdened her soul to the one man who would understand.

"Yes. I feel it all, and it overwhelms me. That's why I run. I hope one day I can run fast enough to leave it far behind." She hit a knot where the tendon contracted the worst.

Ewan sucked in a breath, only letting it out as the tension eased under her fingers. He made a noise in his throat, but she didn't know if it was in response to the pain or her answer. Silence fell for a while before he spoke again.

"Where did you learn this?" he asked. His breath stirred a strand of hair that fell around her face.

She hid a smile behind the fall of hair. "My mother was a very talented witch."

When he didn't reply, she glanced up and found curiosity in his blue gaze. Once a mage appeared in a family, a trace of magic would flow through the veins of their descendants. Since Alice was an aftermage, it only followed that either her mother or father was likewise gifted. People paid extra in Bedlam to stare at the mad witches, as though they expected them to fly around the room on broomsticks or to sprout curly pig tails.

"Why do you call her a witch and not an after-mage?" he asked.

"While mages and their offspring have walked this Earth for over a thousand years, many people still hold to old beliefs and believe our gifts ungodly. Not so long ago, women aftermages were burned at the stake, when fear made men lash out at what they didn't understand. In centuries past, your kind would have been hunted and their fur spread on a floor while their heads were mounted on walls as trophies. " She spoke softly as she worked. "My kind are often called witch behind our backs as country folk make the sign of the cross. They fear us, yet creep to our doors at night to seek cures only we can dispense. My mother's after-mage taint made her a powerful healer. Yet there is nothing magical in knowledge. Like knowing willow eases pain, or to turn a breech babe so a mother doesn't die in birthing, or how to relax a cramped muscle."

One black eyebrow arched. "Magical or mundane, I will take whatever ease you can offer."

She wondered how the silver bullet affected him. As Alice worked, she let her aftermage gift reach out, searching. She gasped—the taint of silver permeated every part of him. "Your veins flow with silver. How do you endure it?"

He ground his jaw. "Simple. I have no choice. Not until I allow our mages to experiment on me, to see if they can find a cure. Until then, you may have at me."

She tapped his forearm. "This was no simple break, especially for a wolf."

He huffed a quiet laugh. "I believe it more shattered than broke. Half a ton of horse landing on you will do that. Quinn does the surgeon a disservice though. He put my arm back together, and he did a good enough job that I escaped a fatal infection."

She scoffed; it looked like butchery to her. Even if the bone had been broken in several places, the doctor responsible could still have tried harder to line every-thing up, to give it the best chance of healing straight. But her attention was needed for what was happening under her fingers. With her eyes closed, she tried to convince the muscles to remember their task. He would need weeks or months of such therapy, but change would occur.

His fingers curled inward and then released outward a fraction more than before.

"Some might call this witchcraft, but I would call it the application of anatomical knowledge. You are a woman of hidden talents." He watched her constantly, at times his gaze unreadable, showing nothing of what he gleamed from his observations.

"If I were a man, I might have studied medicine. An aftermage physician would be greatly sought after. As a woman, I use my gifts to get by, although it has not worked out quite as planned." She had thought her looks and ability to find lost items would secure a wealthy patron who would eventually offer her marriage and security.

She had found a wealthy patron all right, and ended with her mind in shreds. She should have stayed in the village and taken over her mother's role when she died, but she had yearned to see London. She had reached for more like a greedy child, and life had punished her for it.

Ewan lifted his left hand and tucked a strand of hair back behind her ear. "What happened to you, Alice, after we rescued you from Bedlam?"

The unexpected contact made her flinch, but not from fear. A man touching her usually provoked her fear response, but not this man. Why did her body want to press against him rather than shy away?

A wolf protects you, the old mage had whispered.

Alice shook her head to dispel the thoughts clogging up her mind. "Aunt Maggie took me to Scotland to see an old mage, to seek her help in finding the scattered pieces of my soul."

He huffed a gentle laugh. It seemed everyone knew of the formidable Aunt Maggie. "And what did the mage say?"

When Alice thought of Scotland, it seemed a dream. A misty place pierced by silver light and where the veil between worlds dropped. The mage had studied her palm and told her future. She had whispered of a great love, sacrifice, and the potential paths Alice could walk.

"She said there was nothing wrong with me and that the fractures in my soul allowed me to see the world more clearly." Alice picked up the heavy silver necklace around her neck. The wolf's head was about two inches in diameter. Its mouth was open and tiny fangs were exposed as though it howled at the moon. "The mage gave me this necklace then left me to roam, to seek my missing pieces in the heather and valleys."

His gaze flicked down to the emblem of his regiment cast in silver and then back up to her face. "Do you see the world more clearly, Alice?"

She met his intense stare. The blue pierced through her, and he saw all her secrets. But it was a two-way process; in stripping her bare, she likewise saw all of him. She saw what he sought to conceal from others. "When you are broken, it gives you the ability to see the cracks in the façades of others. Will you teach me how you do it? How you shut everything away and don't feel."

He continued to search her eyes and then he looked down to where her hands rested on his arm. "Is that what you want, to no longer feel?"

She wanted to live, to free herself from the dark box where Hoth had imprisoned her. Alice longed to feel the warmth of the sunshine in her bones again. But all her emotions were exposed and raw and everything hurt. "It's so loud in my mind, as though all my emotions are screaming at once. And it's exhausting. Every day I battle constant noise, pain, and pressure. I don't know how much more I can take."

She screwed up her eyes against the tears. Lord, it hurt to simply exist. Despair tainted every breath and burned in her lungs. There were days she wished she hadn't survived Hoth's attentions. Perhaps she should have let him whittle away her soul until eternal sleep claimed her.

Ewan cleared his throat. "You need to build a place that is safe. Furnish it with things that comfort you. Reinforce the walls with stone and steel until nothing can reach you inside. That is your sanctuary. When life becomes too much, retreat to that room and shut the door. Trust that the walls will hold against the barrage."

She thought for a moment, pondering his words. That made a kind of sense. To escape Hoth, she had hidden herself. Except that she had closed the door and shut the monsters in with her, and this time she needed to leave them out in the cold.

"Eilidh. Firstly, my room would contain Eilidh." The terrier's ears pricked up on being mentioned. Her silver head cocked to one side as she listened to her mistress talk. "She is my protector."

He nodded. "Good. But she needs to be bigger. Imagine Eilidh as a mighty dragon. With thick leather scales that can repel any barb or knife, her breath molten flame that coats your enemies until they dissolve into ash before you."

"No. Not a dragon, but a wolf to stand guard." Ever since Quinn had thrust the squirming puppy into her arms, she had known her salvation resided in the dog. The few quiet moments her soul found were when she touched Eilidh. Her light. Only the terrier eased her burden and lit the dark. She assumed that was the hidden meaning in the necklace, that it resembled the terrier's true character.

Now, sitting beside this man, she wasn't so sure.

She continued to work on Ewan's arm in silence, broken only by their steady breathing. Then she declared herself satisfied. "That's all for today. But you need to remind the hand how it should function."

Alice pulled a ball from her apron pocket and Eilidh whined. Alice kept the ball to throw for the dog, but now it would be used for a different purpose. She placed it in Ewan's palm and bent his fingers around it. "Carry this with you, practice squeezing and releasing around the ball. That will work the muscles and tendons in your fingers and forearm."

When he tried to do as she said, his fingers quivered and slid along the ball. "It feels a little better already, but I suspect you will be a hard taskmistress. I have not forgotten my part of the bargain. We can start now if you want, out in the yard."

"But what of your leg?" There was little she could do about the bullet lodged in the bone, but there were herbal infusions that would ease the pain. Alice had a limited herb supply. In her mind, she made a list of plants she needed to procure to aid his recovery. In spring, she could plant a much better range, assuming Ianthe could help her source the seed. Although he would be gone by then, off to Woolwich and the mages' tower.

He unrolled his shirtsleeve and buttoned the cuff. "My hand is the main concern. A limp can be dashing in the right circumstances, but no one wants a useless hand."

Alice rose and washed the oil from her hands at the sink. "Very well, let us begin my transformation into a blade by teaching me how to wield one."

6

_____

Ewan

As Christmas approached, Ewan settled into life with
the people he regarded as family by choice, not blood.
Although technically he and Quinn shared the same
lycanthrope blood, making them wolf brothers. Quinn
only had leave for three months, and he and Ianthe
busied themselves with the horses and spring plans for
Galahad before he had to return to their regiment.
Ewan spent the early mornings with Alice's quiet
company as she massaged his arm.

In the afternoons, they worked with knives. At first,
he drilled her in simply handling a knife. She became
familiar with the different types of blade and the
weight and balance in her hand. When the weather
kept them inside, Ewan made Alice slice vegetables

faster and finer, which brought an amused sparkle to her eyes.

He was satisfied she had good basic skills, so today he would start teaching her to throw with one of his lightweight blades. The weather smiled on them and the sun cast a watery glow over everything, but the temperature was still bitterly cold with the threat of snow in the air. They stood in the sheltered enclave between hill, house, and barn. On the back wall of the barn (and well away from any livestock) Ewan drew chalk circles nestled within one another.

"There are two main aims in throwing a knife: accuracy and getting it to stick in your target. We will start with stance and a relaxed body. You want to hold the knife tight enough that it doesn't leave your hand too early, but not so tight your fingers cramp." That made him smile at the irony of his permanently cramped hand, although he had noticed the smallest improvements since Alice had begun her massages and exercises.

He held the knife in his left hand and pointed to the chalk circles. "Imagine where you want the knife to end up. Visualise it penetrating your target. When you throw, you want to release with your arm extended at the target."

He stepped behind her and placed the knife in her right hand. Even through the thick wool coats they wore, his body tingled with awareness of her. On instinct he inhaled, breathing in her lavender scent and, wolf-like, letting it linger over his tongue. Under the chains of injury and magic, his wolf roused enough to urge him closer. The creature lifted its head to share the taste that filtered through Ewan's body.

Ewan reminded himself he had a task to complete as he corrected Alice's stance and grip. Then he took her arm in his hand and, in slow motion, showed her how to move her body. Over and over, they mimed throwing the knife.

"Your body needs to learn the feel, weight, and movement until it becomes second nature. Now you try." He stepped back, giving her room.

She drew back her arm and threw. The wood gave a soft thud as it was kissed by metal. The blade jutted inside the first chalk circle. Alice had a natural ability with a knife. Ewan had observed a curious phenomenon about women. Most men thought them weak, yet they often showed themselves to be the far more dangerous sex of any species. A woman with soft eyes, lush lips, and six inches of steel was an irresistible —and fatal—predator.

His wolf made another feeble attempt to struggle against its thick bonds. The creature stirred when Alice was near, as though she could free it from the magic holding it prisoner. The sight of her face or sound of her voice roused it from its poisoned stupor. At night Ewan whispered her name simply to prod the beast and reassure himself it still dwelt within him.

In the New Year, he would have to venture to Wool-wich. He worried that if he delayed too long, the silver might irreversibly damage his wolf. While Ewan found elements of the beast distasteful, it was still a part of him. Perhaps even the better half of him, since the wolf understood the bonds of friendship and family on a deeper level than he could ever grasp.

He rubbed his chin, and the stubble returned his thoughts to more human concerns. He managed an adequate job with his left hand, but it was far from the smooth feel of a really close shave. "Good. Again."

Just as Alice was ruthless with her massages and demanding the tendons stretch and yield, so he was a demanding teacher. If she wanted to protect herself, the knife needed to be an extension of her body, as natural to her as using her own hand. He drilled her for over an hour, until her arm began to flag. Never once did she complain or ask to stop.

She simply obeyed.

A chill crept down his spine. Her submission was unsettling, and he didn't want to supplant Hoth in her nightmares.

"That's enough for today. Is it possible to have a bath around here?" His skin itched and his cravats needed more starch. Rural life and a broken body were Hell on his grooming routine.

Alice's green eyes widened and then she laughed, a sweet, tinkling noise that made him smile in response. "I believe we could muster up a bath for you, Captain."

Then the woman had the nerve to salute. As their days together turned into weeks, Alice grew accustomed to him. The skittish horse settled and shook itself loose. In the growing familiarity between them, he spied a mischievous streak. Only when she was most at ease did Alice laugh or smile. The first time Ianthe heard her soft laugh, the woman nearly cried with relief.

"The first in nearly two years together. What a gift for this Christmas," Ianthe had whispered with tears shimmering in her eyes.

To think Alice had endured years without a smile to grace her face or laughter to stroke her throat. At moments like this, he wondered how she bore it. His physical injuries seemed easier by comparison to the emotional scars she carried. Or it might be the thought of feeling so much that mortified him. He had built his reputation on feeling nothing, and only the pain from his body reminded him that he was alive.

Alice found Quinn, and he carried the tin bath from the shed into the kitchen. Ewan watched and pretended to stare at his fingernails while inside he berated himself for being too useless to assist. Once he had been as dashing and capable as Quinn. He might be again one day, if he could strip himself naked before the mages.

They set the tin bath on the slate floor in front of the range, then Alice filled large pots with water and set them to boil on the hot plates. Even better than the anticipated bath, Ewan had talked Ianthe's man, Perkins, into giving him a shave. He sat at the kitchen table while the man wielded a cutthroat razor with an expert hand.

Fortunately, Perkins was the ideal retainer who spoke very little. There was no need for conversation, not that Ewan wanted his Adam's apple bobbing as the steel ran over his jugular. The silence left him time to contemplate his future.

What would he do with his life now the army had no use for him? An injured wolf unable to change form was a liability to his regiment. The Royal Arsenal only wanted him as a curiosity to experiment on. They couldn't even chain him up as a zoological exhibit with his wolf incapacitated.

He would only stay with Ianthe and Quinn for a little longer before he journeyed south. If the mages failed in their task, he couldn't stomach the idea of going cap in hand to beg for charity from his brother, the baron. Not that he could ever darken the door of his ancestral home anyway; his brother had banished him some years ago.

To avoid resting false hope on the mages, Ewan thought it better to assume it wouldn't work and figure out an alternative. As he considered his options, he found himself without direction, occupation, or an immediate source of funds. Although he had some small investments, thanks to the generosity of grateful patrons, they would not last indefinitely.

As much as he hated to admit it, he was going to need a job.

He had spoken to no one about his fears or concerns for the future. Not even Hamish, his closest friend, for to do so would be to expose his vulnerabilities and flaws. Hamish was confident the mages would extract the bullet and silver from Ewan's body and that he would return to his regiment, and the war, hale and hearty.

Perkins wiped Ewan's face with a heated towel. "All done, Captain."

He opened his eyes, ran his good hand over his chin, and then sighed. Better than any shave he'd had in London. "You're a true craftsman, Perkins. Thank you."

"I know someone in the village with a light touch with starch and an iron. I'll take your cravats in when we go for supplies after Christmas." The conversation was a positive soliloquy from the stoic Perkins. Never had Ewan heard him speak for so long. He certainly wouldn't turn down the offer of a proper laundress.

"Ianthe doesn't pay you enough, Perkins, and you are wasted on Quinn. I swear if I make it rich, I shall come back here and woo you away to civilisation."

The older man snorted a laugh and waved his towel. Quinn was a lost cause, more puppy than wolf. Whatever his form, his hair or fur resembled an unruly hedge and he hated anything around his neck. Perkins needed an employer who appreciated his skill and care.

Which led Ewan in a full circle back to analysing his future.

"Bath is ready," Alice said. She poured the last steaming pot into the water. "We'll leave you in privacy."

"Could throw the pup in after," Perkins muttered under his breath as he packed away his shaving kit.

Ewan bit back a laugh. He would pay to see them attempt to wrangle Quinn into a bath. He had spent years on the road with the man, and he was more likely to jump into a freezing cold horse trough than a comfortable bath.

The door closed behind Perkins and Alice. Only once alone did Ewan begin the slow process of removing his clothes. His left hand did most of the work while his right got in the way. Eventually, he had a neat pile over the back of a chair and he climbed into the slipper-shaped tub.

He leaned back and let the heat seep into his bones. Lord, it felt good, and the ache in his leg settled. He flexed and released his right hand. Each day, it moved a fraction further or seemed a tiny bit less stiff.

He ducked under the water and washed his hair. Then, with his ablutions done, he closed his eyes and dozed while the steam curled around him. Instead of considering his lack of prospects for the future, he found himself mulling over a far more pleasant puzzle. One with green eyes, sun bleached hair, and skin the golden hue of honey.

Alice fascinated him. She was a book and he had to keep turning the pages to read what would happen next. He skimmed her early chapters, for they held no interest for him. Fresh, vibrant, and joyful when she arrived on the scene in London, that Alice was too innocent and too full of life for him. He had taken a bet against her, judging how long before the gilded lights of London would tarnish for her and she would grow jaded like the other courtesans.

Never could he have envisaged how terribly events would unfold.

The girl had grown into a woman tangled in

tragedy that added spice to her story. He watched, mesmerised, as she sought to rebuild herself. Shadows and secrets lurked in her gaze that he was determined to know. Every flinch or shudder roused his anger at Hoth and increased his need to see her, if not healed, then in a state that gave her contentment.

He told himself it was merely the deep-rooted protective instincts of the wolf. That he would watch over any woman or innocent so cruelly treated by life. But he knew himself for a liar.

Alice was different.

He would help her transform into an angel of vengeance. In his musings, he stood at her side to always protect and watch over her as she was released on London. Only with Alice could he imagine returning to the glittering salons and endless parties, because he wanted to see her stalk monsters like Hoth and deliver justice for women with no voices.

CHRISTMAS DINNER WAS a raucous affair spent in the kitchen. Ewan had thought they would dine in the dark and dusty dining room at the back of the farmhouse. He'd forgotten this wasn't a grand home with servants waiting to do their bidding. There was also something about the warm kitchen, as though it were the embodiment of the comfort these people gave him.

Tonight, the kitchen was gaily decorated. Alice and Ianthe had strewn green boughs draped with red ribbons about the room. The fresh scent of pine permeated the room and reminded him of nights spent hunting in the forest.

A large duck that liked to attack people's legs had disappeared from the yard and was now roasting in the oven. Quinn muttered something about hot revenge and Ewan swallowed his laughter. The duck had made the fatal error of pecking Quinn's derriere when he bent over a horse's hoof.

Wine flowed and even Alice giggled as she enjoyed her second glass. The meal was simple but delicious, made all the better by the company. Then there was a pudding with brandy for desert.

Ianthe glowed as she raised her glass. "To the merriest Christmas I have experienced in some years. Not only is Quinn home, however temporarily, but we have good friends and good company."

The tapped their glasses and toasted each other. Full stomachs and good brandy had edged everyone's mood to contentment. Quinn produced a sprig of mistletoe from the pocket of his waistcoat and waved it at Ianthe.

The vibrant woman laughed and batted him away. "Since when have you ever needed to wave shrubbery at me to steal a kiss?"

"You're right." Holding the sprig behind him, he cupped the nape of Ianthe's neck and drew her to him for a short but passionate kiss. Then he turned to Alice and held the greenery over her head. "Next."

She suppressed a laugh behind her hand, then leaned over and kissed Quinn's cheek, as a sister would do to a brother.

"See?" Quinn smirked at Ewan. "I am irresistible to women."

Alice stole the mistletoe from his hand and stepped towards Ewan. She held it over his head and laughter danced in her eyes. She leaned forward until their breath mingled, hers sweetened by the wine. Her warm body pressed against his arm.

"Your turn," she whispered.

Desire lit through his body as his gaze fixated on her red lips. How would he ever stop at a single kiss? The heat that flowed through his body demanded so much more. The wolf strained, desperate for a true taste of her to ease its parched throat. Then Ewan pushed his chair back so hard it squeaked over the tiles.

"That would be a mistake, Alice." He strode from the room, his pulse pounding in his ears as he stepped out into the cold night. His breath frosted on the air as he paced, dragging his bad leg through the snow.

The alcohol and the good mood of the evening had simply heightened his feelings. But Lord, he wanted her so badly. A flash of desire burned hot and he thought for a moment that it might ignite the silver in his veins as though it were oil and scorch him to nothing.

7

Alice

THE PLANT in Alice's hand seemed to wilt under her sad gaze. An extra glass of wine created a potent brew inside her. It made her deepest, darkest desires simmer to the surface. She longed to kiss Ewan and see if his lips were as cool as his regard. He was as broken as her, and in a foolish moment she'd wondered if their shattered pieces would fit together.

She had offered up a piece of herself and now she wanted to crawl under a rock and hide. Ewan rejected her and stormed from the house, out into the frigid winter's night. She was a fool to think he would ever be tempted to kiss her, even under the mistletoe.

Ianthe's hand dropped over hers. "We have all consumed a little too much wine, and I am sure Ewan did not mean to offend, but rather sought to protect you. He would not want to take advantage after all you have endured."

"Yes, of course," Alice whispered. Ianthe meant well, but the words cut—she was too broken to be kissed under the festive greenery. She laid the sprig on the table. "If you will excuse me, I think I will retire for the night."

With Eilidh at her heels, she ascended the stairs to her bedroom. The upstairs floor held three bedrooms. Ianthe and Quinn occupied the largest at the front of the house, Ewan stayed in the second largest at one end of the short corridor, and Alice's room was at the other end. She had taken the smallest room, and even that space seemed too big after the closet where Hoth used to confine her.

She didn't bother to light a candle; moonlight streamed across the floor and lit her way. Soon, she crawled under the blankets and pulled them up around her neck. Eilidh turned three times before settling at her waist, her head resting on Alice's hip.

The two glasses of wine had bubbled through her veins and washed aside the broken exterior to reveal a piece of the old Alice. A vestige of the young woman who had flirted and danced with men and had them all vying to kiss her. That woman wanted to kiss Ewan. The older, sadder version of Alice also ached to kiss Ewan and to find the touch so long denied her. But he had pushed her away.

A single tear travelled down her cheek before sleep claimed her.

FOR THE NEXT FEW DAYS, Alice avoided Ewan. She rose early and dressed warmly against the cold. Then she roamed the countryside for hours, only returning at suppertime to warm her bones. In the safe room in her mind, she hid away the tears and shame at her failed attempt to kiss Ewan.

Alice was adept at hiding things. For the woman who hid her soul, hiding a little pain was easy. She would ensure Ewan never knew how his rebuff cut her, and not the tiniest glimmer escaped from the room where she hid her feelings. She craved his companionship and didn't want one foolish moment to jeopardise their camaraderie. Outwardly, their friendship picked up where they had left it off. Bit-by-bit, they resumed their old routine.

After they celebrated the arrival of 1814, Sarah and Perkins loaded up the cart with the first blush of dawn and headed into the village. Dirty laundry needed to be done, whatever the season. They used the services of a laundrywoman, and it was time to drop off one load of washing and collect another. Then the older couple would purchase supplies and check for any post.

Today, Alice stayed close to the house as sleet threatened to fall and it pained her to see Eilidh shivering. She would endure confinement to the house to keep her beloved terrier warm. The departure of Sarah and Perkins did provide an exchange that lightened her heart and brought a tentative smile to her face. Ewan handed over his cravats with explicit instructions about starch and ironing. You would have thought he handed over a priceless jewel to be delivered to royalty the way he fussed over pieces of silk and cotton. He was oddly out of place on the farm; he should have been gracing a magnificent parlour.

Now that the days of January advanced, she wondered how long before Ewan and Quinn left to continue their mission. Not that a man like Ewan would ever last long stuck in the country. He would soon grow bored with the quiet life and need to seek the noise and adulation of society.

Alice would miss him. He saw all her broken bits, and even if he would never desire her, at least he didn't regard her with pity. He had an understanding of her struggles that came from similar experience.

More than that, his touch warmed her body. She relished the few moments when he stood behind her, his chest pressed to her back as he corrected her stance while throwing a knife and his hand wrapped around hers. Or the quiet intimacy that sprang between them during their mornings when she worked on his arm and his breath whispered across her face. Her fractured soul roused from its long winter, and it grew hungry for more of Ewan.

Each day she worked on building the room in her mind where she hid when fear or anguish overwhelmed her. The wolf version of Eilidh guarded that room from demons, and it allowed Alice to keep a calm outer demeanour like Ewan. But more and more, she placed Ewan in that room to hold her when horror threw itself against the walls. In the quiet dark of her bedroom, Alice imagined him doing far more than holding her.

After they saw off Sarah and Perkins, their usual routine was stymied by the weather as a steady, cold fall of sleet arrived. Quinn and Ianthe ran through the freezing slush to the barn to tend to the horses, leaving Alice and Ewan to find some way to occupy their time.

First they sat in the kitchen as Alice massaged his misaligned arm. She closed her eyes as she worked, letting her mage-gift guide her fingers to where they were most needed. Afterwards, they crossed to the parlour. Ewan settled with a book, his damaged leg resting on an ottoman. Eilidh lay at his feet, her gaze on the swaying flames in the fireplace.

Alice roamed the room. She had never been a reader, as it wasn't a skill wasted on young village girls. Knowledge was handed down orally and books were for fancy folk. She arrived in London almost illiterate, knowing only the basics of the alphabet, a few common words, and how to write her name. Then, once she was free of Bedlam, Aunt Maggie had taken it upon herself to teach her to read, all the while muttering darkly about men suppressing education for smart young girls.

Alice reached up to a shelf of the bookcase, took down her prized possession, and carried it over to the large armchair in front of the fire. She kicked off her shoes and curled up with her feet tucked up under her skirts. Terrible breach of etiquette, but as Ewan had once murmured against her hair, creatures like them were exempt from the many rules of society.

She laid the book across her lap and ran a hand over the cover. It was a large botanical book that Ianthe had found for her when she first arrived at the farm. The pages contained gorgeous watercolours of plants, so lifelike she had to resist smelling the flowers or stroking downy leaves.

Alice's fractured mind found it easier to concentrate on the accompanying words when the topic interested her. She memorised the paintings of herbs, flowers, and shrubs with medicinal and healing properties. The text described how the plants could be prepared and lists of ailments they were said to remedy. She absorbed as much knowledge of the subject as she could cram in her damaged head, and at night let it filter to her mage blood.

Alice wanted to expand her gift and see if with practice, she could improve its usage much like Ewan improved his hand flexion. Her finding skill coupled with herbal lore would allow her to pinpoint the right combination of plants to help someone.

As engrossed as Alice was in her book, she couldn't help stealing glances at Ewan. In many ways he was like a wraith, wrapped in shadows that veiled his presence. Raven hair shone in the flickering light like polished obsidian. His long, lean body perfectly filled his exquisitely cut clothing, and an air of quiet menace accompanied his movements, despite his injuries.

She would expire from lack of air while memorising his form, as she forgot to breathe. He glanced up from the small book in his hands and a brief smile graced his full lips. That piercing stare cut through her, and too late she realised he had asked a question while she was contemplating the square line of his jaw.

She dropped her gaze to stare at the peppermint plant with its soft furry leaves. "You must think me foolish to read a book with more pictures than words."

He closed his book and held it in his good hand. "I never judge the intelligence of a person by their choice of reading material. The fact you show such delight in the book tells me you have an enquiring mind."

She stroked the stem of the painted herb. "Ianthe found this volume for me. I want to learn more about botany and its application."

"A noble pursuit. Botany can contribute much to science and medicine." He tried to clench his right hand, but the fingers only curled a fraction before he released them again.

Alice wrapped her hand around the spine of the large book. Others might scoff at her interest in flowers, seeds and roots, but not Captain Shaw. She would never be a doctor or a scholar, but study would enable her to ease the pain of others.

"Might I ask what you are reading?" she asked.

"*Poems, Chiefly in the Scottish Dialect* by Robert Burns. It was my mother's favourite. She used to read from this every night." He rubbed the cover with his thumb.

"Do you see much of her?" Alice found it curious that he spent Christmas in Northamptonshire instead of returning to the care of his family.

"No. I lost her when I was ten. I stole this volume from the pocket of her robe as men removed her body."

A sigh heaved through his chest and then he returned the book to the inner pocket of his jacket, the one over his heart.

"Did you not want to return to your home and extended family?" Alice had left the village where she grew up when her mother died. She could have stayed, but adventure in London beckoned and she had nothing to tie her to the place apart from a few distant relatives. There was no ancestral home; their cottage had been rented. New tenants were moving their pigs into the sty before Alice had finished packing her meagre belongings.

Ewan lifted his leg off the ottoman and placed it on the floor. "No. My older brother has sons and I am superfluous to requirements. He made it clear some years ago that I was not to darken his doorstep again."

Alice always imagined that siblings would stay close throughout their lives. Why would one brother turn away another? Perhaps things were different for the aristocracy. In the village, large families meant more hands to help bring in the harvest or to herd the livestock. Aristocrats might see each other as competition for the coin generated by their estates.

His gaze lingered on her face. "Why don't you tell me what is really bothering you?"

Did she dare? Taking her cue from him, she closed her book and laid her hands flat on the cover, drawing strength from the ornate calligraphy of the title. "You are nobility while I am a mere village girl. We shouldn't even be sitting in the same parlour, but Ianthe insists on treating me as her equal."

"You and I have both whored to put coins in our pockets. We are not so different." He rose by pushing off from the arm of the chair and took a moment to test his leg before walking to the fire and adding another piece of wood. Eilidh's tail wagged once then dropped back.

How could he not see the chasm that stretched between them? He was what her mother would have called *quality*, whereas her sort was bred to labour in the fields or homes of their betters. Ianthe should have employed her as a domestic to cook and clean, but she opened her home and treated Alice as a friend.

"This is not real, here." She waved her hand and stirred the air around her head. "You and Ianthe treat me as though I am like you, but this is a dream full of magic and Unnatural beings. Out there, normal society will see me for what I really am."

There was the truth that hurt in her chest. Try as she might to emulate them, she would never be accepted by others of their class. Better to stick to the things she knew. Life as a village wise woman would not be too intolerable. The contentment found in helping others soothed the jagged edges of her torn pieces.

"Are you forgetting our agreement?" His voice was quiet, a soft whisper against the patter of rain on the window.

She swallowed the lump in her throat. "No. You will teach me to protect myself. But the time nears for you to continue your journey, and I must follow my own path."

Alice would never know why his presence tugged at her or why her mage blood pointed to him when she pondered what was missing in her life.

Ewan leaned one arm on the mantel. "You overestimate society. They are shallow creatures who cannot see past what is before their eyes. I could teach you to be whatever you want to be, Alice. You are naturally an elegant creature. It would take only a little more polish, and the ton would accept you as one of their own and never know the difference. If that is what you truly want."

If that is what you truly want.

She didn't want to be accepted for herself, but for him. In her most foolish dreams she imagined standing at his side, but by day she counted her defects and why she would never be good enough. If she were something else, a woman of quality, perhaps then he might take her in his arms and kiss her.

He teased, saying society would ever accept her. While the demimonde applauded beauty and intelligence no matter their origin, true society was quite a different thing. No noble woman would ever look her way or acknowledge her existence. Breeding would always come through. You practically needed your lineage documented and to hand it over for entrée into most salons.

"You can't make a silk purse out of a sow's ear," she whispered as she stared at her rough hands and split nails.

Ewan narrowed his gaze, about to say something,

when the door burst open and a beaming Quinn and flushed looking Ianthe walked in.

"Who's ready for some tea?" Ianthe asked, tucking a stray curl of hair back into the knot at the base of her neck.

Quinn reached up and pulled hay from his riotous hair.

"Tea would be lovely. I'll help." Alice nodded to Ewan and left the parlour.

Later that day, the afternoon light faded as evening approached. Alice held a cup of tea in her hands as she stood at the kitchen window and thought of the year that waited before them.

As her mind stretched after its long containment, she used the knowledge her mother taught her. She would plant more herbs in the potager to grow her supply of remedies. There were other ways she could use her gift. The trace of power allowed her to find things, but what if she could summon them instead of simply pointing to where they resided?

A swinging light at the bottom of the road drew her attention, and for a moment, her heart paused. But this wasn't more strange men, and she recognised the shape as it drew nearer in the growing gloom.

"Sarah and Perkins are back," she called over her shoulder.

"Excellent timing, supper will be ready soon." Ianthe peered in the oven at the joint of meat and then pushed the door closed with a cloth.

Ewan looked up from his book and placed a marker

at his page while Quinn rose and gestured for him to stay put.

"I'll help them unload. You stay here and brew them some fresh tea. I'm sure they'll be half frozen," Quinn said. He grabbed a jacket and headed out of the door.

Alice placed her cup on the bench and refilled the kettle. Ewan frowned and tossed the book to the table. Quinn and Ianthe wrapped him in cotton wool, rushing to undertake tasks before he exerted himself. Alice could almost see frustration running over his skin, even if his face kept the same bland look.

He needed a purpose in life before he went as mad as her.

It wasn't long before everyone bustled into the warm kitchen and took off wet outer layers. Sarah and Perkins were indeed soaked through. Sodden overcoats were hung on pegs on the wall by the range to dry. Alice poured tea, and once seated with a steaming mug, Sarah pulled a packet from inside her jacket.

"Mail," Sarah said as she handed it over to Ianthe.

Ianthe dropped into a chair and sorted through the mail. She tore open one letter and scanned the contents. "Oh, Quinn, exciting news. We have finally been extended an invitation to visit the Burrow's farm. I hear they have some divine mares."

Quinn smiled. "Excellent. We need at least five more and, dare I suggest, perhaps even another stallion to add to our herd?"

Ianthe clasped the letter to her chest. "Oh, you are a man after my own heart."

She passed the letter to Quinn and then finished sorting the rest of the mail. There was one for Alice from Aunt Maggie and another she passed it to Ewan. "From your major."

He arched an eyebrow as he took the heavy envelope. Then he drew the knife from his boot and slit the seal before he pulled out the sheets within. Two pages were covered in tight, neat script. He leaned back in his chair as he read, as though considering the words in his hand.

"What is it? Is everything all right with Aster and little Rab?" Quinn eventually asked him.

Ewan looked up as though he had quite forgotten they were there. "Yes, mother and child are in excellent health. Aster has been hard at work once more and appears to have found a trace of a certain person of interest who, despite the fact that his heart no longer beats, still causes trouble for us all. Hamish asks that we put off going to Woolwich and pursue the lead instead."

Quinn frowned and the large clock in the corner ticked loudly as he thought. "Forge? But Alick tore his throat out and he disappeared behind a wall of flame when the warehouse burned."

Ewan tapped the letter in his hand. "Vampyres seem rather difficult to eradicate. They're like a red wine stain on your best cravat. Aster has deciphered secret messages that mention him returning to England to distribute something to advance the French cause."

Alice paused on her way from the dresser with a pile of plates. The names meant nothing to her, but the undertone in the room changed. Without shifting form, the men became wolves who had scented their quarry and gone on the alert. Her attention flicked from Quinn to Ewan as some unspoken communication passed between the two men.

"Where?" Quinn asked. A rare hard light entered his brown eyes.

Ewan laid the letter on the table, face down. "Aster found a reference to Seabrook, a small village in Kent. Whatever he plans to *distribute* is going to be smuggled in. This could finally be our chance for justice."

8

Ewan

EWAN STARED at Aster's neatly formed words that marched across the paper. For almost two years there had been no word of the vampyre. With no remains, the Highland Wolves couldn't be certain he'd died in that fire. Once a British agent, Forge had been turned by the French with the lure of immortality and the gold to accommodate his new lifestyle. All they asked in return was a few years in their service. Personally Ewan thought the man did it simply to feed his bloodlust.

The traitor had nearly cost England the war with his plot to intercept the gold payments to her allies. Cutting off the gold would have left England to face France alone, with no allies at her back. There were also rumours that France had crafted a magical weapon to bring England to her knees and Forge was in the thick of that plot.

For his treachery he should have hanged, not that stretching his neck would have achieved anything except making him taller. Add the innocent men he drained of blood, including Aster's father, and Ewan would take great delight in making sure the undead Forge met a grisly final end.

The only question was how to catch the slippery eel who constantly evaded them? He was going to need a better trap this time.

Quinn rubbed his chin. "Forge knows you and he's canny. You would never get close enough to get your hands on him."

Ewan made a noise in his throat and considered his options. As he mulled over possible plans, Ianthe took the plates from Alice and set them around the table.

At length he spoke, a vague idea forming in his head. "He knows the old Ewan, not this damaged one. I could wear a disguise of some sort."

Alice looked up at his words. Transformations were very much on both their minds. Her fingers curled around the cutlery in her hands but she waited for a nod from him before speaking. He needed to work on her confidence; it bothered him that she always waited for permission to do anything.

"Does this man truly know your face or only aspects of you?" Alice asked.

Ewan narrowed his gaze at the young woman. Her words hinted at the same idea he was formulating. "What do you mean exactly?"

She placed the cutlery on the table before she clutched it so tight she cut her hand on the knives. She took a deep breath and let out her thoughts in a tumble. "Does he know the shape of your jaw, the hue of your eyes, and the type of soap you use? Or does he know the preciseness with which you tie a cravat and the impeccable cut of your jacket? The former is a more intimate type of recognition that cannot be hidden, but the latter is readily changed. I could use my hiding gift to smudge your edges and make you less like yourself."

There was a quick mind hiding behind Alice's haunted eyes. Perhaps the conversation veered close to her comment about turning a pig's ear into a silk purse —or possibly the reverse in this case. "What do you mean smudge my edges?"

Heat flared under his skin and he breathed it out slowly. He could imagine her hands on his body working at his edges, and it wasn't an image he wanted to share with the group.

"My mage blood enables me to find things and to hide them. I usually hide objects, but I could apply the same principles to you. It would be a simple ensorcellment to change the shape of your face or colour of your eyes and hair." She waved her hands about his face as though she cast a spell as she spoke.

Ianthe ran a critical eye over Ewan. "Even without resorting to magic, we could play up your injuries. Make your limp more pronounced. Let your hair grow unkempt, keep your chin unshaved. I daresay no one who knew you in London would recognise you."

Ewan shuddered. The idea of not grooming was

anathema to him, and here they were suggesting he play the part of a vagabond. He couldn't imagine a worse torture than telling him not to bathe or shave. They may as well ask him to stop pronouncing his Rs.

"You have raised an excellent point, Alice. It is an idea I can use, no matter how repugnant, to get close to Forge." Ewan held her gaze, wanting to voice his admiration but not wanting to embarrass her in front of the others. Or did he not want to reveal something about himself by praising her remark? He would miss her company when he left for Hythe in Kent. Their time together was nearly at an end, and that made a cold weight settle in his stomach.

"Surely you won't go on your own, though? Will you take other men?" Alice buried her hands in her apron and a frown pulled on her brows.

Ewan shook his head. "Quinn is too well known to Forge, quite apart from the fact he thinks he already killed him. If he recognised Quinn, it would put someone we both care about at risk. Besides, he has his own mission that he has put off long enough and must journey to London for Lady Miles. It is better if I do this alone as the injured and down-on-his-luck war veteran."

"If Forge is working with smugglers, you'll need something to trade to get their trust, apart from your good looks and ability to carry full barrels of brandy," Quinn said.

Ewan curled his right first and unfurled his fingers as far as they would reach. Each day the tendons stretched a smidge more. "If one doesn't possess physical abilities, one must make use of one's mental skills. I shall use our contacts for information on that feared enemy of the smuggler—the excise men."

Ianthe carried the joint of meat from the oven, and Alice slid over a mat to go under the piping hot tray.

"You cannot go alone. Use me. I can be another set of ears and eyes in this endeavour," Alice said, drawing attention to herself. "You can be my injured wastrel of a husband who I must support."

Something in Ewan's chest thumped at the idea of taking Alice with him and keeping her close. In Kent, they could continue her education and he could show her how to be whatever she wanted by changing her voice or posture. But not on a mission like this. "No. This man is a callous murderer. I'll not put your life at risk."

A sad smile touched her lips. "You cannot break something that has already been ruined."

Ianthe gasped, but otherwise remained silent. Perkins and Sarah set about finishing off the table setting and dishing supper into serving bowls. Quinn sat and watched as though he found the whole exercise amusing.

Ewan ground his jaw as he measured her resolve. He understood her need to escape the nightmare world that Hoth had imprisoned her within, but was this the right step to progress the transformation? No. It was too dangerous. If he were truthful, he cared too much for her to risk her life.

"Quite apart from the fact no one expects you to undertake such a mission, you're nowhere near ready for confidential work." He picked up the letter and refolded it back into a neat square.

"Then either make me ready or I will simply follow." Having formulated the idea, Alice seemed quite determined not to let the subject drop. "I will be of use and can disguise your features to enable you to get close to this Forge, but the spell would need to be renewed daily."

Ewan let out a sigh. Was there any point in arguing with a woman who had made up her mind? He couldn't have her following him like a puppy, so it would be better to construct some way to keep her out of harm's way. A small village like Seabrook was bound to have a quiet corner where he could tuck her away. And that way she could *smudge his edges* each morning. "Very well. I will write to Hamish for any further information about Forge and the French weapon. I will also use my contacts for information on the excise men in Kent, and then we shall lay our trap together."

Ianthe dropped a serving spoon with a clatter, her narrowed gaze on Ewan. "You cannot be serious. After all Alice has been through, how can you even entertain the idea of having her anywhere near someone like Forge? Absolutely not. I forbid it. She is one woman, not an agent for the Crown. Let the War Office dispatch someone else to help you."

Alice laid a hand on Ianthe's arm before Ewan had a chance to respond. "If not now, then when? After what I went through, I need to face my demons and slay them. This is an opportunity to take on the role of a fighter, not a victim. And it's not as though I will be chasing the man down the street waving a knife."

Quinn snorted at the image that conjured and Ianthe managed a quick smile. "But he's not a man, Alice. This is a vampyre, and being Unnatural makes him exceptionally dangerous."

The steel crept into her spine as she stood straighter. "I survived two years imprisoned with a soul eater. I think I can last a few weeks in the same county as a vampyre."

Ewan slid his blade back into his boot. "Alice has a point. She survived where other women did not."

"Apart from supporting Ewan, I could obtain a job in the village that would put me near the smugglers' women. We do have a tendency to chat, and anything I learned might be of use to Ewan." For once, Alice didn't falter or back down. She didn't drop her head or sneak out of the room. She stood tall as she told Ianthe of her plans. Whether they accepted her ideas or not, she seemed determined to be involved. "You have given me sanctuary while I heal, for which I will be forever grateful, but now I need to stand on my own feet. The time has come to test my mettle."

Ianthe gripped her hand and met her gaze. "You have become my dearest friend, and I cannot bear to think of you added to the list of victims of this creature."

"I'll be at risk, too," Ewan threw into the conversation, although no one seemed at all worried about his wellbeing.

He appreciated Alice's situation. No one wanted to

linger on the charity of others for too long. Even now, it itched that Ianthe and Quinn provided for him, and he had only been under their roof for two months. He would rather have a purpose than wander around the hills like a lost Romantic poet. And it delayed the time he had to present himself to the mages to become their pet experiment.

"Can you locate Forge, Alice? That might save Ewan valuable time," Quinn asked.

"If we have something he has touched, yes. I would be able to pinpoint his whereabouts." Alice turned to Ianthe. "You cannot protect me from the world, Ianthe. This is what I want, to help bring monsters and demons like Forge and Hoth to justice. Danger does not frighten me, and Ewan will accompany me. I won't walk in the dark alone."

"Alice is quite right. If we place her in a role near the smugglers' women, she can gather valuable information about their operation and reduce my need to expose my face to Forge." Ewan tucked the letter into his jacket pocket. "Perhaps as a barmaid at a pub they frequent, or in a bakery or coffee shop. No one is suggesting she run him down screaming *Die, traitor, die!*"

"You will keep my friend alive—do you promise me, Ewan?" Ianthe had a determined glint in her eye, the one that said she wouldn't budge on the price of a horse.

Ewan saluted the older woman. "Message received and understood."

After dinner, Ewan laboured with his left hand

writing two different letters, one to Aster and Hamish for any information they could find about Forge's activities and what magical weapon the French laboured over. Their return letter was to be sent to a trusted contact in Kent. Then he wrote the retired soldier he knew to alert the man that Ewan would soon travel to Kent and for information of the excise officers in the area. All the while, he constructed a suitable backstory for himself and Alice.

They were to be a married couple with no source of income due to his war injuries. The lure of easy money from smuggling drew them to the eastern coast of England. Their biggest obstacle would be falling in with the right smuggling gang, as Kent was becoming a hot bed of illegal activity. Returned soldiers with no income and in some cases, lacking excitement, were turning to bringing goods into England under cover of dark. He hoped Alice's after-mage gift would help them narrow down the most likely area.

His concern for Alice gnawed at him. He nearly denied her request to accompany him outright. Forge was too dangerous to throw her in his path, and they weren't even sure *how* you destroyed a vampyre. But resolve shone in Alice's gaze. And selfishly, Ewan wanted to keep her near for a little longer.

Her words in the parlour bothered him. To think she saw herself as a pig's ear when he saw only the silk purse. She was wrong. Breeding didn't define a person's ability to be accepted among society. Alick Ferguson was proof of that. He might have Highland aristocracy running through his veins, but that man would always be a beast.

Alice had the potential to be a chameleon, adapting who she was to suit her surroundings. With her after-mage gift of disguise she might yet prove to be a literal chameleon, able to change her appearance. Yes, that was why he would keep her near: to watch her transformation from broken girl to avenging angel.

THE NEXT MORNING, Alice slipped out the back door as soon as she finished his regular massage. Ewan was still sitting at the kitchen table, rolling down his shirt sleeve and staring at the shut door, when Ianthe appeared.

"Has Alice run off already?" she asked as she put the kettle on to boil.

"Yes. Does she do that often?" He had worried she took flight at something he had done. Relief trickled through him to hear it was a regular occurrence.

"Every time it rains. Alice and Eilidh last inside for so long, but first break in the weather, they are off." Ianthe set cups on a tray and then filled the tea pot. "She'll be back at dinner time, soaking wet, and the shadows will be gone from her eyes. Sometimes her pockets will be full of gold coins. She uses her mage blood to find old coins lost centuries ago."

What he would give to lift the shadows from Alice's gaze. If dog and mistress were running over the hills, he had a fair idea where they might eventually end up. He headed to the barn, slipped a bridle onto his horse, and set off on a quiet walk. The sun tried to shine through the clouds, and the landscape was strewn with scattered diamonds as raindrops clung to leaves. Winter would soon give way to spring, and they would make their way to Hythe with the change of the seasons.

He leaned against a tree in the clearing by the waterfall. The serene location was etched in his mind as *their* glade. The farm might be remote, but the residents still cosseted the broken pair. Ianthe and Quinn couldn't help it; they wanted to heal both their friends. Ianthe and Sarah fussed over Alice as though she were an injured bird.

There was a privacy here with only the trees to observe their movements. By the waterfall, they could set aside their patch worked exteriors and be the broken creatures they were on the inside. If they were selkies, they could have peeled off their skins and frolicked in the water as seals. The idea made laughter well up in his chest, but it also had the ring of truth about it. Everybody hid some things until they found the right person they could shed their exterior with and share their darkest secrets.

The horse grazed on the lush grass growing by the water's edge and Ewan waited. She would come. The spot called to her as though it held ancient magic that tugged at her mage-tainted blood.

The babble of the water as it spilled over the rocks held a special charm. He crossed his arms over his chest, subconsciously flexing his right hand. Every day, the fingers obeyed his command a little better. If only

Alice could remove the silver from his blood and reunite him with his injured wolf.

He never thought he would miss hunting in his lupine form. He thought being a lycanthrope made him a beast, but each day he wondered if the wolf was his humanity and the handsome face he wore was the true beast.

A yip echoed through the trees and caught his attention. Alice walked on silent feet, but Eilidh could not contain her excitement and gave away her mistress's presence. The little terrier had to give a greeting when she spotted him and the dog jumped up at his knee for a pat. Then Ewan opened his arms and Alice walked into his embrace.

She leaned her body against every inch of him, her face resting on his chest. They stood like that while time slowed around them. He wondered if he was truly healing her, or if Alice worked arcane magic on him, for he found he needed to hold this broken woman in his arms. Only then did he feel complete, as though she were some missing part of him.

The aroma of grasses and herbs drifted around her as he stroked her damp hair. She must have been lying in the meadow, despite the rain clinging to the foliage and soaking through her clothes. Her body had grown stronger. Muscle and curves enhanced her form. Others would sneer at the faint colour to her face, but he thought it added to her wild appeal.

"Are you sure you want to come to Kent? You could stay here with Ianthe for longer." He had to give her a chance to re-evaluate her decision.

She placed a hand on his jacket and drew circles with a fingertip. "Did you know that despite their delicate appearance, spider webs are very strong? They can be used to bind wounds and stop bleeding. I am like the spider web; others think I am fragile, but my fibres are made of steel. I just need to remember that."

In that heartbeat, he knew she would survive their mission. She had been consumed by fire and then rose from the ashes like a phoenix.

"Very well. I'll not doubt your decision again." He drew her closer and her warmth seeped into his frozen chest. His mother's voice whispered in his mind, repeating the words he heard as he waited to die on the battlefield: *What if tiny shards from a broken woman pierced the cracks in your soul?*

"How do you go, building a sanctuary in your mind?" he asked while he wondered how to protect himself before her broken pieces found their way into him.

A sigh rippled through her body and she turned her face upward to regard him. Eyes the colour of a lush meadow stared at him. "I am finding it easier to calm my mind. When the noise and fear overwhelm me, I am able to retreat and close the door until they pass."

"Good. Your resolve will be tested in Seabrook. Village life can be loud, smelly, and obnoxious." Had he done a good thing in teaching her how to shut away her emotions? Should a creature like Alice be unable to feel? While she needed a way to cope with the events of her past, a part of him wondered if making her an emotionless shell like him was the best course of action.

"I'm ready," she whispered.

Alice might be ready for the challenges awaiting them in Kent, but was Ewan ready to let her into his life?

9

Alice

DEEP WITHIN ALICE'S MIND, the caterpillar stirred in its chrysalis, testing if it was ready yet to emerge. She'd spent two years roaming the countryside and conversing with the shades that lingered after death. She preferred ghostly company to real people, as the deceased couldn't harm her. Or at least ghosts couldn't. Vampyres were probably considered deceased since their hearts no longer beat.

If she wanted to become a blade and be the instrument of downfall to monsters and demons, she would start by hunting this Forge in Kent.

Shame that Ianthe didn't share Alice's convictions. Her friend seemed beset with worry, almost as bad as when Constance had a difficult foaling. Ianthe wrung her hands and looked from Quinn back to Alice. The normally composed woman oscillated between jiggling with excitement and sombre worry.

"Have you had a vision?" Alice finally asked. A vision of her grisly death would explain her friend's concern.

While the mission to Kent loomed, a more immediate concern was what tempered Ianthe's excitement with concern. "No. The sight has not shown me anything, and that is what worries me. Are you sure you will be all right, here on your own?"

February gave way to the promise of an early spring as out in the fields long green shoots from daffodils pushed through the frigid ground. Quinn's three months of leave were over, and he and Ianthe were venturing out to secure more broodmares for their growing enterprise before he had to journey to London and return to his regiment.

Alice suppressed a smile. "I will hardly be alone. Ewan will be here, and Sarah and Perkins are only across the yard in their cottage."

Ianthe embraced her friend and whispered in her ear, "You know what I mean. You will be alone tonight with Ewan, but I promise we will only be gone overnight and back by supper tomorrow."

"I intend to travel to Kent with Ewan as his wife. I believe this will be a marvellous chance to work on our fictitious history. Perhaps I will practice throwing pots at his head to add a touch of realism to our marriage woes." The levity felt foreign over her tongue. If she were truthful, it did worry her a little. Tonight she would be alone with Ewan in the farmhouse. Would she be able to sleep tonight, knowing it was only the two of them under the same roof?

"Go, Ianthe, before Quinn explodes with anticipation. You know he can't resist the offer of a close up inspection of an exquisite mare." Ewan nodded towards the younger man, who was fidgeting with the reins to the horses.

Ianthe tapped him on the shoulder as he helped her up into the cart. "Rogue," she muttered under her breath.

Quinn cracked the reins against the horses' rumps and they trotted off down the road. Ianthe waved and Alice waved back until the curve of the road stole them from view.

"Shall we practise throwing knives in the parlour and leave mysterious marks in the wainscoting for them to puzzle over on their return?" Ewan held out his left arm to Alice.

Alice looped her hand under his arm and they headed back to the farmhouse. The dampness from recent rain threatened to soak through Alice's boots. The dark sky promised still more rain to be released, possibly a thunderstorm. The air was charged and a rumble sounded through the hills.

"I was thinking through the railings on the staircase, to increase the difficulty," she said.

Ewan huffed, as though considering her idea. "If only we had a way to make the railings march up and down the stairs to give you a moving target."

He had such a dry sense of humour Alice couldn't tell if he was jesting or not. Once she had seen a carnival performance where a man threw knives at a spinning wheel that had his assistant lashed to it. That might be a trick to try when she was much more proficient.

He paused and looked up at the gathering dark clouds. "Or perhaps before this weather turns, you could show me the potager?"

Her heart stuttered. Show him the garden? To reveal her love of herbs would be like undressing before him and asking him to pass judgement on her naked form.

"I confess I know nothing about what grows in the earth and I am keen to expand my knowledge. Do you grow vervain? It is one herb that is said to incapacitate a vampyre and would be handy to have on our mission." He awaited her response as though they stood in a ballroom and he had requested a dance.

He appeared genuine in his interest, and Alice had to acknowledge that to date, he had been nothing but curious and understanding despite their differences. "Vervain? We have grown a small quantity but have none at the moment. I will grow it from seed later in spring. My mother used to brew it into a tea for desperate women who wanted to clear their wombs."

They changed course towards the large garden laid out on the south side of the house. Naked apples and pears stood around the edge of the potager. Branches showed off the beginnings of fat buds that would soon be white and pink blossoms. A large quince occupied one corner all to itself, its branches covered in soft green leaves already. Amongst the orderly garden beds,

Perkins worked with a hoe, dragging dirt over low-growing plants. He touched the brim of his hat and then carried on working.

"Why is Perkins burying those plants?" Ewan asked.

Alice pointed to the thin green stalks jutting out of the ground. "He is mounding the leeks. It makes the lower part white, which is the bit we eat. When we need them for a meal, we can dig them back up."

"What an ingenious idea. What else do you grow?"

"Leeks and cabbages in winter with a few left over buried potatoes." Alice ran her hand over a willow frame in a bare bed. "Soon, we will plant the beans and peas that will scramble all over the frames."

"And what of herbs, Alice? What will you grow here that will ease the aches and pains of others?" The blue of his eyes turned darker, reflecting the growing storm over their heads.

Unnatural creature or ordinary man, there was one sure way to ease his pain—laudanum. But somehow she doubted a man like Ewan would embrace the befuddlement that the poppy syrup would wrap around him. There were other remedies that would keep his mental processes clear but still blunt the sharp edge of pain.

She smiled and tapped the side of her nose. "I cannot disclose my arcane art except to another witch."

"Ah, well, I cannot ask you to breach the rules of your sisterhood." They carried on their slow walk around the paths encircling the gardens. Alice pointed out other plants that were covered for winter but would soon be revealed once the late frosts had passed. Strawberries were nestled in pine needles and hay to keep them warm and happy.

"Do you spend much time out here?" Ewan asked.

"Every hour I am not roaming the hills." She had so much to learn, and the more she learned, the more she wanted to do or try. The books Ianthe found fed her thirst for knowledge. They also expanded her horizons about plants and herbs in other countries and used by other cultures. If she could summon as well as find, she could use her gift to obtain seeds from far off lands. "It must seem silly to you, my interest in unassuming little plants."

He stopped and turned to face her, his gaze so serious she had to look away. "Do not make assumptions about what I do or don't find silly. Your blood carries a magical ability, and you constantly display your desire to augment that gift with knowledge to benefit others. That is something I would never regard as silly."

It would be easier to be thought silly and unimportant by Ewan. When he turned that solemn regard on her, it overwhelmed her. To be the focus of his attention made her feel like somebody of importance, as though her thoughts and ambitions mattered. But that was a dangerous path.

Day by day, she longed to be of worth and for him to see her as more than a broken doll. But what if he did? She didn't think she could ever withstand the tidal wave of emotion that threatened to crash through her if he returned just a tiny portion of what she felt for him.

Hoth had broken her with violence, and magic had

fractured her, but Ewan Shaw had the capacity to destroy her with kindness.

~

Ewan

THE STORM BROKE that night as Ewan blew out the candle. Thunder rattled the house and flashes of bright light lit the interior.

"Just like sleeping during a cannon volley," Ewan muttered as he rolled over and pulled the blanket over his shoulders.

His dreams were fractured, much like the rent heavens above his head. Deep inside, his wolf howled at the obscured moon and strained against its silver bonds, desperate to escape the pain.

At one point, Ewan dreamed of a particular widow —a countess much admired by the *ton* for her sombre disposition. In private, she had liked to lick his fingers and toes. Odd woman, but he never complained since she paid him most generously for his company and for the pleasure she received.

Funny thing though, he didn't remember her tongue being quite that small. Or rough. As the tongue tackled the webbing between his fingers, he realised it wasn't so much a dream as a damp reality. He pushed himself up on one elbow and vaguely recognised the small dog sitting by his bed.

"Eilidh?" he whispered her name. Strange that she

came into his room if she needed to go out. Why did she not wake Alice?

A whimper drew his attention as the dog darted to the door and out into the hallway. The cold of the night was nothing compared to the shiver that snaked down his body. Had something happened to Alice?

He cursed his inability to call his wolf forth. He could have used its enhanced senses to feel the night for any sign of trouble. He grabbed a robe to cover his naked body and followed the dog as fast as he could with one uncooperative leg. Thanks to the unleashed weather, cracks of lightning illuminated his way. Eilidh shot down to the other end of the hallway and paced outside Alice's door, waiting for him to catch up. Then she dashed inside.

He paused for a moment before he invaded Alice's room, but if the dog had sought him out, it was for a reason. Ewan pushed the door open, dreading what he would find within. Eilidh had jumped onto the bed and nosed against her mistress.

Another flash of jagged lightning revealed Alice with her arms flung out—to strike the dog? No. The young woman tossed back and forth, her arms held up as though she tried to protect herself from phantom blows. The terrier had been trying to wake the woman in the grip of a nightmare and had fetched Ewan to help.

He padded across the floor to where she slept. Or didn't sleep. Her body jerked in time to the claps of thunder, as though someone rained blows upon her. She made no noise, her teeth gritted together as though she tried to hold in her cries. The storm crashed above the house as another echoed below.

He didn't want to add to her distress, but she needed to wake from the torment that held her in its grip. He touched her shoulder and gently shook her.

Alice cried out as though he burned her. "Alice will try to hold still," she sobbed.

Damn Hoth for what he had done. Not content with peeling slivers from a woman's soul, the demon liked to beat them into submission as well. Ewan wished he could resurrect the creature and kill him anew.

"Alice, it's a nightmare. Wake up." This time he laid his palm against her face and gently stroked her cheek. The dog burrowed in, throwing her small body against Alice. Between the two of them, they should be able to rouse the woman's mind from the dark corner where it was trapped.

Her lids fluttered open in the gloom. "Dark. It's so dark."

That, at least, he could remedy. Another crack of lighting showed him the candle on the bedside cabinet and the small tinderbox. He lit the wick and the gentle yellow flame flickered across her face.

Alice sat up and hugged her knees. Her body shook as though cold and Ewan did the only thing he could think of to help. He climbed onto the bed and drew her to him. The sobs dried up in her throat and her body went rigid.

Possibly this wasn't his best idea, but previously she had sought his embrace. Would she recognise him in her sleep-fuddled state?

If he talked to her, his voice might filter through. "It's dark because of the storm outside. The clouds are covering the moon and stars, but you are not alone. Both Eilidh and I are here for you. Your fierce wolf has guarded your sleep and fetched me to help chase away the nightmare."

He was about to let her go when she let out a sigh and her body relaxed. Her arms slid around him and her head dropped to his chest. He pulled the blanket up over both of them and then stroked her hair.

Eilidh settled next to them, her head on his legs as she kept a watch over her mistress. Minute by quiet minute, Alice stopped shaking.

"Sometimes it helps to talk about it, if you want to," he said.

She was quiet for so long he thought she had slipped back to sleep. The thunder eased away but rain pelted the house. Then she began to talk in a low whisper that would have been inaudible to a man, but his wolf raised its weary head in her presence and listened with acute ears.

"I usually sleep with the curtains open so there is always some light from either stars or moon. He kept me in the dark. That was my punishment when I resisted him or displeased him. He called it the box. A small room with no windows. I would press myself into a corner and cry. Sometimes I was there for days but it felt like eternity. Only reaching out to find the hands of a clock in his bedroom reminded me of the passage of time."

Ewan laid his cheek against the top of her head. "Did he ever rape you?"

Her body heaved with a deep sigh. "No. I used to fight him, and he would beat me until he managed to tear a fragment from my soul. Then, as he savoured the piece of me, he would find release and spill his seed on my flesh as I curled up in pain at his feet. He only wanted my soul, not my body."

Ewan was conflicted. While relieved that she hadn't been raped, he was outraged at how the demon had damaged her self-worth. For that infraction alone, Ewan would have delighted in taking days to shave slices from Hoth. It was cold comfort that Lady Miles' magic had served excruciating justice on the soul eater. She had concocted a spell that whittled away Hoth's flesh and bones for every slice he took from his victims' souls.

"No man could find me desirable anymore," she whispered.

How could Alice think that? He had refused her mistletoe kiss not because he didn't want to, but because with the wine flowing in his veins, he hadn't thought he would be able to stop once he started kissing her. When she had dangled the greenery before him, it had sparked a raw hunger that had charged through his body and roused his wolf.

Thinking back through the years, he remembered the season the young Alice came to London. She had been so fresh and vibrant. Like a flower about to bloom, and men had fought for who would be the one to pluck her. Hoth won and instead of cherishing a rare treasure, he had almost destroyed her.

Alice was still beautiful, but in a different way. The torture had marked her, made her stronger and yet haunting. This was a woman with a past that a man wanted to know. Her history made her appealing and roused his protective urges. The shadow in her eyes called to him. This woman had walked through a nightmare and emerged as something else.

"Tell me your nightmare, Ewan. What makes you wake in the middle of the night in a sweat?" she whispered against his skin.

Could he confess to her? Alice had laid herself bare to him and honour said he should reciprocate. But if he gave her a glimpse, it would be like putting a crack in his wall. One tiny split could undermine his entire defensive structure.

She is already within you. She is the water that breaches impenetrable walls, his mother whispered.

His fingers tangled in her short hair. "My nightmare is loving someone."

She glanced up, a frown creasing between her brows. "How is love a nightmare?"

How to articulate that love was to him what the dark was to her? Something he should fear. His wolf would never have a mate. "We hurt that which we love. If I loved someone, I would destroy them."

She laid a hand flat over his heart. "You don't know that."

"Yes, I do. It is a truth hidden in my bones. I will never love." He had hoped the lycanthrope sickness would burn away the taint of his family. But the monster that always dwelled within him had not budged when he took the bite.

He had seen what his father did in the name of love, and he and his brother were cut from the same cloth. Ewan knew what his family were capable of, so he protected both himself and some unfortunate woman by ensuring his heart stayed dormant. Cold. Untouched.

He could share pleasure. But never love.

10

Ewan

THE STORM RAN its course overnight. The next morning saw a spectacular sunrise, lit with riotous shades of pink and orange as the sun peered over the horizon and chased the clouds away. Ewan stirred from his comfortable position to find a sleeping woman curled up in his arms, a snoring terrier at his side, and a hitherto unknown sense of contentment in his soul. Even his wolf slept, a rarity since he'd been injured.

Ewan had not meant to stay the entire night. He intended to only linger long enough to see Alice fall back into a restful sleep. As he had waited for her eyelids to droop, he had told her tales that his mother used to tell him at bedtime, of daring adventures of mages from history and their magical battles.

Once she nodded off, he found he couldn't bring himself to move. He told himself he didn't want to disturb her. Then he whispered *liar*. He wanted her in his arms. He needed the sense of trust and understanding her slumbering form washed through him. Only holding her close soothed the agony that racked his wolf.

For a little while, he wanted to imagine what it would be like to love and be loved in return. What would it be like to find your wolf's mate, that one person who perfectly complemented your Unnatural soul and who would ignite a passion that would burn until death?

The colours of dawn spilled over the floor in the bedroom as though the window was stained glass. A rug in hues of brown and green covered the bare floorboards and reminded him of the leafy tops of mounded leeks peeking out of the earth. Ewan glanced around, but there was little to learn about the woman from Alice's room.

Sparse, he thought. He had seen more possessions in tents while on campaign. But then Alice had had nothing when they took her from Bedlam, and she seemed to spend her days running through fields and forest. It wasn't as though the young woman spent her days shopping and acquiring fripperies.

It bothered him that she had nothing here that looked worn or familiar. No little trinkets or objects that caught her fancy and nothing used to decorate the room apart from the rug and a vase of grasses and pussy willow. Her lack of personal possessions suggested that she somehow wasn't real and was only temporarily in this world. She was a forest sprite who ran through the woods but who left no footprint in the earth.

He slipped his arm out from under Alice and patted Eilidh, who had cracked one eye open and then closed it again. Then he padded across the worn rug and returned to his room. His mind remained fixated on Alice. Even away from her, he felt the press of her skin against him as he dressed. The faint rosemary and thyme scent of her hair drifted up to his nostrils. Every day he spent with her, she seeped deeper into his soul and mind.

An hour later down in the kitchen, Ewan opened the back door to let out the small, furry cannon ball that had barrelled down the stairs and shot across the floor. Then he sat at the pine table while Alice prepared the fragrant oil to massage his arm.

"Thank you, for last night," she whispered as she took her seat beside him and began the work.

"Eilidh fetched me to wake you. You should thank her." His shoulders dropped as she began with a general massage, working the oil into his muscle before she went deeper into the tendons.

"I do, every day. Just as I thank Quinn for giving her to me. But you gave me a different type of comfort when I most needed it." She poured more warmed oil into her hands as she took longer strokes from wrist to elbow.

He couldn't brush aside her thanks. He drew the woman from the grip of a nightmare, but in return she gave him something infinitely more valuable—a sense of peace and of being needed. "I would ride through Hell to free you if I could."

She looked up, her eyes bottomless pools of deep green that reminded him of the waterfall in their glade, or the finest piece of jade that seduced your hand to caress it.

"We are both in Hell, looking for our way out." She returned to stretching the tendons that held his hand captive.

He would make sure she broke free. It didn't matter if he sacrificed himself, as long as Alice finally made her way to the surface and lived a long and happy life.

His fingers showed the results of her work; each day they curled or straightened a little further. The deep ache in the ulna and radius bones lessened and relieved some of the pressure in his mind. At times, the combined assault on his senses from both the injuries and the silver poison in his blood nearly breached his self-control. He would have to stand still and draw a deep breath while he locked the pain away behind his barricade. Not for the first time, he pondered his decision to put off going to see the mages. He couldn't continue like this. Even if Alice's work helped, it was no permanent solution.

Alice's hands on his flesh created intimacy with her head bowed over his arm and her breath whispering over his skin. What would it be like to have her on her knees, tackling the deep ache in his thigh where the bullet leached its magical venom? Something he thought long dead stirred in his chest. He rubbed the spot in the centre of his sternum with his good hand, trying to disperse the sensation.

Their deal was that he would teach her to protect herself, and she would work on his physical injury to buy him a little more time. He didn't want anyone touching the wounds he carried deep inside. It was better that they were left to fester in the dark. Being incapable of love was safer; it meant no woman would ever suffer his family curse at his hands.

But this woman was rain on parched earth, and she seeped into the cracks to reach far below. Like the seedlings she tended with such care in the garden, she had planted a seed within him that unfurled and reached for her warmth.

He rubbed at his chest again as he remembered her asleep in his arms. Why couldn't he leave last night when he should have? Curious, but he would remain resolute to avoid any emotional entanglement. He simply felt a kinship with Alice after all she had been through, and it was nothing more.

In the very back of his mind, his wolf sniggered as though it knew something he did not.

LATER THAT DAY, Ewan rummaged in the tack room attached to the barn. Quinn had told him that what he sought would be found out there. Eventually, he spotted what he needed slung over a saddle on a high rack: old saddlebags. He used a broom to knock them down, and then headed back inside to find Alice.

He dropped the bags on the table. They were battered and worn, perfect for their needs. "We must think about our journey and what to pack. The nights are getting warmer and we should leave soon. We can only take what you can fit into the saddlebags."

Alice rubbed her hands down her apron. "I have very little, and the one thing I cannot leave behind would never fit in there."

He frowned. What could she want to bring that wouldn't fit in a saddlebag? He could only think of the large botany book, and that would be safer in Ianthe's parlour and would still be here when she returned. She wasn't a woman for jewellery or fine dresses, so he doubted it was an item of clothing. Although since they were heading to a larger town, perhaps he could take her shopping one day to buy something frivolous.

Then a flash of silver under the table caught his eye and he grinned. "Ah, of course. Eilidh."

He was a little relieved, too; the dog was a fierce protector of her mistress. The terrier would guard Alice when Ewan wasn't around. Alice's skill with a knife grew daily, and he suspected she used a touch of her aftermage gift to help the blade *find* its target. Ewan had no doubt any man who tried to harm her would find himself breathing through a new hole in his chest.

She bent down and fussed with the terrier. "Eilidh won't be any trouble, I promise. I will share my meals with her, so she won't take any extra food."

The lump in Ewan's chest moved and ached. The wolf pricked its ears, for it claimed the little dog as part of its pack and no member ever went hungry.

There were brief moments when he thought Alice had found her way out from the dark, and then she let something slip that tumbled everything around her. Did she really think he would begrudge her the dog's company or the small amount she would eat?

"Alice." He murmured her name. What could he say to quiet the demons that attacked her mind? "I would not dream of depriving you of Eilidh's company. Of course she must come with us."

Her head shook and one hand wiped at her face before she stood. "Thank you."

"Here." He held his arms open and she stepped to him. Her body gave a shudder and then she sighed. Not for the first time, he wondered for whose benefit he sought to hold her—hers or his?

After a moment, she pulled away, the faint trace of a smile on her lips. "I'll go pack now. It won't take me long."

Ewan stood immobile even after the kitchen door closed on her retreating form. Partial ideas struggled to coalesce in his mind. He had come to Northampton-shire to lick his wounds while he figured out his future. Now he added a new item to his list of objectives—a future for Alice.

He had joined the army at sixteen and knew no other life. The work as an agent of the Crown had suited his temperament, and then he found a new sort of brotherhood in the Highland Wolves. While his injuries removed him from active deployment, he hoped to show the War Office that a crippled spy could still be an effective one. Finding Forge was an opportunity to prove he could still undertake covert assignments outside of his regiment, even if the mages failed to cure him.

That left the issue of finding a path for Alice. Ewan knew wealthy matrons who might offer her a post as companion. But his mind baulked at the thought. Carrying another woman's parcels and reticule for the rest of her life would condemn Alice to a submissive role. Perhaps with her interest in plants and botany, she could find work with an apothecary?

Being mage blooded meant she could always find work using her gift, but that often meant a life on the fringes of society. While mages were ranked equivalent to a duke, it was an honour conferred to only the mage and did not flow to their descendants. The mage blooded were only accorded the position they were born with, meaning the village girl would always be seen as a poor, working class woman.

Any possible avenues of employment he came up with seemed too constrained to suit the new, emerging Alice. There was a wildness about her, and she needed to be free whatever she did. Perhaps a course of action would present itself while they were in Kent.

Thoughts were still circling in his mind as he went upstairs and packed his saddlebags. He took little, for what would an impoverished soldier have? Their wealth would rest in the two horses Quinn would procure on their trip to view the broodmares. The fewer physical possessions they had, the easier it would be to pass themselves off as persons in need of employment, either legitimate or not.

Ianthe and Quinn returned late that afternoon. Ianthe drove the gig with three horses tied behind. Quinn rode a plain-looking bay and led another near identical horse from it.

Ianthe beamed as she pulled her procession to a halt by the farmhouse. "I managed to procure two of the most amazing broodmares and one horrid thing that Quinn insisted on having."

Ewan held out his good hand to help Ianthe down while Quinn dismounted.

Quinn scowled at his mate, and then pointed to a gangly-looking chestnut that would have resembled a giraffe if you painted patches on it. "Look at her legs and deep chest. She'll breed winning racehorses, that one. You wait and see."

"The day you can win a race without killing yourself on one of these mad horses you seem Hell-bent on breeding, that will be the day I agree to marry you," Ianthe said.

Quinn grabbed her hand and kissed her palm. "There is a bet I most readily accept."

"And horses for us, I see." Ewan nodded to the two solid bays and curtailed the display of affection before the lovers got carried away.

"Plain and cheap, as you asked. And with an absolutely horrid, jarring trot, so it's just as well you don't have any plans for a family." Quinn winced as he walked. "There's also the clothing you requested."

"Let's get this lot settled and then we can all go inside for a drink. Quinn can regale you with how he's going to eat his hat when his horrid mare whelps a pup instead of a foal." Ianthe winked at her partner and untied her two broodmares.

11

Alice

THE DAY finally dawned when they would depart. Alice sat on the bed in her room and stared at her blank walls. A vase on the window ledge held bracts of pussy willow left over from winter. Their fat, furry heads made her smile. Would she return to this room to pick more pussy willow next winter?

Of course she would, even though they ventured to capture a dangerous creature. Both Ewan and Eilidh would guard her. Her fingers curled in the quilt—what was she doing about to embark on a dangerous mission with a man she had known only a few short months?

She rose and paced back and forth, debating with herself. She had spoken with such conviction about being included and going as support to Ewan. Now the day had arrived, and cold dread swirled in her stomach.

You need to do this to be free, a voice deep in her mind counselled. *You need to face what frightens you most in order to defeat it.*

"Yes," she whispered, and stopped before the window. The face reflected in the thick glass was no longer the face of a terrified girl. This was the face of a confident woman. Leaving the protective shelter of Ianthe was the first tear in her casing, and soon the new version of her would emerge.

Alice's hand went to her neck and the silver wolf, its head warmed by the contact with her skin. Each day she had tried using her mage blood to summon an object. So far she had managed to make an acorn on the table tremble but not move. It was a start, but would she ever be strong enough to draw a bullet through flesh and bone?

When you are free, you will be able to free Ewan, the voice said.

Strange, she would've thought at a time like this it would be her dead mother who offered her counsel, but this was the voice of another.

Turning the words over in her mind, Alice picked up her saddlebags and left her room. Her resolve waned as she descended the stairs and then helped saddle the horses. Doubts ate at her conviction and tore holes in her determination. Perhaps it was too soon. How easy it would be to run and to hide in the glade for another year or two. The idea of returning to village life with its crowd of people made her chest constrict, as though someone squeezed her lungs.

"The others don't think I can do this," Alice said to

Ewan as he double-checked the contents of his saddlebags.

Ewan glanced at Ianthe and Quinn and then back to Alice. "I think a bird doesn't know if it can fly until it leaps from the nest. You just need a little faith as you jump."

How did this man understand her so completely? His words rippled through her body, and a small piece of Alice's soul fell back into place. It didn't quite fit back into the shape where she had torn it from because the edges were worn and the patch was visible, but bit-by-bit she rebuilt herself.

No, transformed herself.

Ianthe broke away from the others. Tears shimmered in her eyes as she embraced Alice. "Do be careful. I will never forgive myself, or Ewan, if anything happens to you."

"The sight still has not given you any sign of our success?" Alice asked.

Ianthe shook her head. "I am blind and it terrifies me. I wish I had not ignored my gift all these years. Then I might have been able to command it to show me your safe return."

"We will prevail." Alice kissed her friend's cheek. She borrowed strength from Ewan and the unknown voice that whispered from the depths of her mind; they both believed she could undertake this journey, and that assuaged her doubts. "Thank you, Ianthe, for rescuing me and giving me a chance. Now I need to spread my wings and see if I can fly."

Ianthe held her at arm's length and screwed up her face. "Why couldn't you test your wings here?"

How could she explain it to her friend? She needed to embrace danger, to dare life to strike her down and to see what happened. If she faltered and fell, then she would pick herself up and try again. No one would beat her down this time. "Because it is too safe here. We will keep in touch; I am not going forever, after all. Only for a little while. And Seabrook is not *so* far away."

Ianthe stroked Alice's face, her brows pulled together and furrows on her forehead. "I just don't want to ever see you hurt again."

Alice smiled. "I know. But imagine if we can save other girls from what befell me. We both know Hoth was not the only demon in London. I will not stay tucked up here while such monsters prey on innocent women."

"You are a beautiful avenging angel, and I wish you luck." Ianthe kissed her and embraced her again.

Quinn gave her the gentle hug of an older brother. Then he whispered in her ear, "Believe in yourself, Alice. You are one of the strongest people I have ever met. Forge is no match for you."

She smiled, unsure what to say, and then Quinn gave her a leg up onto the saddle. She dropped a hand to the saddlebags and patted the contents—her mortar and pestle and a bag with herbs. She had one change of dress and little need for anything else, but she was determined to ease Ewan's pains.

A tiny part of her thought if she could only grow her

gift strong enough, she could cure his wolf that lingered near death inside him. She had seen Quinn shift into his beast, and she longed to see Ewan's powerful creature shake off the sickness and run free over the hills.

Alice settled in the saddle. Her brown plaid dress was made of plain, rough wool that would be able to withstand the harsh life they were about to lead. The skirt was fuller than what the fashionable set wore, and it allowed her to ride astride without exposing her whole leg. A large shawl could be wrapped around her upper body or used as a head scarf and would provide extra warmth. A battered bonnet of Sarah's now sat at a crumpled angle on Alice's head.

A pair of laced boots on her feet had nearly been the cause of an all-out battle. Alice liked to run barefoot through the fields and rarely wore shoes. Ianthe and Sarah insisted that if she were trekking across England in search of a traitorous vampyre, she simply had to wear boots. Alice sulked all afternoon, hiding in the barn with Eilidh, but had relented at length.

The clothes itched and she wore far too many layers after her life as a forest sprite dancing through the trees. She dimly recalled wearing expensive silk and the finest muslin when she had her brief time in the sun as a pampered courtesan. But now she knew only rough and dirty linen.

Their horses were as unremarkable as their clothing, the sort of lower class mounts that two down-on-their-luck types could afford. In deference to Ewan' injury, they would ride to their destination as no one expected him to walk across England.

Alice wondered that they didn't make do with the one horse. It wasn't uncommon for the man to ride while the woman trudged behind, carrying a load.

"Why two horses? Isn't that quite extravagant?" She wriggled her feet in the stirrups.

Ewan's back straightened in the saddle and he arched one black brow. "Did you really think I would ride and watch you walk?"

No. From the little she knew of him, he didn't seem to sort to let a woman trail behind his horse. Not unless there was a crowd of them and he was attempting to out-ride their pursuit.

"Are you ready?" Ewan picked up his reins in his left hand.

A bird doesn't know if it can fly until it leaps from the nest. Alice drew a deep breath, nodded, and jumped from her proverbial nest.

Ewan put heel to his horse, and the placid gelding walked down the road. Alice's mount followed as though an invisible rope tied the two together. Ewan waved once then kept his gaze on the middle distance. Alice turned in her saddle to watch the farmhouse and Ianthe until they both disappeared. It would always represent a safe haven to her, and she hoped they would return before too long.

Eilidh thought they embarked on a great adventure. She ran back and forth across the road, and when her little legs grew tired, Ewan picked her up to ride in front of Alice's saddle.

It was nearly a hundred and fifty miles from Ianthe's secluded farm in Northamptonshire to the small coastal town of Seabrook, just up the coast from Hythe in Kent. It would take them at least three days on the road to reach their destination. Days they would use to grow into their pretence of a married couple. It also allowed time for Alice to work on Ewan's disguise as she practised concealing his handsome features.

To minimise how much magic she had to use, most of the disguise hinged on him embracing a scruffy appearance far removed from his usual immaculate grooming. He grumbled and scratched at the growth on his chin.

Alice wondered how he would cope after a few days on the road without bathing and had to suppress a laugh. "You know you cannot shave. You are supposed to look rough and dirty."

He narrowed his gaze at her. "I hate it. It itches."

"How long did it take you to dress when you were in London? I can't believe I married such a dandy." She rolled her eyes and giggled, then slapped a hand over her mouth. Where did that noise come from? There were days when her mosaic soul seemed lighter in Ewan' presence and she could laugh.

He narrowed his eyes but stopped his hand as it was about to scratch his chin again. "You'd complain if I kissed you. Women prefer a clean shaven man, not one who leaves a rash on their skin."

Why did he have to say that? It reminded her of Christmas night when she had tried to steal a kiss from him. Her heart raced a little faster and she stared at Eilidh as she imagined being the woman he swept into his arms and kissed. Alice remembered pleasure, and a man like Ewan Shaw knew exactly how to deliver it. She recalled the talk that swirled around the handsome cavalry officer and heard of the notes slipped from the hand of wealthy women into his pockets.

They rode all day with only occasional stops to spell their horses. Ewan set a hard pace and the light was fading before they decided to seek shelter for the night. They were far from any village or tavern, but spotted a rickety old barn just off the road for their first night alone.

They unsaddled the horses and let them loose in an overgrown yard. Alice found an old bucket and filled it with water from the well. Meanwhile, Ewan found a discarded sack and stuffed it with mouldy hay. Then he propped it up against the far wall inside the barn.

"Target practice," he said when she asked. "We have time for a small amount before we lose the light."

She threw the knife and Ewan made a campfire in the barn doorway. Eilidh stretched out by the flames and promptly went to sleep. Soon, the light faded and the target blurred into the wooden planks of the wall. Alice put away the blade and sat by Ewan on the ground. He had unrolled their blankets and laid them close to the fire, but inside the barn in case of rain.

They ate a cold meal of bread, cheese, and meat that Ianthe had packed for them, and Ewan tossed slivers of beef to Eilidh.

"You are quite turning her head," Alice said. The little terrier was becoming devoted to Ewan and her ears pricked up whenever she heard his voice or slightly uneven tread.

Ewan tore the last piece of meat in half then popped one piece into his mouth and held out the remainder to the dog. "It is the wolf way, to share all we have with the pack."

"Are we your pack, Ewan?" Alice's heart constricted. *Pack* held connotations that seemed as strong as family.

"We are for this journey." He tossed another piece of wood onto the fire.

Dark soon descended, and there was little to do except watch the flames dancing in their small fire. When Alice lay down on the rich smelling hay, she could watch the stars through the holes in the barn roof.

"How we have both fallen from being fêted as London's darlings," Ewan murmured from beside her.

Alice didn't miss those days. She preferred the silence of a forest and the protective embrace of an ancient tree to a noisy assembly room. "I would far rather have stars over my head than any painted ceiling."

"What made you seek your fortune in London?" His voice was quiet in the dark.

So many things were softly spoken between them. Whispers of secrets were passed back and forth as glimpses into their broken souls that would never be shown to anyone else.

Alice smiled at long ago memories. It didn't seem like a lifetime ago, it seemed like someone else's life entirely. As though she read the tale of that doomed young woman in a book. "There are few employment prospects for the daughters of witches. Society applauds mages, but the mage blooded are as welcome as bastard offspring."

He exhaled a deep breath. "Aftermage or Unnatural, we are all rejected by society. Parliament only recently gave us the same rights as other British citizens. Until the Unnatural Act passed in 1812, we were less than human under the law, cursed creatures to be hunted and shunned. Although not burned at the stake like your predecessors."

There was an intimacy to lying beside Ewan, gazing at the midnight sky above as she continued to narrate her downfall. "If I am not too bold in saying so, I was a somewhat charming girl, but also a practical one. After mother died, I set out to capitalise on the best asset I possessed—myself. I intended to use my gift to find a wealthy patron, live in a lavish townhouse, and have servants."

"Sometimes our plans go awry." His voice dropped in tone.

Alice found comfort in Ewan, but no pity. What had happened could not be undone. Not even the most powerful mage could reverse time, and there was no benefit in dwelling on past events, wishing things had unfolded differently.

"Indeed. My plans went awry. I thought Viscount Hoth the answer to my prayers, but he turned out to be a nightmare in disguise."

But the demon taught her a lesson. Never again would a man, mage, or Unnatural hurt her.

"What of you, Ewan? What was the dashing cavalry officer doing in London, and how did you become a lycanthrope?" She was curious how he came to walk a path like hers.

"I was an officer in the Scots Greys, but we languished on home duty. I made my own excitement by volunteering for confidential assignments. Charming, wealthy, older women allowed me access to a number of conspiracies and secrets crammed into the parlours of London. My captain and I were approached about being the first of a new regiment to be made of Unnaturals who would fight for England on foreign soil. All I had to do was hold still while a crazed beast tore half my throat out."

"Why would you volunteer for that?" It sounded horrible and gruesome. What man would sign up for such a fate . . . but then what woman would blindly agree to belong to a soul eater?

"Because I sought escape." He fell silent and said no more.

What extremes they had taken to escape their situations. They lay side by side and watched the stars twinkle above. Alice thought it would be impossible to sleep with his body so close to hers. But at some point exhaustion crept up on her and whisked her away to slumber.

The next thing she knew, Eilidh's wet nose pressed into her cheek. She opened her eyes on the faintest blush of pink chasing the stars away as another day dawned.

12

Ewan

DAYS on the road would make the most placid person grumpy. It wasn't the time in the saddle that ate at Ewan, for he was used to long hours on horseback. But the itch between his shoulder blades nearly made him lose his temper. Blasted clothes probably had fleas or lice. Quinn would have thought it highly amusing to purchase infected attire for the mission. Even in wolf form, Ewan was fastidiously clean and spent as much time grooming his fur as a bored house cat. He longed for a hot bath and a stout brush to scrub himself clean.

This particular mission couldn't be over soon enough for him. Then the clothes would be tossed on a bonfire, and he would run naked to the closest bath house and barber. He cast a sideways glance at Alice.

The woman never complained or uttered a cross word. She simply bore everything without complaint.

Guilt gnawed at his insides. He had tried to escape his heritage and didn't want to become a hard man like his father who would push a woman too far. Or worse, did Alice feel unable to complain, afraid of his reaction? The fragile woman had never spent so long in the saddle, and each time they stopped, she clung to the neck of her horse to slowly lower herself to the ground.

She caught his gaze and smiled. "Stop fretting about me. My bottom went numb the first day and I haven't felt anything since."

He shook his head. Her appearance fooled him. She was nowhere near as fragile as she looked. As she'd said, she was the spider web that appeared delicate but could hold a struggling insect fast. "I'm sorry for the pace of our journey, but we should make Hythe today."

"I know this is no relaxed jaunt. I won't break down on you or dissolve into tears." She rode with a weary smile and her hands held the reins limply. Not that there was a need to direct her mount—it mimicked Ewan's horse in pace and direction.

Her lack of complaint worried him. She would say nothing as he drove her into the ground. If a woman didn't give a man limits, how did he know when he pushed too far? There was something for him to mull over as they rode. Even Eilidh was subdued. The dog rode with her mistress more often than not as the terrier's seemingly boundless energy hit its limit.

Finally, their hard pace was rewarded when Hythe, the small coastal market town on the edge of the

Romney Marsh, appeared in the distance. Cottages and houses appeared at more regular intervals on both sides of the road. People walked, rode, or drove carts around them.

"Hythe," Alice murmured. "Ianthe said it means 'haven', or 'landing place'. I wonder which it will prove to be."

Ewan halted by a large tree that offered dappled sunlight. Alice had worked a low level enchantment to change his hair from pitch black to a dark brown and his eyes to a similarly muddy hue. She also added flesh to his lean, muscled form. It shocked him the first time he stared into water and a stranger stared back. "Why would you marry such an ugly fat brute?" he had asked her.

"Since it is my working, I can see through it." She looked at him so intensely he wondered if she didn't see right through him to the wounded wolf cowering in his gut. "Don't forget it will wear off over the course of the day. I do not have the ability to make it last longer."

Her claims to simply smudge his edges were more effective than he thought. His own mother wouldn't recognise him now. "I need to see my contact first. Why don't you wait here with Eilidh? I won't be more than an hour."

The town was a mishmash of medieval and Georgian buildings, overlooked by a Norman church perched on the hill. The picturesque place even boasted a charming seafront promenade. The fortunate town had benefited from the war with France. The Royal Military Canal was constructed as a defence and brought much-needed employment and capital to the area.

Ewan left Alice and the terrier sitting under a tree and walked to a cottage on the edge of town. He identified it by its white picket fence that had one grey picket, a signal that the occupant used to be a member of the Scots Grey, Ewan's former regiment.

Ewan exchanged only the minimum number of words with the man who opened the door. Enough passed to identify himself, then the retired soldier fetched a letter for Ewan and shut his door again.

As he walked back along the road, Ewan opened the letter and scanned the contents. The excise man knew of several smuggling gangs operating along the Kent coastline. Most brought in the usual smuggled spirits, but one group had dark rumours swirling about it, even for a band of smugglers.

A drunk local muttered one night of his boss having an unnatural appetite for blood. His drinking buddies scoffed, but next day he was found dead on the beach with an ugly neck wound and his body drained of blood.

Ewan tucked the letter into his jacket and returned to Alice. "We are nearly at our destination. We only need to ride about another three miles up the coast towards Seabrook. We're looking for a tavern called the Dancing Sow."

The tavern was where the dead man had been drinking before he met his fate, and it was where Ewan would start his search.

Forge had been an odd man even when alive. He

preferred to frequent the lowest class of tavern he could find, preferably the sort full of cutthroats and thieves. By contrast, vampyres were known as French dandies with their love of fashion and the high life. Did stilling his heart give Forge a new taste for luxurious living, or would he stick to his old proclivities?

The tavern they sought was far enough from Hythe to offer seclusion but not too far that it would affect distributing contraband to other counties. It was the sort of quiet location ideal for smuggling in a magical weapon to use against the British on home soil. The problem with the monstrosities created by the mages was spotting them. The weapon was unlikely to be a large and unwieldy cannon or a type of land battleship. It could be something tiny and unassuming like buttons for men's clothes or the pitcher used to pour your ale.

Alice picked up the dog and placed her in front of the saddle before hauling herself back up. "At the risk of pandering to your cleanliness obsession, I do find myself longing for a hot bath."

Ewan laughed. "Watch out, you'll be hankering for clean clothes next."

His body ached as though he had travelled through the bowels of Hell, and he suspected Alice hurt just as bad with muscles unused to days in the saddle. A bath was a fine idea, except the sort of establishment they were seeking probably wouldn't have one on offer.

It took hardly any time to make Seabrook and they soon found the tavern, a two-storeyed building with a Tudor whitewashed façade and thatched roof. A pig dancing a jig graced the sign swinging over the front door, the paint faded from years of rough weather rolling off the ocean.

The smoke curling from the tavern's chimneys could have appeared warm and welcoming, but this establishment had an aura of neglect. The whitewash was long overdue a repaint and the walls were sooty and grey with dirt. The small windows were dim and lined with grime and gave no clue of what lay inside. The bare dirt yard around the inn looked like it would turn to mud with the lightest rain. Chickens scratched through the dirt and a mangy cat stalked behind them.

"I think the horses will be slaughtered for meat before we cross the threshold," Alice said as they dismounted.

"Keep your knife close," Ewan whispered in her ear as he took the reins and looped them over the hitching rail. It seemed Forge stuck to type even as a vampyre. Or more likely he needed to remain invisible while on English soil. Leasing a fine house and hosting regular dinner parties would rather call attention to him. But then so did leaving a drained man on the beach. Mayhap he had thought the tide would carry the body out to sea.

"Stay with the horses, Eilidh, and bark if anyone approaches." Alice held up a hand and waited until the dog sat on the ground by the geldings.

Ewan played up his limp, dragging his left leg as they entered the dim interior. A smoky haze clung to the upper third of the room and over time had stained the whitewash yellow. Candles dripped from a variety of mismatched light fittings hanging from the ceiling. Conversation rose and fell from the few patrons huddled in dark corners. Tables around the edge were set into booths with built-in bench seats. Railings emerged from the top of the seat backs to create the illusion of privacy.

Several large tables occupied the main floor with long bench seats for communal dining. A bar of ancient wood ran the length of one wall, the surface blackened from decades of hands and filth crossing its surface. Ewan leaned his good arm on the bar and peered over.

"Can I help you?" a woman asked. She wore a cream apron over her dress and wiped a glass on one corner before setting it down. Her face was lined with years of worry, and the stray wisps of hair peeking out from under her cap were as grey as the exterior of the tavern. Deep lines radiated away from the corners of eyes the colour of chocolate.

Ewan was relieved to see she appeared clean and tidy, even if the outside of the inn was not. "My wife and I are new to the area and we're looking for rooms. Do you have any space available?"

She narrowed her gaze and assessed Ewan and Alice as though she could tell the contents of their pockets by the way their jackets hung. "How long do you plan on staying?"

"We plan to settle here if we can find work. We are looking for a fresh start now that Sean has been discharged from the army." Alice stepped closer to Ewan, tucking herself against his side. Alice retained her name, but they decided on Sean for Ewan, since he was known to Forge.

The woman's face lightened with interest. "A fresh start? Well, you're a pretty wee thing—are you also a hard worker?"

Alice glanced at Ewan before answering. "I certainly am."

The older woman pursed her lips then seemed to make up her mind about something. "We're short-staffed here. One of the girls got herself in the family way and had to leave. It's hard work but honest, if you're willing. There's a small cottage out back if you want it. I can deduct the rent from your wages, if you can pay the first week up front."

Ewan laid some coins on the counter and slid them over. "That ought to cover our first week."

The money was swept off into her hand and disappeared into the woman's pocket. "Welcome to the Dancing Sow family. I'm Mrs McGaffin, but most people call me Gaffie. I run this place with my boy, Jimmy, and his wife, Daisy."

Alice held out a hand to Gaffie. "Thank you for the opportunity. I'm Alice. And this is my husband, Sean Evans."

"You wouldn't happen to have a bath, would you? We've been on the road for days." Ewan plastered his most winning smile on his face.

The innkeeper blushed and seemed lost for words for a moment or two. Apparently his smile worked even when his usual features were made coarser by Alice's spell. That was reassuring to know. He was tempted to try it on Alice just to see if she would blush too.

Gaffie nodded. "You'll have to heat your own water, but there's a tin bath out back you can take into the cottage and a good supply of coal and wood for your fire."

"You are a goddess of comfort, Gaffie." He took her hand and placed a kiss on her knuckles.

The woman giggled, a noise quite at sorts with her appearance. "Get on with you. I'll have Daisy show you where things are."

"Thank you, madam." If he kept charming the locals like this and winning their support, he could have Forge captured by suppertime tomorrow.

"Daisy! Come show these folks to the cottage out back. And find the bath," Gaffie yelled through a doorway by the bar.

A woman no older than Alice appeared from out back. Daisy was on the slightly short and plump side, with long, lank hair tied back at her nape and a tired expression in her brown eyes.

"This way." She led them through the main room of the tavern and around the side. Out the back of the tavern were the stables laid out in an L-shape and making two sides of a large courtyard. In the middle of the yard was a stone well. Horses stuck their heads over the half doors of their stables as they passed, and one stall was home to a cow. A squat pigsty ran along the end wall of the barn, and squealing and snuffling came from behind its walls.

Ewan prayed they weren't going to be situated next

to the pigs. He might be undercover, but he still had some standards. Thankfully the lass took them to the small wattle and daub cottage next to the stables. It only had one room, but the fire would heat the space and they would have privacy out here. In a tavern, all the walls had ears.

"I'll fetch clean blankets for the bed, then I'll help you carry the bath over. There's both wood and coal stored behind the stables that you can use for your fire," Daisy said then retreated back to the main building.

"I'll set the fire first, then find pots and draw some water," Alice said.

A bath was on both their minds. The more Ewan thought about bathing, the more his body itched as though lice ran over his skin. "I'll fetch the horses and Eilidh."

It took time to make the cottage passably comfortable. First, the dirty floor needed sweeping. Alice did that while the fire built its base of embers. Daisy returned with a pile of blankets, and then she and Alice carried the tin bath over from the stables.

Alice filled pots with water from the well and set them on the cast iron plate of the stove to heat. That gave them time to unsaddle and brush the horses. Eilidh sniffed in all the corners of their new home, and then sneezed.

"Not the cleanest, girl, but we shall make do." Ewan ruffled the dog's ears.

Alice continued the monotonous work of pouring one pot into the bath and then heading outside to refill it with cold water from the well. By the time the bath was full and ready, they had seen to the horses, swept the cottage, made the bed, and almost settled into married life.

Almost because Ewan was left contemplating the awkward bath question. In another lifetime, he quite enjoyed watching a woman bathe, but that was when he could recline on a divan with an exquisite glass of wine and watch the show.

Honour dictated that Alice bathe first, but it didn't seem right to stay in the room while she did. The tiny cottage lacked sufficient space for them to avoid each other. Even the sole bed was barely big enough for two, but his bones ached at the mere thought of sleeping on the hard ground for weeks on end.

He was still watching steam curl off the water when she returned.

"Are you mesmerised by the thought of being clean?" she whispered from beside him.

He huffed a quiet laugh. "It will take several baths, a massage, and a shave at the best baths in London to ever make me feel clean again. But no, I was thinking I would go for a walk while you have your bath."

She poked at the fire and tossed on another scoop of coals. "It's cooling off out there, and I doubt a walk would be good for your leg. You need a decent soak for the heat to work through to the bone. I won't be long; a quick dip, and I shall report for work in the tavern."

"I wanted to afford you what little privacy I can." He gestured to their cramped quarters.

She gave that sad little smile that made his chest

ache and his wolf whimper. Then she reached up and started to unbutton her dress. "I am no stranger to being naked in front of a man. And I would feel safer knowing you were close by."

Well, he certainly wasn't going to stare at her like a fifteen-year-old boy encountering his first naked woman. He turned his back and studied the scant contents of his saddlebags until he heard the splash of water and her soft murmur.

At least the tub was small. She had her knees pulled to her chest, so there was little flesh visible. But what he did see was slick perfection. He had expected to see her back laced with scars from her time with Hoth. But she was unmarked.

She looked around as she reached out for the soap and flannel sitting on the nearby chair. "He was always careful when he beat me. Cuts, bruises, and even small breaks all heal—anything too deep would permanently damage his property. It wouldn't do to be seen out with something that appeared less than perfect on his arm. That would reflect badly on him."

"I'm sorry, I didn't mean to stare." Yet again, she peered into his mind and plucked out his intent. Was this what it felt like when he read the thoughts of others that they had written so clearly in their faces?

One shoulder lifted in a shrug as she ran the soap over wet skin. "We both have histories we seek to conceal, but in hiding we only make others more curious."

If he was going to stand around and talk, then he may as well perform a useful task. "I'll wash your hair," he offered. Then he found a small jug and pulled up a chair behind the tub.

"Thank you." Alice scrubbed at her hands and fingernails while Ewan poured water over her head.

Hairdressing would never be his forte, especially not with his injured hand. He managed to wash and rinse Alice's short hair well enough to satisfy his own standards.

He took the hint when she wrapped her hands around the edge of the bath and looked around. He fetched a towel and held it up like a screen as she stepped from the bath, and then he wrapped the cloth around her.

Her smile of thanks was shy and a tiny bit awkward, but they were coping with the intimacy. Coping? He lied to himself constantly. Her presence gave him quiet contentment. Alone with Alice, he could breathe; she saw beneath his façade and he had no need of his practised looks. If he dared an honest inspection of his motive, he knew the truth he would find—he enjoyed the intimacy between them. Relished it, even, savouring every moment.

There was danger in becoming too comfortable with their roles; he might not want it to end.

13

Alice

ALICE WONDERED why she even bothered having a quick dip in the tub; the very air in the tavern was dirty and dank and would surely coat her clean skin by the end of the night. The clientele looked like they marinated in filth. The men had worn faces, greasy hair, and blackened hands as they clutched their tankards of ale.

How she would survive in this world? The dark nightmare that destroyed her sanity had come to life and spread to her waking moments. In her rising panic, every man was potentially an Unnatural demon who would torture her while whittling away her essence.

Then a man entered the tavern with a small black shape attached to his leg, and she knew how she would find her way forward. Man and canine took a seat in a corner and the pressure in her mind eased, and she let out a long held breath.

Find my sanctuary, she asked of her gift, and it centred on Ewan and Eilidh. No matter where she moved in the tavern, she felt their presence and it soothed her panic. This Unnatural man would protect her from any threat, and if she needed further reassurance, she had only to touch the wolf's head around her neck.

Ewan opened his small poetry book, and while he appeared to read, from under his brows he tracked Alice. He was her wolf protector if she needed one. Eilidh huddled close to his legs under the table. The little terrier might hate the tavern, but she would not leave her mistress.

Alice drew a deep breath and prepared for the battle ahead. More than bringing a traitor to justice, she fought for the inner peace that would only come when she found the last piece of her soul. She also fought for the touch of the man who hid in the gloom. There was the truth she had come to learn over their days travelling together. Her body and soul craved the quiet moments when Ewan held her. Yet he seemed unmoved by her, as though she pined for the attention of a marble statue.

Was she a foolish girl, pinning her affections on the first man who showed her kindness? *No*, the voice whispered. She understood him in ways others could not. Ewan hid from his past, and Alice peered into the cracks others didn't see. Just as she needed to face her demons to reclaim her life, so Ewan needed to confront whatever lay in his history. He just didn't know that Alice intended to free him as well as herself.

A tiny piece of her had hoped she would be the mate to his wolf. It seemed an extraordinary type of thing when Ianthe spoke of the deep bond between her and Quinn. Yet from what she recollected, Ianthe said the wolf always knew innately and was single minded in securing the love of its mate. Ewan showed no romantic interest in Alice. Did that prove she could not be anything of significance to his wolf?

As she returned to the bar with her tray full of empty mugs, another presence gave her comfort. The slight weight of the knife strapped to her ankle. Ewan frowned when she suggested putting it higher up her thigh. *Too hard to reach in a hurry*, he had said, and then pointed to her calf instead.

Not that she wanted to think about having to use it. There was a world of difference between throwing a knife at a barn wall or sack stuffed with hay and plunging it into the warm, living body of another person. She wanted to become the blade, but could she use one in a pinch?

She dropped the tray on the bar and wiped her brow on the corner of her apron. Her first night was proving to be quite a trial. She didn't know if it was the hot, crowded tavern making her sweat or the need to constantly reinforce her mental armour just to make it between tables.

Daisy joined her at the bar as Gaffie refilled the pitchers.

"I wish my Jimmy would look at me the way your

man does." Daisy sighed and leaned her elbows on the counter.

"I'm not sure what you mean." Alice turned and glanced at Ewan. While she saw the handsome man, others saw the nondescript fellow she blurred over his features. Did they give themselves away by how he kept watch?

Gaffie chuckled. "Your man reminds me of the farmers who drag themselves in over autumn. Those lads work all the daylight hours getting in the harvest before winter hits. After dark they come in here, exhausted and parched. When you drop a full tankard in front of them, they have the same look in their eye as your Sean. They savour it for a moment before drinking deeply to satisfy their thirst."

"Oh," Alice said. Her mind slowly processed the comparison. Then her eyes widened, for surely they must be mistaken. Ewan didn't look at her like *that*. Did he? She snuck another peek.

Daisy sighed. "He looks a fine fellow too. I bet he has quite the form under those clothes, despite his injuries."

Alice wondered at the state of Daisy's marriage that she was casting eyes at Ewan and making such comments after their brief acquaintance. She hoped her hiding spell was holding up. Daisy shouldn't see the lean, handsome man but the nondescript, fleshy one. Although there was something about the way he carried himself. Whatever his outward appearance, he emitted an aura of quiet menace, and a man who exuded trouble had an intoxicating appeal to some women.

Now that Alice thought about it, she didn't want other women mooning over Ewan, even if their arrangement was pretend. She had so little in this world and would jealously guard her moments with him. The tug on her ankle reminded her of the knife's presence. That would entertain the locals if she drew a blade and told the other woman to stay away from her man.

With some effort, Alice returned her mind to why she was now a barmaid in a dingy tavern. They were in Seabrook for one particular reason, and there was no time like the present to guide conversation in the needed direction. "The injuries have affected Sean's pride, though. It's hard for him to sit there while I work to put a roof over our heads."

"Even able-bodied lads are finding the going hard. Many a man has returned from the war only to find honest work thin on the ground." Gaffie dropped two full pitchers on the trays.

Alice smiled and met the tavern owner's gaze. "Waiting around for honest work won't put food in your stomach. Sean is resourceful with a keen mind, and he would do anything to provide for us. Legality doesn't matter when a man's self-worth is at stake."

Gaffie made a noise in her throat and shared a look with Daisy. Then her gaze narrowed on Alice. "I'll talk to Jimmy. He may know of something that would give your man a task to keep his mind off his aches."

The first step to finding the smuggling ring might now be under way. "Thank you, you are so kind to us."

Alice picked up the full pitcher and launched herself back into the crowded floor. Part of her job was to ensure the men's mugs stayed topped up. The other part was navigating a clear course through an ocean of grasping hands. The men resembled octopi, for they seemed to have hands everywhere as she brushed past.

Alice wondered if one among them was Forge. Quinn and Ewan had struggled to give her a description, the man nondescript and average as though he wove his own hiding spell to conceal his appearance. He could be any one of those crammed inside the tavern or, more likely, none of them. The vampyre wouldn't have any need of ale or a plain pub meal, and a man sitting with nothing before him would stick out in the tavern.

She wanted this mission over and done with so she could return to Northamptonshire, but she also wanted to keep the pretence going. If it took weeks or months to track down Forge, would Ewan grow used to calling her his wife and climbing into bed with her at night? Would the line between reality and the fiction they enacted blur?

Could an injured wolf learn to love a broken witch?

"Come on, lovely, spend some time with ole Pete," one man said as he reached out and grabbed her waist. His friends laughed and waved their mugs.

For a brief moment, panic bubbled in her chest at the unwanted contact. Then Alice remembered Ewan's words. She retreated to the safe haven in her mind and shut the fear and loathing outside. That enabled her to ignore the creeping touch and smile kindly on the foul-smelling gent. Then she brushed his hand away.

"I'm afraid you would turn my head and ruin me for other men," she said.

"Turn your stomach more like!" another man shouted, and the table burst into laughter.

The men held out their tankards and Alice filled them from the pitcher before she moved on to the next table.

As night lengthened outside the grimy windows, more men tramped through the front door. Some looked weary, as though they had worked hard all day. Others sought escape in the bottom of a bottle. A few women spun through the crowd, looking to earn a few coins. One peddled her aftermage skill of reading palms, and another offered to talk to dead loved ones. If that failed to elicit any pennies, they were open to a quick swive up against the wall outside in the chill night.

A few men stopped at Ewan's corner to find out more about the stranger in their midst. It was past midnight when the crowd began to thin. Men staggered home to waiting wives, some draped an arm around a local girl who would keep them warm for an hour or two, and others trod the sagging stairs to the upstairs rooms.

As the tavern emptied of the last few men, Alice took off her dirty apron and ran a hand through her hair. The thought of dropping exhausted into bed had never seemed so appealing.

"Do you need a hand cleaning up?" Alice asked of the owner, fervently hoping Gaffie said no.

"Not tonight, love," Gaffie said. "You're worked hard today, why don't you see that man of yours off to bed now?"

"Thank you, I will. Goodnight," she called.

"See you in the morning, love. You'll find us in the kitchen out back, when you're ready," Gaffie said as she piled mugs on a tray to be washed.

Alice followed a waiting Ewan out the door. He leaned heavily on his walking stick, dragging his left foot as Eilidh danced on ahead. The dog ran on and wove amongst the trees to one side of the tavern as they headed to the little cottage across the yard.

Alice didn't mind the cramped room they shared, or the trek across the yard in the chill night air to reach it. Their isolation away from the main building afforded them the privacy to discuss their plans without people in the next room overhearing.

Once inside, Alice lit a candle, Eilidh darted over to the warm fireplace, and Ewan dropped the bolt across the door. The room held a bed, a table and three chairs, and little else. The furniture was tired and worn, like the occupants of the tavern. Eilidh settled and watched with her head resting on her paws.

Alice dropped into a chair and slipped off her shoes. She wiggled her toes as Ewan blew on the embers to revive the fire.

"Tonight I think I walked as many miles as we rode to get here." Alice lifted one foot onto her knee and rubbed the spot that ached in the sole.

Ewan took up the poker and prodded the remains of the fire, stirring the embers into life before tossing on a shovelful of coal. Eilidh wagged her tail and showed her approval as the growing flames threw out warmth. Satisfied with the fire, Ewan took a seat opposite Alice.

"Remember they cannot harm you, Alice." Ewan' voice was low, almost a whisper in the near dark. The single candle flickered on the table and cast his face in shadow.

"I'm sure it will become easier with time, and it helps to know that you and Eilidh watch out for me." After her years of isolation, the press of the tavern had nearly overwhelmed her. Ewan was her anchor, the constant in the corner of the room that kept her from fleeing. The fear had clawed up her gullet when the first man had smacked her bottom. Memory flooded back and she had had to bite back a whimper. Then she had looked up to find Ewan's steady gaze on her and she knew she was not alone.

No more fear.

"How was your first night? Did you learn anything?" Local men had come and gone at his table. There had been a few laughs and even more quiet conversations.

"I have put out the word that I am looking for work. Preferably of the questionable and not entirely legal sort that earns more coin. I also dropped into conversation that I happened to know a customs man who had money troubles." Ewan flexed his arm. His fingers moved much easier now, and the tone was returning to his forearm. It would never be perfect, and his body constantly battled the silver taint inside him, but the strength in his hand improved. "Tomorrow I'll ride along the coast and see who I encounter."

The Kent coastline had developed a reputation for smuggling as men returned from war with empty pockets and no employment to sustain them.

Alice's feet ached. She could roam barefoot for miles over the countryside, but put her in boots and treading floorboards, and her feet protested. Earning your coin on your back was less exhausting. "I had a quiet word with Daisy and Mrs McGaffin and mentioned you were looking for any sort of employment, legal or not. Gaffie is going to talk to her son, Jimmy. I have the impression he is on the wrong side of the law."

"Let us hope the hints we drop lead us to the right smugglers. Ours will be less concerned with French brandy than importing the enemy's magical weapon— whatever it may be." Ewan dropped his jacket over the back of a chair and pulled off his Hessians.

"But if it is magical, the weapon could very well be the brandy. Wouldn't that be the perfect disguise for it?" Alice struggled to keep her eyes open as bed called her name. "I think I will turn in. I need to sleep since I will be walking a hundred miles again tomorrow night."

Hour by hour they learned to live together. Such a cramped space forced intimacy, and it was hard to undress without seeing each other. Ewan turned his back as Alice slipped off her dress and short stays. Likewise, Alice averted her gaze as he removed his shirt.

Well, she looked a little. He was a finely crafted specimen. To ignore a disrobed Ewan would be akin to ignoring a statue from ancient Rome. It just didn't seem right.

Ewan refused to take the bed, leaving that for Alice. He laid out his bedroll by the fire and settled down. Alice carried the candle over and set it on a chair positioned by the bed.

"Good night," she whispered as she slipped under the blankets. Eilidh jumped up and took her usual position next to Alice.

She didn't hear if Ewan answered; exhaustion had already swept her away.

14

Ewan

EWAN AWOKE to a flashback of a dead horse tumbling over him, pinning his wolf to the ground as pain engulfed his body. Then the pressure shifted. As he opened his eyes, he saw Eilidh get up from his side and pad to the door. No dead horse, just a terrier who felt like one. How did Alice sleep with the dog burrowed against her?

The damn floor was harder than the cold ground they had slept on for days, and his damaged body took exception to his position. He sucked in a breath as he tried to roll over and fire radiated out from the bullet lodged in his leg. He needed to find a mattress, or he would be a cripple by the end of the week.

"Tonight you either sleep in the bed with me, or I

will lie on the floor next to you." Alice's voice came from outside his line of sight.

He would have grumbled, but his mind was distracted trying to dampen the pain coursing through his body. "Very well."

With a Herculean effort, he managed to sit up. He rubbed his hands over his face. It was probably too early to seek relief in liquor, although that would add to his seedy reputation.

"I'm going to make you something for the pain." Alice poked at the embers in the grate and revived the fire. Then a few strides of shapely ankles went past his view as she went to the door to let out a patient Eilidh.

"No laudanum." He hated the stuff. He'd seen people give up the will to live, lost in a haze induced by the poppy syrup.

"It won't be laudanum." She pulled the bag of herbs from a shelf and then fetched the tiny pestle and mortar. The morning light through the window illuminated her outline in the thin shift as she ground a handful of herbs.

He pondered how well a spider web described her. At first glance, one would think her delicate with her slender build and not enough flesh on her bones. But then one would see the curve of muscle, the way she walked like a fluid cat, and would realise she was all hidden strength.

What would it be like to run his hand up naked skin, over the hill of her hip and into the valley of her waist before cresting a firm mound? She was made for pleasure, like him, and what heights they could reach together. His wolf uttered a rasp of agreement. Even as it fought its own battle with agony, it roused at the idea of naked play with Alice.

Ewan shook his head to dispel the vision before she turned around to find him staring. Again.

Alice had known last night when his gaze roamed her bare back. Perhaps her finding gift allowed her to latch onto wayward thoughts flung from his mind.

He pulled his legs further under him to discover his left leg wasn't the only stiff part of him this morning. That would teach him, although contemplating more pleasurable activities had distracted his mind from the ache deep in his bones. He levered his body up into a chair and tried to dislodge the cramps in his neck and shoulders.

Alice unhooked the kettle from its spot over the fire and poured steaming water into a mug. A quick stir and then she placed the concoction on the table in front of him. Fragrant vapour wafted up that reminded him of how her hair smelt after she had lain in the meadow.

"It's mainly white willow, which will ease the pain but won't affect your mind. There are other herbs I would give you, such as devil's claw, to help bones heal if I can find a source. I wish I knew a herb to counteract silver." She dropped a hand on his shoulder, then her fingers dug into his flesh. She clucked her tongue in a disapproving noise and her other hand joined the first. "You're as stiff as a board; it's a surprise you even managed to get off the floor."

While he nursed the drink, she eased some of the tension in his tight shoulders. When was the last time a woman looked after him? *Not since mother*, the small boy in the back of his head whispered. His cold soul basked in Alice's ministrations. Normally whenever a woman showered him with attention, she expected something in return. Not Alice. She gave of herself completely and never expected anything from him.

His mother would have liked Alice. She approved of an enquiring mind and had always been fascinated by aftermages and their talents. Even the wild aspect of Alice's character would have delighted his mother. No doubt she would have applauded the plan to exact revenge on brutes like Hoth and might have suggested a particular specimen to start with. If she had lived long enough.

The cold ache settled again in his chest. He wished he could give Alice something in return. Something worthy of her. Love—a word he understood on an intellectual level, but it was a thing he could never extend to a woman.

The wolf whimpered, *mate.*

Impossible, Ewan dismissed the creature's thought as the mad raving induced by the silver wrapped around it. He had seen three fellow wolves find their mates and an extraordinary type of love, but that was not his path. Better he and his beast remain lone wolves.

Alice's hands stilled and then dropped away. "I'm going to help Daisy and Gaffie in the kitchen today. We have bread and stew to make for dinner tonight."

He rolled his neck. The woman really did have magic fingers. "I'm going up the coast. I can take Eilidh, if you don't mind? That way she won't be underfoot in the tavern."

Alice dropped into the chair across the table from him. She wrapped her hands around a cup of tea and lifted it to her lips for a brief sip. "She would like that. It also means you will have company while I gossip with the other women."

"I'll be back before the tavern gets busy tonight." He drank his herbal tea. It tasted somewhat bitter, but if it eased his aches, he would swallow it by the gallon.

After breakfast, Ewan took his time shaving while Alice dressed. Four days of growth was driving him to distraction, and he could not live as a shaggy mutt any longer. Shaving was a fraught activity using his left hand and the spotty job irked him. Not for the first time he wished for sufficient income to lure Perkins away from Quinn. The lout didn't deserve a man who could offer the closest shave in England—not to mention his cravat knots rivalled Ewan's own.

"I could do that, if you like?" Alice offered.

He stared at the cut-throat razor in his hand. "You do so much for me already; I feel like an imposition on your time."

"I enjoy my time with you and I would happily prolong it. Shaving is a skill I was taught by the madam who swept me off the London streets. It's such an intimate act." She took the blade from his fingers and moved to stand behind him. "Especially since we were taught to do it naked while straddling the man."

He was glad she held the blade, because he would have cut himself on hearing those words. Her mischievous streak crept out at times and lightened his dark mood. There was something to fuel his dreams tonight, a naked Alice on his lap while she shaved his chin.

She placed one hand under his jaw and tipped his head back. "This gives me time to hide your features again. The spell must be reinforced each morning or it will drop completely."

Alice wielded the razor the same way she massaged his arm—with long, confident strokes. In no time, she had his chin smooth enough to satisfy his exacting standards. With practice, she might even rival Perkins.

"Thank you." He ran his good hand over his skin. A glance in the mirror showed that he no longer stared back. The other man, with eyes the colour of mud and too much flesh to ever be a cavalryman, met his gaze.

Once they were both dressed, they left the cottage together and Ewan pulled the door shut behind them. "I'll see you tonight."

"Until tonight," she whispered. Then she leaned up and kissed his smooth cheek before running across the yard to the tavern.

For the second time that morning, he stroked his face, imagining he could feel the impression her lips left. What would he do with her? Or the more accurate question, what would he do without her?

He stood in that one spot until the terrier yapped with impatience and broke his reverie. Ewan took his time saddling the horse, playing up his limp and crippled hand. You never knew who watched, and he wanted to ensure the locals thought of him as the wounded soldier. Outside, he walked the horse to the well and used the low wall to climb into the saddle.

Then man, horse, and dog headed north. He rode up the coast and Eilidh ran beside the gelding. At times, she would disappear into the longer grass and he would pull the horse to a halt until he caught sight of her silken ears bouncing up and down as she chased some rabbit or field mouse.

Somewhere along the isolated stretch of the edge of England he would encounter his contact, far away from prying eyes and eavesdropping ears. He hoped for information on the smuggling gangs that operated along the coast and which one was being used by the traitor.

Aster had decoded the French messages relaying that the weapon was ready to be shipped into England via known smuggling routes. A rare lapse by Forge had resulted in the discovery of the drained body, and that in turn led to the Dancing Sow. It was too coincidental for another vampyre to be in the area. It had to confirm that Forge hid from the sunlight somewhere in the region.

But what was the French weapon? British intelligence had failed to turn up any whisper as to what they planned to unleash. They only possessed one clue— that it could be unloaded by small boats under the cover of night. Ewan's money was on something contained within brandy barrels. Poison, perhaps?

He sat and looked out over the ocean. The water was calm, with only a few fluffy white peaks breaking the expanse of dark blue. Grey patches on the surface were echoes of the clouds high above. Far off, as a distant smudge on the horizon, you could just see the shadow of France.

Was there a boat out there, even now sailing towards England with a magical cargo meant to injure decent English folk in their homes? The men working for Forge probably had no idea they did the bidding of France. But at least one knew he followed the commands of a vampyre.

A yip from next to the horse's hooves pulled his thoughts from the miasma rising off the ocean to the grass underneath him.

"What is it, girl?" he asked the little terrier. Her ears rose as she gazed back down the road.

Ewan glanced at the approaching rider then turned back to watch the seagulls wheeling over the water. He feigned disinterest but relied on his senses other than sight to tell him if the horse would approach or carry on past him.

The regular pound of hoof on solid earth slowed and then stopped.

"Evans?" a voice called out.

Ewan turned. The other rider was better dressed than most ruffians, so this was no smuggler. He was also clean shaven with a bright blue jacket.

"Yes," Ewan answered. To those in this county he was Sean Evans, he couldn't risk his true name being overhead by dead ears.

The other man rode closer so they could talk without raising their voices, but not so close you could lunge at the other without falling off the side of your mount. The stranger dropped his hands to his horse's wither and, while he appeared relaxed, he kept a tense set to his shoulders. "We have a mutual interest in this coastline."

"It does grow a fascinating selection of flowers; I believe that one is an Aster." Code phrases were often somewhat embarrassing, but it was no coincidence that this one contained a reference to both an ordinary purple flower and an unusual woman.

The other man smiled. "A flower that many think unremarkable because they do not know how truly remarkable it is."

Quite so. Aster had been disregarded until Hamish glimpsed the keen mind hiding behind her darkened glasses. Now that the War Office had her wielding that intellect in their favour, they had no intention of giving her up. When not deciphering coded messages for the war effort, she worked to advance their knowledge of Unnaturals.

It seemed fitting that she was their way of identifying each other, although talk of plants had him wondering what Alice would see in the natural carpet spread out on the cliff. Were there cures for various ailments scattered around that none would see except her? Did he ride over something that could battle the silver in his blood?

They should come for a ride together, so she could explore nature's bounty. Thinking of things to do outside made a very natural, and nude, Alice flash through his mind. Ewan dragged his mind away from the memory of naked Alice hugging her knees in the cramped tin bath. "You have news?"

"Aye. There's a gang operating somewhere along this stretch of coast. We've had deuced trouble trying to find them, and the man in charge seems but a wraith. We think they have tunnels somewhere." His contact was an excise man, charged with stopping the smugglers and collecting the king's taxes on goods and liquor entering England.

"You suspect it's him?" Ewan couldn't bring himself to say the demon's name aloud, although it would be handy if he could be summoned in such a fashion. That was another way Alice could help. Once they had something Forge had touched, she would be able to locate his hidey-hole.

The excise man shrugged, the action carried out by his shoulders and lips in unison. "We found a dead man on the beach not far from here. His throat ripped out and his body drained of blood. Folk round here whispered of vampyres and everyone is growing garlic in their garden. Talk is the night before he was in the Sow, drunk and muttering his boss' blood thirst turned his stomach."

Ewan swore under his breath. Vampyres were considered a European Unnatural and none were, as yet, known to have made it to English shores.

"It must be him, unless we have a rogue vampyre dining on the locals. I may have need of you, to gain their trust. If I can offer them notice of the excise officers' raids, I can get closer to them." This was the intelligence he had to dangle before them. It didn't matter if they smuggled brandy, a magical weapon, or lace, they still needed to know when the king's men were in the area.

A frown drew the other man's dark brows together. "You'll stop them?"

"I'll cut off the head and leave the rest blind for you to dispose of." Ewan meant it literally. Forge was already dead and he had instructions on how to ensure the vampyre was eternally sent to Hell. Aster told him to remove and destroy the liver, but Ewan was taking his head as added insurance.

His contact nodded. "Done, then. I'll meet you here same time, every three days, for an exchange."

Ewan let the excise man ride away. Eilidh still waited by the horse. "Well, girl, we have progress on that issue. Shall we see if we can find the local witch so Alice knows where to source her herbs and such like?"

The dog barked and Ewan took that as agreement. Then he turned the gelding's head and rode back towards the small settlement that encircled the tavern.

15

Alice

ALICE DONNED her apron and tied the ends behind her back as she walked across the yard. She approached the rear of the building and pulled open the door. Inside, she was relieved to see the kitchen had moved on from the Tudor era of the building's exterior and looked to have had improvements made in Georgian times.

One wall had three brickwork ovens, with embers glowing underneath and cast iron plates above that held kettles and pots. The adjacent wall had a large fire-place with a half carcass of meat on a spit. A wiry-coated turnspit dog ran in his wheel, and a chain from wheel to spit turned the mechanism to cook the roast evenly.

Daisy sliced vegetables at an enormous table in the

middle of the room. Gaffie fussed by the ovens, stirring a pot that looked large enough to bathe a child.

"Good morning." Alice called to the women as she walked over to the dog's workspace.

"Morning," Gaffie and Daisy chimed in unison.

Alice's heart broke for the ugly little canine. Turnspit dogs lived thankless lives, working endlessly with only short breaks to keep the meat revolving. Often they laboured without so much as a name, not even recognised as living creatures. No one spared a thought for the little animal that cooked dinner.

The dog paused for a breath, and she reached between the spokes of the wheel to scratch his ears. Mournful eyes fixed on her as he leaned into her touch.

"What can I do?" Alice asked, giving the dog one more pat before returning to the long table. She tried to make sense of the array of items spread before her.

"Can you make pie?" Gaffie said, waving a wooden spoon in the air. "The lads love something sweet after their stew."

Alice ran an eye over the ingredients stacked on the table. There was flour and butter to make a pastry, and berries that would make a filling. A little cinnamon or spice would add to the flavour, if she dipped into her tiny supply. "Leave it to me; I'll concoct something."

Gaffie beamed and moved down the row of hot plates to stir another pot. "You're a good girl, Alice. What's your man up to today?"

Daisy took her chopped vegetables to the stove and scraped them off the board with the large knife. They dropped into the pot with a faint plop.

"He's going for a ride up the coast. Always looking out to sea that one, trying to find a way to earn a living." She hoped her hint wasn't too obvious.

Daisy picked up a parsnip and waggled it at Alice. "Jimmy says he'll have a chat with Sean. He might know of something."

"That would be wonderful, thank you." Alice found a bowl and added flour and butter to begin making pastry. Once she had rubbed the butter through, she would add a pinch of salt and then enough water to make the pastry into a pliable dough that she could roll out.

The women chatted as they worked. Alice had never been much of a talker, but she tried since the other two went out of their way to include her. She had spent long stretches in total isolation as Hoth's pet, and then in Bedlam her fellow inmates had been more inclined to talk to the walls than to each other. It was odd to talk of trivial things and local gossip when there were deeper issues affecting the world.

By the time the other two were speculating on the father of another woman's child, Alice had two large pies baking in one of the brick ovens.

"Oh, that smells delicious," Gaffie said.

The turnspit dog was allowed a break and Gaffie lifted him down for a drink of water.

"Does he have a name?" Alice asked. She found an offcut of meat and slipped it to the dog. With a long body and short, crooked legs, he was an ugly thing, but he gave her a grateful look as he wolfed down the titbit.

"No." Gaffie frowned. "He's just the turnspit dog."

"Oh." Alice loved Eilidh, and it ached her heart to think this creature never saw the smallest scrap of affection. Here at least was something she could do while in Seabrook. She had a dream of liberating abused women like she used to be; her plan now expanded to rescuing turnspit dogs.

There was also a wolf she longed to set free. As Alice worked, she exercised her gift, locating the ingredient she needed and trying to summon it to her. When the salt pot bumped an inch along the table to her outstretched hand she nearly shouted in triumph.

With the pies baking, Alice helped Daisy wash and dry the used pots and utensils. As the pastry on the pies began to turn golden brown, the sweet aroma wafted through the kitchen.

The door banged open and a large man filled the space. He stopped and sniffed, hands on his hips. "Outdone yourself today, Ma. Smells grand."

"That'll be Alice's pies you smell." Daisy rushed over to the hulking stranger and stood on tiptoe to kiss his cheek, an action he ignored.

So this was Jimmy, son of Mrs McGaffin and Daisy's husband.

He turned to narrow his eyes at Alice and she shrank inside. Timid Alice, the one who was afraid of men, ran and hid in her reinforced room. She slammed the door in her mind so hard the walls shook. The other Alice, the new bolder one, met his gaze.

"Blackberry pie with a touch of cinnamon. Hopefully the patrons will like it tonight." She brushed down her apron and glanced at the knife resting on the table.

If he got too close, she'd reach the knife long before he could reach her.

He pushed the door shut behind him and walked across the floor. "Ma and Daisy told me about you and your man. Sean, is it?"

Now Alice knew why Daisy looked at Ewan with longing. Stand the two men side by side, and even with the hiding enchantment that concealed Ewan's features, he was still a finely crafted work of art compared to this great clay beast who looked ready to pull a cart.

Jimmy was big and broad with the flat, crooked nose of a man who liked to brawl. He also emitted a pungent odour that battled the sweet tang of pie. That would be why the bath looked largely unused. This man certainly seemed unfamiliar with the concept of washing.

She glanced sideways at Daisy. Her new friend could also do with a good scrub and hair washing. Then her attention shot back to Jimmy. "Yes, Sean was injured fighting the French and is having a devil of a time trying to find work."

Jimmy scratched at the stubbly beard attached to his face that merged with enormous sideburns that swept from his jaw up to his hairline. "A fellow soldier. You're lucky he returned at all. Our da didn't."

Alice glanced at Gaffie. "I'm so sorry, I didn't realise. I am thankful that I have Sean back, even in his injured state."

The older woman busied herself wiping her hands on her apron. "Well, he was a gruff old bugger, but I loved him just the same. He wouldn't have Jimmy going off to war on his own and insisted on joining up, too. I swear he thought it was a grand adventure."

Jimmy dropped a hand to his mother's shoulder and gave her a gentle squeeze. "He did us proud, Ma, not that the bloody government cares. We're all just cannon fodder to them. Those Unnatural freaks are treated better than good, honest Englishmen."

Alice noted that Jimmy didn't care for Unnaturals. Not that Ewan would shift into a wolf before him, but it was better to know a man's prejudices when talking to him. Jimmy's regard for his mother made Alice wonder if a softer side lurked inside the great brute, although it didn't seem that Daisy saw much of it. The other woman looked as starved and hungry for affection as the turnspit dog.

"Sean says much the same. Those in charge abandon soldiers who served our country once they are of no use," Alice said.

Dull brown eyes regarded her, and then he grunted and reached a hand down the back of his pants to scratch his bottom. "Every man has to look out for himself, but we take care of our own around here. If your Sean is a good one, we'll find a way for him to provide for you both."

Alice smiled. Her role on this mission was no different than as a fledgling courtesan. Be interested in the man—attention was as attractive to a man as a fine form. A small amount of flattery and downcast eyes could work wonders for loosening a tongue. "Thank you. In the meantime, I shall do my bit by helping your mother and Daisy to keep all the men fed."

He took another sniff and winked at her. "If your pie is anything as good to eat as it smells, I think Ma will be happy to keep you around."

"Right, girls, stew is all done and the pies won't take much longer—let's tidy up the tavern before the boys all start to drag themselves in for supper." Gaffie waved them towards the next room.

"I'll bring up another keg, Ma." Jimmy lumbered away to the doorway that led down to the cool cellar where the ale was kept.

Daisy grabbed two buckets and handed one to Alice. "Let's fill these outside to wipe the tables down."

They walked out into the sunshine to the well. Alice grabbed the rope and let it down with a splash.

"Your Jimmy is a fine, strapping man," Alice said.

Daisy took the rope and hauled up a full bucket of water and tipped it into one of the pails. She had a faraway look in her eye as she worked. "That he is, and he loves his ma ever so much. I just wish he was more loving with me."

"What do you mean?" Alice sent the empty bucket back down to fill far below.

A sad smile curved Daisy's lips. "I feel as though I've lost his love."

Alice laid a hand on Daisy's arm. "Tell me to mind my own business if you want. But I am an aftermage and can find things. Usually people seek my help to find lost jewellery or trinkets that have meaning to them, but I could try to find your lost love."

Daisy rubbed a hand over her belly. "I want to find more than his love."

Alice glanced at the gesture, looked around and leaned in closer. "My mother wasn't just an aftermage, she was a witch. She had a reputation in our village for her spells that helped women conceive."

"A witch?" Daisy's eyes widened and she drew in a sharp breath. "Do you know a spell that would help me?"

Alice hid her humour. *Witch* evoked a stronger response than *aftermage* ever did. One seemed capable of no more than parlour tricks, whereas a witch was a woman of arcane power to rival the feared mages.

Alice hoped that friendship with Daisy would reveal a large amount of local information, particularly since she shared a bed with one of the smugglers. This seemed the ideal opportunity to offer her help to advance their friendship. "I know many spells, but my strength is finding things. I need to know what is lacking so that I know what needs to be found. Does Jimmy need to find your love, or does his seed need to find your womb?"

Daisy dropped the bucket and sat down on the edge of the well. Tears formed in her eyes. "Both. He seldom lays with me, and when he does, it is rather ... brief."

Alice sat next to her, draped her arm over Daisy's shoulder, and pulled the other woman close. "Leave it to me. I will concoct a spell for both of you. One half to rekindle Jimmy's love and the other half to help you quicken. You can see by how he treats his mother that he is a man with a large heart. All he needs is a magical nudge to remind him why he married you."

Alice didn't need to be a witch to know what spell would work; it involved hot water, soap, and a good dose of lavender oil. They both needed to bathe and wash their hair. Currently the only thing breeding was the lice on their bodies.

"Do you really think a spell will work?" Daisy blew her nose on the corner of her apron and then wiped her face.

"Of course. My mother was a third generation witch and quite powerful. While I am a fourth generation and not as strong as her, my talent allows me to target exactly what is needed." Alice would also work her hiding gift on Daisy in a similar fashion to how she did on Ewan. Except she would do the opposite and make the woman's feature's finer, her cheek bones higher and her eyes wider. Jimmy would find his wife irresistible by the time Alice was done with her.

Daisy wiped her face on her apron. "You must think me daft, blubbing on you when we have only known each other for a couple of days."

"I hope we can become firm friends, and isn't this the sort of thing friends share, talking about their men troubles?" It was no hardship to like this woman; she was lost in her own way and needed a push in the right direction. Already Alice's hand itched to hold the herbs that would form the base of the spell.

With buckets filled, the women headed back into the tavern. The rest of the afternoon and evening was an endless round of running to the kitchen for food, serving the men, and running back again. Alice thought she would be as fit as a racehorse before their time in Seabrook was over. Ewan appeared as dusk fell and settled into his corner with Eilidh.

Only past midnight as the patrons said their goodnights did she take off her apron and wait for man and canine at the back door. They walked in silence across the yard to their cottage. Once inside, Alice undressed and then hopped between the sheets. She slid over close to the wall and leaned on one elbow as Ewan undressed by the flicker of the lone candle.

He removed his shirt first, and she watched the play of shadow over his skin as he folded the item and draped it over the back of a chair. Then he sat and removed his Hessians, standing them at the end of the bed.

"Are you sure about this?" he asked without turning around.

"Yes. You either sleep here with me, or I join you on the floor." She patted the blanket next to her.

His shoulders heaved in a sigh as though the prospect of sharing a bed with her was something unpleasant.

"Whatever is the problem?" Alice asked.

One black eyebrow arched. "I normally sleep naked, and I do not want you to think I plan to take advantage of you during the night."

She laughed. "If anyone can control themselves, it is you. I have no fear of anything happening without my express consent. You also forget that while my time as a courtesan ended in a catastrophic fashion, I did nonetheless see a few naked men in my short career. You will not shock me by being the first."

He huffed a gentle laugh. "If you are sure."

He eased his trousers over his hips and folded them with the same care and attention as his shirt received. Then the items joined the neat stack on the chair. At last Ewan turned and stood naked before the bed.

Alice couldn't help it. She had invited the man who made her heart race to join her in bed. Naked. Nerves welled up in her chest and she giggled. She sat up and slapped a hand over her mouth.

Ewan frowned and put his hands on his hips. "Did you just laugh at my splendid nakedness?"

Alice dropped her hand and tried to control her pounding heart. She desperately wanted to drink up the sight of him and linger over certain areas. "I'm so sorry, I swear I couldn't help it."

He climbed into bed and pulled the blankets up his body. "I'll have you know some women swooned on first seeing me *au naturel.*"

She could well imagine it. Her knees trembled under the bedding and probably would have buckled if she hadn't been lying down. He would probably think her as foolish as the women who had paid for his time if he knew how strongly she reacted to him. "I've probably seen a few more naked men than your average society matron."

He huffed. "So in your experience, I don't compare favourably?"

She bit the inside of her lip to keep from smiling. For all that they boasted of being the stronger sex, men had delicate egos when it came to a particular part of their anatomy. Alice schooled her features to maintain a frown, a practice that had become easier under Ewan's tutelage. "Perhaps it is other men who suffer from the comparison, and my giggle was one of nervous relief that I don't have to lie outrageously to inflate your ego. I was never good at pretending."

Ewan gave a low chuckle as he settled in the bed. "Men do like to hear they are the biggest a woman has ever seen, even if their appendage is the size of a baby's finger."

Alice lay on her side to study his face as they talked. "Some men take a gasp of surprise as amazement at their endowment, when in fact we're shocked at how small it is and wondering where we put the magnifying glass."

His chuckle turned to a bark of laughter. "Let us agree to be honest with each other, Alice, and not resort to the gilded lies that courtesans peddle."

Alice's heart stuttered in her chest. How could she ever be honest with him? A small lie was better than revealing the true extent of how he affected her. "Very well. You are not malformed despite your injuries, and some would go as far as to call you pleasing to the eye."

He rolled towards her and stroked her cheek. "And you are an ethereal beauty such as I have never seen before. You are a forest sprite who steals my breath as she casts her magic over me."

He rolled back over, blew out the candle and darkness settled over them.

Alice swallowed, his words still echoing in her

mind. She was more confused than ever. Warmth radiated from Ewan's body and Alice couldn't stay away from him.

He lifted his arm and she nestled against him, one hand on his chest. This was what her soul ached for all day: time in his arms while her mind wrestled with all her burgeoning thoughts and ideas. With her hand on his skin, she reached out to find the traces of silver within him. Each day it seemed to sink deeper into his bones. How long before it consumed all of him and even the most powerful mage wouldn't be able to reverse the damage done by the French magic?

She would not lose him or the wolf she had never seen. That thought gave her more reason to work harder on expanding her gift. Her hand sensed the bullet deep in his femur, but she dared not try to summon it until she was sure it would work. Better to concentrate on the mundane aspects of her life before she was tempted to try and make the bullet wriggle.

"Daisy is having marital problems with Jimmy and burst into tears on me today. I have offered my after-mage skill to find their love for one another. He is a great beast of a man. I wonder if he is an ox-changeling."

"They must make a grim-looking couple." Ewan stroked her upper arm with his thumb.

"Grim or grime? I had to bite my tongue before I suggested they both start with a bath."

His chest shook as he laughed. "I see my attention to personal grooming is rubbing off on you."

Eilidh settled on the bed down by Ewan's feet, with one eye on the door.

"I plan to concoct a spell that involves a large quantity of hot water and soap. Jimmy is going to talk to you about employment prospects." Alice couldn't keep her eyes open and let them drift shut.

"Good. I believe I have something to trade that will be of value to them," Ewan whispered against her hair.

16

Ewan

BIRD SONG WOKE Ewan early the next morning. Long before colour appeared in the sky outside, birds left trees and hedges to find their breakfast in the damp earth. In the quiet that enveloped the room after the nearby birds had flown off, Ewan gave himself over to his deepest thoughts about the woman asleep in his arms.

If you took a jug full of rocks, it seemed impossible to add anything else to the container. But if you poured in water, it would find all the gaps between the rocks. Ewan was the rocks and Alice the water. She flowed through his cracked soul and filled all the empty places.

He had meant what he said to her the previous night—she was a beauty unlike any other and he was falling under her spell. His growing need for her worried him. Even in its tortured state, his wolf rumbled with possessive thoughts. The need to join with her tortured the beast as much as the silver.

How would he ever let her go? Their broken, jagged edges fit together to form a new and different whole. Then he remembered a darker beast that lurked inside him, the opposite to his wolf. Both creatures fought for control of his unconscious self.

One would protect, the other destroy.

His family blood coursed through his veins and wrestled with his lycanthrope side. He couldn't keep hold of Alice, no matter how much he wanted to. If the demon ever broke free, he would squeeze the life from her where Hoth had failed.

He needed to clear the muddled thoughts clogging up his mind and to find a way forward. Careful not to wake the sleeping woman, he slid his arm out from under her. He would miss his morning massage, but he needed to exercise a different muscle—the one in his head.

His covert mission to exit the cottage undetected was undermined by the dog who needed to go outside to answer a call of nature and a non-cooperative leg that gave out on him, causing him to crash against the chair as he dressed.

"What are you doing?" Alice sat up, rubbing her eyes.

"I'm heading out for an early ride." He righted the chair and then shrugged on his jacket.

"So early?" She peered at the dim window. The

light that filtered through was caught between moon-light and dawn.

"I find watching dawn creep over the ocean helps me think. Go back to sleep."

"I must rework the spell in case someone sees you," she murmured.

She was right, of course. It was too great a risk to have someone see his true face. He sat on the edge of the bed, took her hands, and pressed them to the sides of his face. With closed eyes, Alice whispered words under her breath that made a shiver wash over Ewan.

Once done, she slid under the blankets, revealing only an exquisite collar bone and the arch of her neck and shoulder. He longed to follow the curve with his tongue, but he had to leave before he stripped off his clothes and crawled back to her inviting warmth.

Alice thought he had control, but at times it was as fragile as spun toffee. One tap and it would shatter. Funny how others thought she was breakable, but she had the hidden strength of steel. The same people thought he had an iron control, but when it came to this woman, it would dissolve in a heartbeat if he thought he could truly have her.

Once outside and with the horse saddled, he rode up the coast to watch the waves crash as the seagulls circled. He sat for a long time watching the sun come over the horizon, but still his mind was turmoil. He rode up and down the stretch of coast, as though he expected to find the answers he sought somewhere along the beach.

As the sun rose higher, he stopped at a busy cove.

Down below, women and children were picking through the rocks. There must have been a shipwreck recently and they were searching for anything that washed ashore. Another rider approached from the direction of the village. He matched Alice's description of an ox-changeling—Jimmy McGaffin on a sturdy beast, one bred to pull a plough or carry his weight.

"Hard work, that, if you're thinking about giving it a go," Jimmy said as he reined his horse to a halt by Ewan.

So many people struggled to eke out a living, many right under the noses of the wealthy. How much went on beneath their noses that the aristocracy never noticed? Or did they know but simply pretended not to notice, like the Unnaturals in their midst?

Or like the abuse of women, his mother whispered from a distant memory.

Ewan shook his head, pulling his attention back to the scene below. "I somehow doubt my leg would appreciate me scrabbling over rocks. I'm not as nimble as I was as a lad."

A small boy held up a flask he had found and a woman, presumably his mother, snatched it from his hands. It was a hard life picking amongst debris, looking for anything of value that the sea gave up.

"Hear you're looking for work," Jimmy said.

Ewan nodded. "Anything that would produce a coin or two. It doesn't sit right that Alice is the one putting a roof over our heads. That's my duty."

Jimmy pulled a filthy-looking handkerchief from his pocket and blew his nose, a noise that startled

Ewan' placid horse and gave Ewan a flashback to the bugle signal to advance.

"I might know of something. There's an old woman in the village and rumour has it she keeps a pile of coins under her mattress. Me and another fellow were going to pay her a visit and have a peek."

Ewan shuddered. These men had no honour if they would rob an old woman who had probably hoarded coins to see her through her old age. "No, thank you."

Jimmy narrowed his gaze. "You too good for thieving?"

Ewan turned and pinned Jimmy with a cold stare. "No. But I have a problem with taking coin from someone as down-on-their-luck as me. There are far deeper pockets out there."

"Oh, like who?" Having absorbed a quantity of snot, Jimmy's cloth now wiped sweat from his forehead before he shoved it back in his pocket.

Ewan suppressed a shudder at the action. He swept a hand over the stretch of beach and the ocean beyond. "Rum, brandy, tea, and tobacco are all to be had in exchange for a bit of hard work and enterprise. Those are profits that would feed and clothe several families and benefit the entire community, and the only pocket hurt would be the Exchequer."

"You're talking about smuggling." Jimmy laughed.

Ewan shrugged. "Why do you think I brought Alice to Kent? I know the opportunities available to men out here. I just need to find those of a like mind to make it happen. I might not be able to lift a barrel, but I have other skills. I can read and do arithmetic."

If the lummox didn't take that hint, then Ewan didn't know what else to do. He might have to start a rival smuggling gang just to have something to do and in the hope that he and Forge would be boats that met in the night.

Jimmy scratched his bushy jaw. "If you're of that inclination, I'll talk to the boss see what he says about bringing in someone new. We lost a man recently and could do with one more. We're a small and tight crew, though."

With that said, Jimmy turned his horse and rode off, leaving Ewan hoping the boss mentioned was Forge. Otherwise, he would be scrambling over rocks for a clue that Alice could use.

THREE NIGHTS LATER, Ewan sat in what he now referred to as his corner, tracking Alice as she moved amongst the patrons in the dim interior. At the same time, he kept a look out for a particular type of man. The sort who turned their faces from the authorities and made their own way under cover of dark. He made some progress as each night more men stopped to chat with him.

Trust was slow to build, but one contact led to another as he made it known he was familiar with an excise man with expensive habits. He couldn't offer the smugglers physical strength, but he could offer them inside knowledge of when the officers would be out.

Men would sit opposite him, he would buy them a

tankard of ale, and they would judge each other while they talked of inconsequential things. While discussing the weather or recounting war tales, they weighed up how much to trust each other. Tonight had not seen any progress and yet an expectant air hung in the tavern. More than once, he caught other men staring at the door, waiting.

Ewan would lay money on something happening tonight, and it made him grind his teeth to not know *what*. He needed a breakthrough. He needed to find the one person who would crook their finger and let him close to the gang Forge was using to advance the French cause. He needed to find the weapon created by the French mages before it was unleashed on an unprepared England.

The door banged open as someone threw their weight behind it. Everyone looked up as a group of six men spilled into tavern. One tumbled forward, obviously the man who crashed into the door. The others laughed and pointed as he lost balance.

Ewan's heart tightened as the over-balanced fellow dove onto Alice. The large man's hands went around her as he used her to stop his fall. She gave a yelp and Ewan rose from his seat. The blackguard better not harm her. Then laughter broke out as the man righted himself and held up his hands in horror.

Alice met Ewan's gaze across the room and she shook her head slightly. No rescue needed; she was all right. The man and his friends apologised loudly to her.

"Drinks are on us!" one said and scattered gold

coins on the bar.

The door closed on the last man, one who stuck to the shadows even at night, but Ewan's blood ran cold as the nondescript man skirted the crowd to seek out his own quiet corner.

Forge.

Plans were constructed and abandoned in Ewan's mind. As much as he hated inactivity, his mission here was more akin to fishing than direct battle. He had thrown out his bait; now he needed to exercise patience, play out his line, and wait for Forge to take a bite.

Conversation erupted in the tavern as men bombarded the new comers with questions. Ewan caught snatches of, *how did it go?* Another man's mouth made the shape for *barrels.* Much to his frustration he stayed on the edge, trying to piece together what he overheard. From the corner of his eye, he saw men tug the brims of their caps at Forge. A quiet signal of acknowledgment and respect.

A man with an accordion sat on a table and began playing a fast tune. Another man grabbed a fiddle and joined him, and soon the tavern echoed with fast and cheerful music. The women in the crowd were quickly claimed for dancing and couples whirled around the hurriedly cleared space.

The man who bumped into Alice approached her with his tweed cap in hands. Ewan couldn't hear what he said over the music as all words were washed away. After a short conversation, her gaze sought his and she cocked her head to one side, asking a silent question.

He shrugged and tried to look disinterested. It was up to her if she wished to dance or not. Ewan couldn't take her out on the floor, but he didn't think she would want any man but him touching her. He was surprised when she let the man take her fine hand in his enormous one.

Just as he worked his hand each day to stretch the tendons and remind his fingers of their job, so each day she reclaimed another piece of herself and moved a little easier amongst people. Round and round, the dancing couples spun. So intent was Ewan on keeping track of Alice that he didn't hear the man slide onto the bench opposite him.

"Your wife is a pretty, wee thing, Evans."

It took seconds for his distracted mind to register the use of his false name. He turned with a practised smile in place. "That she is."

He flicked his gaze over the man while pretending disinterest. This fellow had burst through the door with the others with spare gold in his pockets. Tall and skinny, he looked the sort who would eat like a horse and never lay down a spare ounce of flesh. His haggard face had a long nose and deep-set eyes. Dark hair was cropped so short that pink scalp showed through in places.

"What does she see in a maimed soldier like you?" his new acquaintance asked.

While his hand grew stronger every day, admittedly the limp did bother him and labelled him *cripple*. Still Ewan could ignore the jibe. Others saw only the glamour Alice used to hide his true features. "There are other ways to keep a woman satisfied that don't involve standing up or dancing."

Ewan kept his gaze on the other man as he widened his grin and winked. Let him work through what that comment meant. Like most men, this one thought size and strength were what appealed to a woman. But a woman could be blind to a man's appearance if he knew how to put her wants and needs before his own.

That was the real reason he had made such an impression on the older matrons in London. True, his handsome face added to his appeal, but his real skill was knowing exactly what lonely women wanted after years of cold, empty marriages. Then his nose wrinkled as he caught a whiff of his companion. His tendency to bathe regularly was also part of his popularity.

The man barked in laughter and even snorted beer out his nose as he finally understood the comment. "Guess you didn't lose that in the war, then?"

"I am quite intact where it counts." Ewan poured more ale. These oafish men with their crude comments weren't his preferred type of company, but he would make do for a chance to plunge his hands into Forge's torso and pull out his liver. This time he would make sure the fiend was permanently laid to rest.

His new friend leaned closer over the table, not that they needed to whisper with the loud music and raucous laughter around them. "Jimmy says you know an excise man."

Ah. Finally, someone asked the right questions of him. Had Jimmy sent him or their silent master in the corner, the one looking as disinterested in Ewan as Ewan was pretending to be in him?

"Yes. A particular one with a fondness for gambling and who keeps a lovely mistress. He has expenses, you see, that his pay doesn't always meet." Ewan held his tankard in one hand and stared at the malty ale. The brew wasn't bad, given the low status of the tavern. He'd certainly had worse that tasted as though they strained it through old stockings.

"Poor fellow. Perhaps we could help him meet his expenses, if he could help us."

The question hung between them. Here was the moment Ewan had been waiting for, to be taken into the smuggling ring in return for delivering information on the excise officers.

"I'm sure he would do all he could to be of assistance." Ewan raised his mug in a silent salute to the poor excise man.

The other man nodded. Satisfied, it seemed. "I offer a proposal then, to see if we can trust him. And you. I'm Crufts, by the way."

A test. Luckily, he was prepared for such an outcome. "Pleasure to meet you, Crufts. I shall go see my friend tomorrow for a friendly chat. Perhaps we will talk about how his garden grows or if he has any favourite fishing spots."

"You do that. And you let us know if he has anything to pass on tomorrow night." He drained his ale and nodded to Ewan. Then he left, stopping at the far corner for a brief conversation in the shadows before he joined his friends at another table.

The atmosphere grew louder as the ale flowed freely and the music kept playing. Ewan caught sight of Alice with the large man's arms still around her. The oaf held her a little too close for Ewan's liking, one beefy hand on the side of her waist as he guided her through the throng.

Fire flared through Ewan's veins as the wolf fought the silver to growl and snap at the man holding *his* Alice. The poison in his system tore through his bones and stabbed into his chest as he struggled against it, trying to shift form. Ewan dropped his tankard to the table as the wave of agony crashed through him. His hand spasmed as claws tried, futilely, to break through his skin.

Alice caught the sudden movement and left her partner to rush over. She laid a hand over his clenched and shaking fist. "Are you all right? What happened?"

He could lie. Say he was fine. He could tell her to go back to the dancing. But for once he was going to be selfish. He didn't want another man touching her. He wanted her quiet companionship all to himself, and he wanted them both out of the overloud inn and away from the all-seeing gaze of Forge.

"My injuries pain me. Would you help me back to the cottage?" he said.

"Of course." She stepped aside as he rose. Alice slipped her arm around his waist and he drew her close as he leaned over her shoulders. They walked around the edge of the crowd and towards the door. His limp was heavy and, for once, he let the grimace of pain show on his face. May as well put on a good show for those who watched. No one would reconcile the crippled man with the creature who used to glide across a ballroom floor.

It might have been petty of him, but it felt so damn good to have her pressed against him. Lavender and sage wafted from her silken hair next to his cheek. Eilidh shot out of the tavern and ran yapping after moths. The terrier dodged back and forth as they walked across the yard.

A question burned through Ewan, as hot and bright as the pain coursing through his veins. "How did you find dancing?"

She paused and looked up at the pale sliver of moon. A cloud covered part of it and shadowed half her face. Then she flashed a brief smile. "I rather enjoyed it, once I shut myself in the room where fear could not reach me."

"I'm glad you had a good time." He smiled, and it came so naturally to the muscles of his face. But he wasn't glad. He hated every second of it. It rankled to see another man holding her. No one should lead her across the dance floor but him.

They carried on to their cottage. He drew the large key from his pocket and unlocked the door, then gave a bow to Alice.

With a murmured *thank you*, she headed inside.

Ewan locked the door once Eilidh had raced inside and scooted under the table. Alice lit the candles on the table with a match, and Ewan dropped heavily into the chair by the fire.

She poked the embers with a poker and tossed on a

fresh scoop of coals. "Now will you let me apply a hot poultice to your leg? I want to try drawing the silver out with herbs."

He rolled his shoulders. His whole body ached and almost made him wish for the peace of death. Almost, but not quite. "I can see resistance would be futile. You may have at me."

While Alice fetched a bag from under the bench, Ewan tugged off his boots. The pain down his leg amplified once free of the constricting leather. He ground his teeth to hold in his reaction as he slid off his trousers and stockings. Given how high up his thigh the bullet was lodged, there was no other way to do this except mostly naked. Only the hem of his shirt provided a small amount of modesty.

He dragged the other chair out and rested his right foot on it. Then he tucked his shirt around his manhood. Never before had he felt so vulnerable and exposed.

Alice worked at the bench, grinding herbs with a mortar and pestle. Once satisfied, she tipped the ground herbs into a larger bowl. Using a cloth wrapped around the handle, she carried the boiling kettle over and added it to the herbs. She stirred for a few minutes and then spread the hot mixture over a cloth. She folded it into a rectangle and then came to sit on the floor beside him, the fragrant poultice in her hands.

She looked up at him. "This will smart as it's very hot. I don't know if it will work, but I am hoping the poultice will attract the silver and draw it from your body."

At a nod from him, she laid the cloth high on his thigh and pressed it around the sides so it encompassed as much of the area around the bullet as possible. He sucked in a breath—it was hot, but not unbearably so.

"What's in it?" he asked, to distract himself as his body acclimatised to the poultice.

She smoothed a hand along the cloth, ensuring the herbs were evenly distributed. "A number of things of my own creation. Firstly wormwood, otherwise known as Artemisia, after Artemis, the Greek goddess of the moon. I thought her a good starting point for any spell to be worked on a wolf."

Alice sat back on her heels at his side. "Next I added yarrow, associated with Achilles and said to heal soldiers."

Ewan chuffed at that one. She had carefully thought of legend and mystical associations as she wove her spell.

"Then sage, or in Latin *salvere*—"

"To heal or cure," he finished her sentence. Plants meant as much to him as he was sure rattling off munitions would mean to her. But the ancient lore she knew about the herbs she selected fascinated him. "Where did you learn this?"

"I read whatever books Ianthe could supply me with that covered botany. The three ingredients I selected are all known as silver plants, and I hoped their affinity for that element would help draw the substance from your blood. I have woven a spell upon them, asking the silver within you to *find* the poultice."

She smiled, a haunting thing that stole his breath. She was more than outward beauty. Her soul sang to him with a refrain that he found irresistible. He might be an Unnatural, but she was unearthly. A creature from another world dusted with grace by the moon.

"You said to create a room to keep myself safe when the fear attacked, but I have found other rooms within me, as though I explore a house I had forgotten I owned. As I found pieces of my soul and stitched them back together, it has unlocked more rooms. One contained the knowledge my mother passed to me of how to weave herb lore with our gifts to heal others." She ran her hand along the poultice, helping the heat to seep through.

He shifted in the chair. The heat sank through his flesh and deep into the bone, but he felt a pull and tug in the opposite direction as something was eased free of his body. Inside him, his wolf let out a deep sigh. "I'm finding I am rather fond of witches and all they can do."

He reached out and cupped her face. She possessed such haunted eyes that he saw them in his sleep. He stroked her cheek with his thumb. Then he leaned forward and drew her to him. She rose up on her knees, her lips a hair's breadth from his. He took a moment to judge her demeanour. He didn't want to cause her distress or ask for something she was unwilling to give.

For months she had tested his control, and now he would toss it all aside to know the taste of her sadness.

While he pondered what to do, Alice closed the gap between them and kissed him.

17

Alice

ONCE BEFORE, and emboldened by too much wine, Alice had tried to kiss Ewan. But a combination of their friends watching and trying too soon in their acquaintance had contributed to a humiliating rejection. He had pushed her away and stormed off into a snowy night. Now, that attempt seemed a lifetime ago. Since then, he had called her an ethereal beauty and said she cast a spell on him. Surely that meant he felt something for her?

Their time together nurtured familiarity into a sense of peace with one another. For Alice, over the past few weeks that comfort had transformed into something deeper and stronger. An ache took root in her belly as night after night she lay in his arms with nothing more than a stroke of his hand to feed a growing hunger. Sitting at his feet, willing the poultice to ease some of his pain, all she could think about was having his body pressed next to hers.

When his hand tangled in her hair and he drew her to him, her heart stuttered and her limbs tingled. Finally he signalled that he, too, felt the heat growing between them and was ready to act upon it. Then he paused.

That would never do.

What if he changed his mind?

She leaned up and kissed him.

Her lips glided over his, teasing, hoping he would respond. His hand tightened at her neck, holding her to him as he deepened the kiss. Ewan's touch was a lightning strike that destroyed a dam. A flood of emotion poured through Alice.

She was a child drunk on her first taste of liquor as she pressed into him, her arms winding around his neck. As they kissed, never had she known such desire. The ache inside her bloomed in fiery life and flowed outward through her body.

As a lass, she had tasted enough pleasure to be easy with it and had moved to London to find her fortune as a courtesan. She had experienced a few dalliances before Hoth seized her. The men who went before Ewan were flickering candles compared to the power of the summer sun.

She moaned, wanting more. The taste of him in her mouth was sweeter than any wine and far headier. He used practised flicks to drive her mad with longing in the briefest of contacts. Her hands slid down his chest and her fingers curled in the bottom of his shirt, intent on removing it from his torso. Her body screamed for his naked skin next to hers.

Then he captured her hands in his good one and lifted his head. "We cannot do this, Alice."

Her fuddled mind didn't understand. They desired each other, so they most certainly could do it. Indeed, they *were* doing it, right up until he stopped.

"Yes," she whispered, still catching her breath. "Yes, we can."

He leaned back a few inches, but it may as well have been miles, such was the distance in his eyes. "No. We cannot be, Alice. The pain this evening has fuddled my thinking, and I am sorry if I led you to believe there could be something between us."

Of course. She was a fool. Sleeping in his arms was part of their pretence, the mirage they threw up so that the people of Seabrook believed them to be a married couple. In actuality, it meant nothing to him.

For a second time, he had refused her.

How many times did he need to reject her before the message made its way through her dense skull? He was the son of an aristocrat and she a mere common girl, good enough for a brief diversion but nothing more. Wolves found their mates among ladies of breeding, not rubbish dumped in Bedlam. One Highland Wolf was even married to the daughter of a duke!

They played roles within the walls of this cottage and nothing was real. Did it prove her mad that she thought the pretence was something tangible? She followed her part as an actor, but like a simpleton, she had believed what happened on the stage and she had forgotten her lines were scripted.

Her soul curled up and wept, but the stronger Alice nodded her head and never let her internal agony show. "Of course. I understand."

"No, you don't. Alice, look at me, please." His hands cradled her face.

She wanted to look away, to hide the pain simmering within her, but a tiny part of her still obeyed a command and she raised her eyes to his.

"Never doubt the strength of my attraction for you, Alice. But I do not want to take advantage of our situation. I would never use you." He searched her face, seeking her understanding.

But she couldn't understand. It made no sense to her. Her body craved his touch, her soul calmed in his embrace, and he understood her as no one else ever could. The trace of magic in her blood tugged, telling her that what she sought was within him.

Ewan claimed he was attracted to her and yet pushed her away at the same time. His actions said one thing but his words another, and her mind couldn't make any sense of it.

"I need to go back to the tavern. Daisy will need an extra set of hands with the mood the men are in." She rose and held her back stiff as she walked towards the door.

Behind her, the chair creaked as he moved but there was no shuffle of his feet. He did not attempt to stop her leaving or follow her. "I never want to hurt you, Alice; that's why we need to stay apart. You would be harmed if you got too close to me."

But he had hurt her. Like a knife slicing into her stomach, his rejection cut her open.

Alice unlocked the door and walked out into the dark. She headed across the yard, not wanting to be near the cottage, but she couldn't bring herself to walk back into the loud and crowded inn. She paused at the halfway point and took a moment to embrace the silent night.

The moon hung low in the sky, as though it weighed down the heavens and would tumble to Earth. Alice held up her hand and wrapped her fingers around the glowing orb. It appeared that it should be easy to pluck the moon from the stars, like taking a jewel nestled in velvet. Yet the celestial body resisted her attempts to grasp it, just as Ewan gave the appearance that he welcomed her touch and kisses and then turned his head from her.

"Would you capture the moon?" a voice whispered from the dark.

Alice gave a start and jumped. "Who is there?"

A man detached from the stable wall and advanced a step. "I was enjoying the peace and quiet out here when I saw a woman trying to grab the moon."

"It's so full tonight that at times, I think it is within reach, only to have it dance beyond my fingertips." She dropped her hand. He probably thought her mad. Did one suddenly become sane when one left the lunatic asylum, or would the taint of Bedlam linger within her forever?

She glanced back towards the cottage and the man hidden within its walls and sighed. So many things were unattainable and yet she kept trying over and over, even when it was pointless. She was like the turnspit dog, running like mad in its wheel but not going anywhere.

"You set yourself up for failure. I prefer to keep my sights on things I know I can grasp." He walked to the edge of the well and sat down.

He was an odd man, with nothing remarkable about him. Of average height and build with regular features and short, cropped dark hair. At least he didn't smell like Jimmy. There was a soft edge to his voice, as though he never raised it but expected others to fall silent to hear him.

"It seems I have always pined for the unreachable." She thought affection had built between her and Ewan. He admitted he felt something, but it must be a scant thing that he could so easily deny his feelings. She didn't want to live her life in disappointment. Didn't she deserve a small measure of happiness after all she had endured?

The man crossed his ankles and glanced up at the stars. "Perhaps you need to lower your sights and stop gazing at the moon. Try reaching for something closer to hand."

"Perhaps." A stranger reinforced what she already knew deep down. Stop wishing for Ewan when the most she could hope for would be a rough man like Jimmy. "Thank you for your insight, but I must return inside. Daisy and Gaffie will need a hand in the tavern."

"You're the new girl, Alice." He still pitched his voice so low that she strained to catch his words.

"Yes, I am." It was no surprise he knew her name. In a small community, word would spread like wildfire that a new couple had moved into the cottage behind the Dancing Sow. Two weeks were a long time in village gossip.

"I saw you serving tonight, and I am told you are responsible for the delicious pies my men can't stop talking about." A brief smile touched his face, and his teeth flashed in the dark. Oddly long and sharp teeth that flashed a warning through her brain.

"I am glad the men like them. It's good to be useful." Her pies disappeared in short order once they were placed on the counter. The men fell on them like hungry wolves on a rabbit.

"Oh, I suspect you have many talents the men would appreciate, Alice." He crossed his arms and watched her with a predatory stare.

Shivers washed down her spine. His black eyes were dull in the moonlight and flat as though there was no life behind them. Just what did he mean that the men would appreciate her talents—did he know of her history? Another question rose in her mind. "May I know your name, since you are familiar with mine?"

"You can call me Callum, and I look forward to getting to know you better, Alice." He stood up and melted back into the dark like a shadow that moved with the shifting of the night.

Chills washed over her skin and she brushed her hands up her arms to dispel it.

Callum? Why did that name niggle at her mind and make her wish that Ewan stood at her back?

Callum Forge. The vampyre they sought to capture.

Alice drew a deep breath to dispel the fear that raced over her. She rotated one ankle simply to feel the weight of the knife on her leg. She reinforced her mental defences and then flung open the door to the tavern. Inside, the atmosphere had become more chaotic. Men were cheering and yelling as couples danced to a manic tune. Daisy raced from table to table topping up tankards, and even Gaffie was doing her bit.

"Oh, Alice, everyone is so thirsty with all the dancing," Gaffie said as she pushed the pitcher into Alice's hands. "You keep pouring and I'll draw off more pitchers."

The evening became a blur of music and laughter. Alice worked until her feet ached and her hand cramped from carrying full jugs of ale. She still managed to sneak one quick trip to the kitchen to feed meat scraps to the exhausted turnspit dog, who lay slumped in front of the fire.

At long last, the musicians grew tired and dropped their instruments. Men drank themselves from raucous to sleepy and heads nodded. One by one, the men staggered to their feet and headed out the door.

Alice dropped to a bench as the last few people were ushered either out the front door or up the stairs to their rooms. Gaffie locked the front door and then turned and leaned against it.

"Well, that was quite the night," the tavern owner said.

"Everyone seemed in a celebratory mood. I was too busy to ask the occasion." Alice wiped her face on her apron and then she fanned herself with the edge of fabric.

"Jimmy's crew had a good day." Daisy sat next to her.

"Oh? What do they do?" Given that Jimmy didn't own a boat, Alice was pretty sure his *crew* weren't a bunch of sailors or fishermen.

Gaffie flicked a towel at Daisy. "They had an excellent day at market and all that spare coin was rattling around in their pockets." The older woman smiled broadly. "Now it's rattling around in *my* pockets."

Alice bit back her retort. She assumed the men took their contraband into Hythe for sale or distribution. That was a type of market, she supposed. "I think there will be quite a few sore heads in the morning, judging by the amount of alcohol consumed."

Daisy nudged her with an elbow. "How's Sean? He looked like he was hurting."

"His leg is bad." His leg and her heart—both ached with no cure in sight. "I need to find some herbs to ease his pain. Something stronger than willow bark."

"You want old Nelly." Gaffie lowered herself to the bench. "She lives along the inland road, at the edge of the forest. Grows all sorts of things out there."

No matter what county one travelled to, there was always an aftermage healer or witch around somewhere, living apart from others and growing all kinds of herbs and plants. "Thank you. I'll visit her in the morning if you could do without me here for a couple of hours?"

Gaffie reached out and squeezed her hand. "We'll cope. You find something to help Sean feel better."

Alice wondered if their local witch knew a spell to harden her heart so it no longer bled. "I'll find some more berries for pie while I'm out."

Daisy winked in her direction. "Why don't you toddle off to bed? That man's probably waiting up for you."

Alice sighed. If only he was.

18

Ewan

EWAN WAS STILL awake when Alice returned in the small hours of morning. Yet again, he had hurt the young woman when he only sought to protect her. How did someone with his charm with the fairer sex manage to make such a pig's ear of things? It should have been easy to explain to her that he denied his feelings to shield her, yet the words twisted on his tongue and gave the flavour that the fault was hers.

He couldn't sleep knowing she laboured in the tavern. Having no purpose weighed on him. Was this what his life would become if the mages failed to heal him—relying on others to provide, while he did nothing?

At least there were signs of progress with his mission, and tonight he'd spotted Forge. He suspected

Forge had sent Crufts to talk to him and that Jimmy was just a mouthpiece for the group. Ewan was confident of being admitted to the gang, so long as Alice's spell concealed his true identity from Forge.

Clothing rustled as Alice undressed in the dark, and then silence.

Her poultice had brought him some relief, and he was able to rouse his wolf enough to use its vision to see her outline in the dark, standing immobile at the end of the bed. He let the wolf go to sink back into oblivion, before a headache threatened from the exertion.

"You know the rules. We're either both in the bed or both on the floor," he said.

A sigh came in answer and then the bed dipped as she climbed over the end and crawled in against the wall. She didn't move towards him, and the hollow in his chest began to freeze like the water of a pond in winter.

"Let's not argue, Alice, please. The defect is entirely my own, not yours, and I cannot sleep unless you are next to me." He walked a dangerous line. He needed her companionship and warmth as much as his lungs needed air, but at the same time, he had to keep her at arm's length.

"We are an odd couple," she whispered. "I push, you pull. I want too much and you have nothing to give."

"Alice." The ice around his heart cracked at her mournful words. He murmured her name again and then reached for her. Finding her form, he wrapped his arm under her and pulled her tight against him. "I would give you everything, but I cannot."

He needed to protect her from the most terrifying thing the world contained—him. Deep within him lurked a monster more evil and destructive than Hoth. His wolf kept that creature at bay, and they both worked to ensure it would never rise to the surface and hurt someone.

But Alice crept into all his hidden spaces—what if, in reaching for his wolf, she inadvertently touched the other beast instead? He couldn't bear the thought of hurting her or of seeing her flesh bruised and broken like his mother's. Alice needed to stay far away, even as he needed her skin pressed against his.

With a sigh, she settled against him. "There was a man in the yard earlier, he said his name was Callum."

Ewan froze. "What did this man look like?"

"That is the strange part, there was nothing remarkable about him except for his eyes. They were black and dead with no spark of life within them. We talked for a little while, and then he simply disappeared back into the shadows."

"Forge." He hissed the name between his teeth. "Do you think he was watching us?"

He could only hope they hadn't somehow given themselves away. The man had watched him in the tavern but not a flicker of recognition had passed between them. But then, Forge hadn't survived this long by being overt. Did Forge know Sean was really Ewan, come to bring him to justice?

If Ewan had a heart, it would have stopped as he

considered the risk to Alice. He bristled that she had stood outside their door, alone with the murderous vampyre. Forge could have drained her body and tossed her down the well and no one would ever know. His wolf snarled and twisted, trying to break free to protect Alice.

Her body relaxed against his side even as his stiffened, prepared to fight for her.

"He didn't seem to be paying any notice to the cottage. He said he wanted to escape the noise in the tavern and that he heard the men talk about my pies."

"Be on your guard, Alice. He is dangerous, and if he suspects our true reason for being here, both our lives would be forfeit." He had been a fool, thinking he could protect Alice, but what could a crippled wolf do against the much stronger Unnatural?

"I am going to visit the local witch in the morning, and I will ask her about vervain." Her arm stretched across his chest as she snuggled closer.

"Good." He kissed the top of her head. He would make her a dress of the herb if it kept Forge far away from her. Perhaps with a garlic necklace and hat to match.

Oh, the irony. He had hoped they were in the right place to find the smuggling ring Forge used, and now he wanted to snatch Alice away and send her back to Ianthe and safety. "Promise me you will never again be alone with him or get too close."

"I promise," she murmured as her head dropped to his chest.

Her breathing became deep and even as she fell

asleep. Ewan still lay awake, running through scenarios in his mind and trying to unravel an impossible puzzle: how to have the woman at his side without destroying her or getting her killed.

ANOTHER MORNING ARRIVED FAR TOO SOON. One thing Ewan had always loathed about army life was their insistence on springing from bed before dawn. No one needed to be awake that early unless you were returning from the gaming dens, delivering coal, or collecting nightsoil. He missed the indolent London lifestyle where one didn't have to rise from bed until after noon.

What would it be like to linger in bed all morning with this woman? The ache in his chest moved lower. He may be injured and defective, but he wasn't dead. Nor was he a saint. Having the nubile woman he desired draped over him reminded his body of a thirst that had gone too long unquenched.

He needed to douse himself with cold water before she saw that his resolve not to touch her dangled by a burning thread.

"Eilidh wants out," he whispered, and then he reluctantly moved away from her warmth and grabbed his trousers.

The terrier rushed off to the field behind the cottage. Ewan left her to tend her needs while he saw to his. He pulled a bucket of water from the well and shoved his whole head in. Holding his breath, he tolerated the frigid water until his lungs nearly burst, then he stood up and shook icy drips down his naked torso. The heat burning on the inside dissipated somewhat. As long as Alice had dressed by the time he returned, the fire shouldn't reignite.

Eilidh reappeared, and damp man and canine walked back to the cottage. Alice had risen, dressed, and was making tea. Ewan let out a relieved breath; he wouldn't be tortured by the silhouette of her naked form within her shift.

"I could have heated some water for you to wash," Alice said as she poured from the kettle into the smaller pot.

"I find cold water quite invigorating." He found a shirt, dragged it over his head, then cast around for his waistcoat. He always felt naked until he had a certain number of layers buttoned up around his body. Fine clothes were his armour that allowed him to lock everything inside.

"We are running out of tea. If you find the smugglers, do see if you can steal a small quantity of it." Alice set two mugs on the table.

"I shall make the procurement of more tea a priority mission for today." Ewan eyed his grubby stockings before he pulled them on his feet. What he would give for crisp, clean clothes.

Alice removed a pot of porridge from the grate over the fire and dished it out. Breakfast was simple, but kept them both sustained until suppertime.

"I have my own mission to visit the local aftermage healer today. Apart from acquiring vervain and a few other herbs I need, I shall find more berries for pie. It's a battle to find the ripe ones before the birds gobble them all up," she said.

Her pies were made from ambrosia. The sugar and spice balanced the tart blackberries, and the crust was light and flaky. Night after night, the patrons devoured as many as Alice could make.

Ewan patted his stomach. "If you keep making pies like that, I'll never be able to lever myself back on a horse. You also won't need to spin an enchantment to add flesh to my bones."

She flashed him a brief smile before dipping her spoon into the hot porridge. "We need to earn the trust of these people, and pie seems to be my way."

Knowing Forge lurked in the shadows only increased Ewan's concern for her. At least she rode inland, whereas Forge would be hiding from the sunlight in a dank cave somewhere near the coast. "Be careful, and take both Eilidh and your dagger."

Alice lifted the hem of her gown to reveal the short brown boot and the knife strapped to her lower leg. "Easy to reach, just like you showed me."

The sight of her leg was like blowing on the embers in his gut, and the flames threatened to sweep through his body. He dropped his gaze to his spoon. "I am riding out to see my contact. The gang is going to make use of me if I can offer something of value. I plan on delivering them the movements of the excise officers, and I shall obtain tea in exchange."

A brief smile touched her lips before she fell silent once more. Events lay unresolved between them. It was easier in the dark to hold each other while they whispered of secret things. In the daylight, it was harder to hide what burned behind your eyes. He had to do something to break the impasse, but what?

Alice renewed the spell to disguise his features and then left without her customary kiss to his cheek. Ewan watched her ride out of the yard and rubbed his face. The itch was only the growth of his beard, not his skin missing the touch of her lips.

He took his time saddling his horse and then rode north. At the same spot along the coast, he stopped and watched the ocean as he waited for his contact. Before too long, he appeared and the men had a brief conversation before going their separate ways. That left Ewan with a new problem—how to find the smugglers?

He should see if he could steal an item belonging to Jimmy that would enable Alice to locate him with her gift. Until then, he would try his own reconnaissance. Their sort didn't usually erect signs to their secret caves and passages, which made them rather difficult to stumble upon.

If he were a smuggler, which cove would he pick? He rode the coastline, pondering the available choices and contours of the land. They needed a cave to hide the contraband until it could be moved. A flat expanse of beach was visible from inland and wasn't very desirable. They would want a bit of a shelter at their backs, perhaps a small cliff that might conceal secret tunnels or entrances.

He paused at one such spot, although he could easily find a dozen such locations if he kept riding. For once, fate smiled upon him. Jimmy rode up on his broad draught horse.

"The very man I was looking for," Ewan called out as he neared.

"And now you have found me," Jimmy replied as he pulled his horse to a halt.

"I have spoken to my man and he had information to pass along." Ewan kept a smile on his face while inward he hoped Jimmy appeared because he had stumbled upon the right stretch of beach.

Jimmy fidgeted with his reins and looked around. A complex internal battle played out across his face. Either that or he was constipated, by the way he screwed up his eyes. Then the situation appeared to resolve itself and he dismounted from his horse.

"You may as well come with me," Jimmy said.

Ewan leaned on his horse's neck as he slid to the ground, then the men tethered their mounts to a nearby tree. Jimmy led the way down a worn path to the beach.

Below, tucked in the sheltering embrace of the over-hanging cliff, were two dinghies. The timbers were worn and covered in barnacles and Ewan wondered how watertight their hulls were. A familiar man coiled a rope by one boat. Crufts.

"He one of us, then?" Crufts said as they approached.

"I reckon, if the boss agrees," Jimmy replied.

Crufts dropped the rope into the bottom of the closest boat. "I want to see this; could get entertaining if you're wrong. We both know what he did to Jones."

Jimmy paled under the layer of grime covering his face, and Ewan had a flash of sympathy for the big man, assuming *Jones* was the drained corpse found on the beach. Jimmy would be quite the banquet if the vampyre decided to feast upon him. Daisy might have far bigger concerns than the marital bed, like picking out her widow's weeds.

Jimmy shrugged as though he didn't care, but he swallowed several times as though his throat had gone dry. "Evans is solid and the boss will see that."

Jimmy walked up another path, invisible from above, that was cut through the rock. Ewan followed and Crufts went behind. A little way up the path, Jimmy headed into the shadows cast by an outcrop. Ewan rolled his shoulders, his way of checking the location of his knives before he followed Jimmy.

The shadow turned into the entrance of a cave that led inland along a narrow tunnel. At points it was barely wide enough to roll a barrel, but it was concealed from prying eyes above. A light flickered up ahead, and soon the tunnel widened out into a natural cave. In the middle, opposite the entrance, a lantern sat atop a barrel. A man sat beside it at a small table, reading from a large ledger.

Shadows reached to either side of the cave, as far as the scant flame would allow, and revealed row after row of barrels stacked at least four high before they merged with the dark and disappeared. Ewan couldn't count how many in total, but he guessed a hundred or more. Why would Forge stockpile liquor?

"Boss, Evans has some information to pass along." Jimmy quickly side stepped to reveal Ewan behind him.

Forge closed the ledger and looked up. His piercing black gaze narrowed on Ewan, though he spoke to Jimmy. "And you thought to bring him here and reveal our location?"

Jimmy took off his cap and wrung it between his hands. "I . . . umm . . . I met him just by the path and didn't think—"

"No. You seldom do think, McGaffin. He is here now. Let's hear what he has to say, and then I will decide his fate." Forge dismissed Jimmy with a wave of his hand.

Ewan noted how Jimmy rushed to hide behind him, and then he limped a few steps closer to Forge. He prayed Alice's spell held and that the vampyre didn't have some way of seeing through enchantments. "I know a customs fellow. He told me the men would be out in force along this stretch tonight. They'll even have a ship patrolling the coast to stop all incoming boats."

Forge stared at him, his dead features unreadable. Then he nodded. "My thanks. Tonight we'll light the beacon so my ship knows to stay away. You could be handy." Forge's hand rested on the ledger, one long and sharp fingernail tapped the cover. "Can you read and write?"

"My mother was a gentlewoman and saw to it that I knew my letters and numbers. But my hand is not as tidy as it once was." Ewan held up the injured arm, still stiff but useable since Alice had worked her magic. "I can write with my left; it just takes a little longer."

Forge grunted. "A man of talents. Good. If you can keep the ledger of what comes in and payments, that would free me to concentrate on other matters."

"Since we are to be comrades, you wouldn't happen to have any tea going spare, would you? Alice ran out this morning." Ewan grinned.

Forge laughed and then pointed to Jimmy. "Find the man a small measure of tea. He has saved us far more by letting us know the customs men will be out tonight."

19

Alice

ALICE RODE INLAND, following the road and Gaffie's directions. Before long, she spotted a cottage that seemed to have grown out of the surrounding forest. Trees entwined their branches with the thatch roof and wild roses scrambled over the walls. But that wasn't what drew her eye. It was the riot of plants running from cottage to road that took her breath away. The pages of her botany book were crammed before her.

Dismounting, she left the horse at the roadside and told Eilidh to stay put. Then she walked up the path, pushing aside plants that sought to claim every piece of ground for themselves. It was only spring and already everything here looked in full bloom.

A woman emerged from behind a soaring artichoke. "Can I help you?"

"Yes." Alice pointed to one plant with a tight cluster of white flowers on a tall stem. "Do you have any valerian root for sale?"

"Ah. A sister witch are you?" The old woman narrowed her eyes and stared at Alice as though she could see the trace of mage power flowing through her veins.

"One of little power but with a thirst for knowledge," Alice replied.

The woman cackled, and Alice could imagine her toiling over a large pot by a moonlit night and throwing frog's legs into a bubbling concoction. "That's the best kind. Being open to learning will get you further than raw power."

Alice wished for just enough power to make a bullet move about six inches. "I try to meld my gift with herbs to help others. I have quite a list of things I need, if you can help?"

"Old Nelly can help you, lass." She beckoned Alice closer and the two women wandered through the fragrant landscape.

Alice could have spent all day talking to the old woman. She was a living, breathing textbook with a scattering of outrageous spells to bring revenge down on the head of an unfaithful lover. Not quite the remedy Alice needed—she'd need a tonic to make Ewan her lover first. Not that she would ever want to compel him. If he could not freely love her, what was the point?

Soon her basket was full, and Nelly even supplied early raspberries and their small leaves for making tea.

Alice promised to return as soon as she could, then climbed back onto the horse and waved goodbye.

At the Dancing Sow she unsaddled the horse and placed her herbs in the cottage. Then she took her basket of raspberries to the bustling kitchen. As Alice donned her apron, Jimmy rose from the table muttering under his breath about *man's business*, picked up his jacket and hat from the hook by the door, and walked out.

Daisy's face fell when her husband left without so much as a kiss on the cheek or a glance in her direction. Alice's heart constricted for her friend. Both of them were in a pickle with men. Why was it her gift allowed her to brew a spell for Daisy and Jimmy to find the spark of love, but Alice had no cure for loving an untouchable man?

"What did you find, love?" Gaffie asked as she picked up the turnspit dog and placed him in his wheel. After a rusty groan from the mechanism, the spit started to rotate as he ran, turning the haunch of meat for supper.

Gaffie was in a fine mood, and Alice suspected the popularity of her pies had much to do with it. Men were flocking for a slice washed down with a fine French brandy. Strange how barrels of the stuff materialised just when they were needed most. The combination of pie and liquor saw more coins disappearing into Gaffie's sagging pockets each night.

"Early raspberries. It will be a much sweeter pie for the men, and let us hope it puts them all in a sweet mood." She gathered together flour, butter, salt, and water to make the pastry. Her mind formulated and discarded a number of spells as she worked. She also worked on summoning items and managed to make a fork, needed for pricking the pastry, almost move three inches to her hand, but the effort left her exhausted.

By the time the pies were filled, tops crimped on firmly and dusted with sugar, she had the beginnings of a plan. It took another long hour before most of the work was done to prepare for supper and to ensure there was sufficient food to feed the hungry men who would pile into the tavern once the sky started to darken. Gaffie waved her away for a break, and Alice seized the opportunity to put one part of her plan into effect.

She checked and double-checked that she had everything needed to perform the arcane ritual she intended to inflict on Daisy. Only then did she set off in search of her fellow barmaid. She found Daisy wiping down tables in the main room.

She took the cloth from Daisy's hand and dropped it back in the bucket. "You are coming with me."

"I have work to do," Daisy said.

"It will wait for an hour, and then I will help you catch up." Alice pulled Daisy towards the back door.

"Mrs McGaffin will be ever so mad if the chores aren't done." Daisy chewed her bottom lip and her gaze went to the closed kitchen door.

Alice paused for a moment, wondering about the nature of Daisy's relationship with her mother-in-law. Then she discarded that thought as a problem for another day. Today's challenge was reigniting the flame of love in Daisy and Jimmy's marriage.

"An hour is all I ask. I want to start to weave a spell around you to make you irresistible to Jimmy. We are performing powerful magic and it might take several days before it reaches its full effect." Alice winked and hoped her friend would comply.

Daisy's eyes widened and her mouth made an o-shape. "You promise to help afterwards with my chores?"

An easy promise to make—Alice wouldn't leave her friend to work on her own. "Of course. Four hands will easily have this place tidy by tonight."

Out the back and across the courtyard, Alice led a nervous Daisy. "I've never dabbled in spell work before. We're not going to kill chickens or something like that, are we?"

"No chickens will be harmed." Possibly a few lice might drown, but they needed to go. Ewan would laugh. His fastidiousness had brushed off on Alice, and she found her body longed for a bath if she went longer than a week between them.

Alice drew Daisy into the cottage and shut the door behind them. Eilidh had scampered in and took her spot by the fire. In front of it, with fragrant steam rising from the surface, was the tin bath.

"A bath?" Daisy glanced at Alice as though she had gone stark raving mad.

Alice knew mad and had been that way for many months—bathing was not an act of insanity, despite what some folk thought.

"There are fragrant oils in the water that will scent your skin. Then we will wash your hair with a secret formulation my mother handed down to me." There were herbs swirling in the water that would adhere to Daisy's skin and help the finding spell Alice would cast. But the only secret to what she planned to use on Daisy's hair was that it contained soap.

Daisy still kept a suspicious eye on the bath.

"I am not very powerful, and finding Jimmy's love will take time. Think of this as the first step." Alice intended to work on Daisy's features while she bathed. She couldn't alter them much, not like she did with Ewan. But she could enhance what nature had given the other woman. She could add lustre to her hair and a sparkle to her eye. A light spell would improve her skin, highlight her cheek bones, and plump out her lips.

"Do I have to take all my clothes off?" Daisy stared at the water as though she suspected it would rise up and plot to drown her.

"That is the most effective way to bathe, and the spell will work better if it has direct contact with your skin." Alice started on the buttons of Daisy's dress.

"This does feel ever so . . . forbidden," Daisy whispered.

"Because that is what frightened men would have us believe. They tell us such things are dark or forbidden because they do not understand a woman's power and they do not want us to wield any," Alice said as she helped Daisy from the dirty dress.

Alice shook her head over the garment. Such a

shame to make Daisy put it back on when clean. Perhaps tomorrow they could undertake laundry.

Daisy laughed, a nervous sound, as her gaze darted around the room. "It's not evil is it? Casting spells?"

Alice remembered sitting at her mother's feet while she spun stories of their ancestors. How ignorant men would burn women aftermages as witches while bowing and scraping to men who were mages. Being feared or revered was based solely on gender. "No. Once men thought women with the trace of magic in their veins were evil and they called us witches. Now we are more enlightened. It is not the spell that is good or evil, but the person's intent. We are finding your love, and that is a noble cause."

Despite the fact that mages and their offspring had walked the Earth for thousands of years, many people were still uncomfortable with things they couldn't see or touch. It made it easier for them to sleep at night if they dismissed practitioners of magic as witches and shunned women's abilities as ungodly.

There were days when Alice remembered all too much of her time in Bedlam. Other aftermages had shared her cell because people couldn't comprehend what they did. Like the woman declared mad because the ghosts of her dead children tugged at her skirts, and her husband didn't want to answer awkward questions about what happened to them.

Alice averted her gaze as Daisy stepped into the bath and then sat down with her knees pulled to her chest. Alice pulled a chair within Daisy's reach and set down a steaming mug. "That's raspberry leaf tea. My mother always said it was good for a woman on the inside."

"Do you think the spell will be strong enough to really make Jimmy want me?" Daisy asked with a wistful tone as she laid her cheek on her knee.

Alice picked up the jug she would use to wash Daisy's hair and thought about her next words. She had faith the spell would work for Daisy and Jimmy, but she couldn't cast one to make Ewan love her. Such was the curse of being an aftermage, the gift could be used for others but not for your own benefit.

She wondered what it would take to breach the wall that surrounded Ewan's heart. Why did he think he couldn't love? Given he thought her delicate, he probably just said it to assuage her feelings, thinking she couldn't bear to hear the truth.

"I am sure it will work. The problem is not such a big one. Jimmy does love you, but sometimes men get lost in their problems and forget to see what is in front of them. The spell will simply remind him why he married you. What was it like, when you first met and he wooed you?" She wet Daisy's hair and then picked up the soap to work into her scalp.

"He was ever so sweet. I worked in the dairy and he used to turn up clutching handfuls of daisies—that's my name, you see."

As Alice washed and rinsed Daisy's hair (and washed and rinsed it again), Daisy told the story of a bumbling lummox who had courted a simple dairymaid. From her tale, it seemed they had genuine affection for each other, but lost their way after Jimmy and his father went off to war and only one returned. Alice suspected he paid more attention to his mother to make up for her loss, and in the process neglected his wife.

A simple enchantment was all this relationship needed.

"What about you and Sean, how did you meet?" Daisy sipped her tea as Alice rinsed her off for the last time.

What to tell? She had never been particularly adept at lying and needed to stay as close to the truth as possible. "Can you keep a secret?"

"Oh, yes. Is it terribly scandalous?" Daisy turned to stare at her with wide eyes.

"Not really, but there are parts of my history I would rather others didn't know."

Her torture at Hoth's hands and her time in Bedlam were truths only a select few would ever know. But Daisy could hear an abridged version.

"I was born and raised in a small village in Somerset. It was just my mother and me, and I used to help her brew remedies and spells for the villagers who came to our door. Then she died when I was seventeen. I could have continued as village healer, but I wanted excitement. Instead, I travelled to London to seek my fortune." That part of her narrative was entirely true.

Daisy finished her tea and placed the empty mug back on the chair. "I thought only lads undertook mad journeys like that. I can't imagine going to London all on my own."

Alice hadn't thought it mad at the time. She had

trodden the road full of wild hope, expectations, and gilded dreams. "In my youth, I was told I was a pretty thing, and on my first day in London, I was approached in the street by a very well-known madam."

Daisy gasped. "You never went into whoring, did you?"

Alice winked. "In a way. The madam ran a very high-class establishment, the sort aristocrats paid dearly to visit. She trained me to be a courtesan. We were educated, taught social graces and how to treat a man as though he were a king."

"Is that where you meet your man?" Daisy's hands tightened on the edge of the bath as though Alice's story was gripping.

She remembered seeing the dashing lieutenant at soirees and dreaming of such a man to sweep her off her feet. There was no need for Daisy to hear of the man who shredded her soul. Only one man mattered now, the one who protected her and held her close at night. "Yes. Sean was in London with a few of his fellow soldiers. We met, and my life has been entwined with his ever since."

A faraway look descended over Daisy's face. "And then he went off to war and was injured."

"Yes. A horse rolled on him. But I would love him injured or whole, makes no difference to me." She kept quiet that he was a lycanthrope. Given the Highland Wolves were the only shifters in the army, it would give away his true identity to reveal that detail.

"Do you love him so terribly much?" Daisy asked.

That was what pained Alice so. She would patch

together her heart and give it to Ewan, but he had pushed aside her love. She wiped the back of her hand across her face. She hadn't even noticed the tears falling down her cheek. "Sometimes love is uneven. Perhaps that is the curse of women, that we love far more than we are ever loved in return."

Daisy took Alice's hand. "You're wrong. I've seen how he looks at you. That man's love for you is so vast it would span the ocean."

A stone fell through Alice's empty torso. If only that were true. Ewan was simply a far better actor than her. They needed these people to believe they were a married couple, and it seemed he had convinced those who watched them.

"Perhaps," Alice whispered.

Daisy stepped out of the bath, and they towelled her body and hair dry before she put on her dirty clothes once again. Then Alice set to combing her hair and plaiting it into a thick tail that hung down her back. As Alice fussed with Daisy's hair, she wove a simple enhancement over the woman's features.

"Jimmy loves you, too, Daisy. I think he is trying to help his mother through her loss." Alice surveyed her handiwork. The bath and spell combined wrought a transformation over Daisy. Her long hair had its lustre restored, there was a glow about her cheeks, and her eyes twinkled.

"In case the spell needs a little more help, take this token and place it under your pillow tonight." Alice handed her a tiny cloth pouch.

"What is in it?" Daisy's hand hesitated over the diminutive parcel.

"Some herbs to aid his memory, that is all. The scent should remind him of his love for you." Alice also planned to add a little extra spice to Jimmy's ale when he turned up this evening. Sometimes a love spell needed a good prod to get it working.

Daisy took the pouch and tucked it into her pocket. "Now, shall we finish cleaning down the tables and preparing dinner for all the lads? I suspect they'll be hungry when they return this evening."

Arm in arm, the two women walked back across the yard. As they took their cloths and set to work, Alice pondered her relationship with Ewan. How sad that their deception was so convincing that she believed herself the loving bride of an ordinary injured soldier. Instead of moping, she should she cherish the days or weeks they had before them, and prepare for a life without him.

This mission was a test. Was the broken and shattered woman capable of moving amongst people again? On the surface, it would appear she could. Ewan had prepared her well and taught her how to master the fear and pain that overwhelmed. But now she wanted a different type of lesson from him.

Alice wanted to remember the touch of a man.

She wanted to learn of pleasure.

20

Ewan

EWAN HAD BECOME the thing he feared the most—a bureaucrat. Or was it a bookkeeper? He wasn't sure where the line was drawn between the two, and in his mind they merged into one crooked-backed, pasty-faced, emaciated scribe. An Unnatural creature with a dour wardrobe and the ability to drain the vitality from the world around him. He'd rather lie trapped under a dead horse than spend his life scribbling numbers onto paper and only wearing black.

When he was sixteen, his brother the baron offered him a choice: the army or university. Ewan thought if he were going to spend his life taking orders someone else, he'd rather do it with a weapon in his hand, not a quill. It also helped that women swooned over cavalry officers. No one gushed over the appearance of an accountant or lawyer.

As it transpired, life in the army suited him, especially once he caught the attention of his superior officers looking for men to undertake covert missions. The brotherhood he found with his fellow soldiers was augmented when he took the bite and became one of the Highland Wolves. He trusted his pack with his life, and his brother lycanthropes had his back in any fight.

Now, his pack had shrunk to Alice and her terrier, and the thought of relying on them if anything went wrong made his blood run cold. The woman was untested and the dog was easily swayed by a meaty titbit.

For the second time in his life, he would be grateful if Alick bounded into view as his great red furred wolf with saliva dripping from his fangs. Instead, Ewan pushed thoughts of rescue aside and tried to concentrate on his battle with a column of numbers.

Ewan had spent the day sitting on a tea chest at his impromptu desk made from a brandy barrel. His eyes ached from working by the pallid lantern light as he tallied up the inventory. Forge operated an odd system. Tea and tobacco were sold on directly. But for every four barrels of liquor snuck into the country, his men were allowed one to sell with the gold being split between them. The vampyre kept the other three barrels for himself.

Over two hundred barrels were stacked in the cave. Waiting.

Every now and then his gaze would slide sideways

to the stacks while he pondered what deadly surprise lurked within. Ewan suspected Forge stockpiled the French weapon until such time as his masters gave the order to release it. That meant he still had time to eliminate the vampyre and get rid of the threat to England. Somehow.

As he calculated the latest profits from the delivery sold in Hythe and then each man's share, he swore he heard his mother chuckling in his ear. He had been a horrid student and hated every second of mathematics. English was different; he inherited his mother's love of language and the flow of poetry.

The mission in Seabrook gave him a chance to reclaim his chosen career as a spy. If he failed here, he might be forced to seek a career as a tutor. There was a horrifying thought—trapped in a schoolroom teaching children as ungrateful as he had been. His mother's laughter echoed louder in his mind.

If he failed to destroy Forge and whatever hid in the barrels, he would seek an honourable death rather than take up a quill as a scribe or bookkeeper. Or perhaps he could walk out into the ocean and let the sea claim him. No. For that would leave Alice alone. While part of him knew he had to release her to live her own life, the wolf muttered that they should keep her forever.

Blast. Distracted, he had tallied the wrong column of numbers. He let out a sigh, dipped the nib of the quill in the ink, scratched through his carefully penned total, and started again. It was laborious work, not because of the mathematics. His quick mind did that easily enough. Rather, it was concentrating on forming the correct strokes with his left hand. While he could write with both hands, it took more effort to make his penmanship acceptable to his critical eye.

Objectively, he admired the way Forge hid treacherous activities within an illegal one. Smuggling was highly profitable, and coin bought silence from the men involved. Those involved were well paid by selling their share, and they just shrugged when Ewan asked about the brandy left to sit in the cave.

Not that the men would talk anyway, since they faced jail or deportation if caught by the excise men. Or a worse fate from Forge. One man had muttered that he worked for a vampyre but the others stayed tight lipped on the subject. No one commented that they mostly saw him at night and that he never ate or drank when he appeared in the tavern.

Jimmy slapped Ewan on the shoulder and made the quill jump. "How are the numbers? Will you be done in time to pay out the men tonight?"

Ewan frowned at the blob of ink that formed as a result of Jimmy's friendly greeting. He really was becoming a bookkeeper, because the smudge annoyed him and made him want to rip the entire page out and start again.

"Assuming Crufts returns with payment from Hythe, then yes. The men will have ample to spend in the tavern tonight."

A perfect situation for Jimmy. The men were paid and then promptly spent their coin in the tavern run by his mother. He should really cut out the middleman and issue them chits to spend on alcohol and food.

A wind blew down the tunnel and ruffled his pages. Just as he reached for them, a figure appeared in the entrance to the cavern. Forge. Ewan ducked his head and curled his spine so he hunched over the work. Every morning Alice altered his features, but Ewan wouldn't know if Forge saw through it until the moment the game was up.

Jimmy headed over to the man and touched the brim of his cap, a reflex when his boss appeared. Ewan thought it would be better to make the sign of the cross in the vampyre's presence and drape garlic around one's neck. It was highly unusual to see Forge during the day, but it was overcast outside and the sun hid behind the clouds.

"Evans here has tallied all the stock from the last shipment and worked out each man's cut. We just need the coin to pay everyone," Jimmy said.

For once, Ewan was grateful for his unkempt appearance. He had forgone shaving for the last few days as he didn't want to deal with the intimacy of Alice scraping away the hair. He couldn't think of shaving and Alice without imagining her straddling his lap as she groomed him.

"Good to hear Evans is proving his worth." Forge approached and picked up one of the sheets. His attention seemed to be on the neat columns of numbers, and his act might fool another man. Not Ewan. He saw the sly way Forge's eyes tracked sideways under his brows, studying the newest member of his group.

Ewan let his injured hand curl, the jagged scar that decorated his forearm visible under the edge of his pushed up sleeve. "I do what I can. Did my information prove useful?"

"Indeed," Forge murmured. "Two crews south of Hythe were caught and lost all their goods, boats, and their freedom. They now languish in gaol waiting to be sentenced to deportation in the colonies. Thanks to you, we shall be able to keep your lovely wife supplied with tea and company."

Ewan stared at the quill and wondered how far it would go into the other man's eye socket. The wolf roused to hear Alice's name cross the traitor's lips, and the creature longed to wrap its jaws around the man's thin neck. Instead, he mentally tugged his forelock and remembered his place. "She is most grateful for the tea you gave us and to see me gainfully occupied."

Forge made a noise in his throat and his gaze drifted back to the tally. "We're doing well. We are on track."

"You have quite a quantity of brandy stored here. Might I ask why?" Ewan took a risk and threw out the innocent sounding question while he squinted at the quill as though deciding if he needed a new nib.

A dead black gaze turned to him. One corner of Forge's lip curled upward and revealed a sharp canine. "Not that it is any of your concern, but I have been waiting for the right moment to release my stock."

"Of course sir, I was simply curious as to the long term strategy." Ewan screwed the lid back on the ink pot. "I'm certainly grateful for the work. It will enable me to provide for Alice, rather than her having to work every day." Words of gratitude nearly choked in his throat, but he would say them to play his role.

Forge placed the sheet back on the barrel. "Oh, don't be in such a hurry for her to quit the tavern. The men do like her pie."

Jimmy laughed and the tension broke.

"With the last shipment, I believe I have enough to move forward. Soon we'll start moving my stock to my contacts. We'll need all the men when we do that. I want it dispatched as quickly as possible." Forge stared at Ewan for a moment longer, then he gave a brief nod. "Evans."

One word and he left, dissolving back into the shadows.

Soon we'll start moving my stock. Ewan was running out of time. Earlier he had feigned his leg giving out and crashed into one of the barrels. Whatever was sealed within didn't move with the fluidity of liquid but the thump and slide of more solid items.

DARK FELL EARLY on a gloomy day, and evening found Ewan in the same corner, watching Alice work. Each night, she moved a little easier among the tight pack of patrons. Each night, she grew a little more into her new skin. Ewan marvelled at the changes time had wrought. He remembered the frail creature Aunt Maggie and Ianthe had helped from Bedlam. Her very nature had been insubstantial, as though she were an apparition made of mist and dust.

Now she grew in confidence. She learned how to handle the attacks of panic that threatened to overwhelm her. And more importantly, he'd taught her how to protect herself both mentally and physically. Alice was no longer a victim, but a confident woman who drew men to her.

Other changes occurred around them as Ewan settled into his new role as bookkeeper for the smugglers. More men stopped to talk to him, to trade war stories, or simply discuss the political climate. Bit-by-bit, or slice-by-slice of pie, the locals drew them into their embrace. Alice's kind nature allowed her to make friends with Gaffie, Daisy, and the other women. The men who frequented the tavern certainly appreciated a pretty face, and her pie added to her reputation.

Ewan had his place in the gang now and had met Forge without any flicker of recognition passing between them. He would assume Alice's spell worked, up until the point he found himself tied to an anchor and feeding fish. His plan advanced, and all he needed to do was lay a trap and to find a way to be alone with the vampyre without the hulking mass of Jimmy at his back.

Alice approached his table with a plate in her hand. She set it before him. "The last slice. I nearly had to pull a knife on a man who tried to take it."

Before she could dart away, he took her hand and kissed her palm. "Thank you for gallantly defending my pie."

She stared at her hand. Then she turned it over and tucked it into her apron pocket. "You're my husband; of course I would make sure you have the last piece."

There was so much he would say to her, but words dissolved on his tongue and slid back down his gullet. He wanted her. The need burned through his veins, and the thought of possessing her was all that kept his wolf clinging to life. It took all his control to stop himself from having her. She had endured too much to be used by another man.

But where was the line between pretend and actual feelings? They acted their parts, but each morning when he awoke with her pressed against him, he had trouble remembering that he must not love her. He would gladly dip himself in silver if in exchange she were happy and cherished. And pleasured.

Other men in the tavern cast her sideways glances, yet she seemed unaware of them. A new and strange emotion clawed into existence in his chest—jealousy. Never before had Ewan wanted something he couldn't have, and it made his teeth ache.

What if there was a way? His wolf whispered. *What would you do to keep her?*

Ewan picked a fork and teased loose a bite of pie. He knew the answer to that question. If it were at all possible, he would do anything to keep her.

21

———

Alice

As Alice walked away from Ewan, her palm itched. His kiss was such a gentle, intimate act that it stole her breath. She had struggled to find something to say to him as her mind tried to decipher what his action meant. He tortured her with gentle words and soft caresses, all the while saying they could never be together.

She wanted to ball her hands into fists and burst into tears. The infuriating man would send her screaming back to Bedlam if he carried on like this. Something needed to change between them. As a first step, Alice needed an honest explanation from her *husband* as to why she wasn't suitable to be with him. In her opinion, their broken pieces seemed to fit together perfectly. Or was she deluded?

Alice was yanked out of her musings when Daisy grabbed her hand and pulled her into the kitchen. The woman glowed and her brown eyes sparkled with vitality that wasn't from Alice's glamour, but entirely natural.

"It worked." She practically squealed the words, bouncing on her toes with excitement.

Alice smiled. At least someone was receiving loving attention. "I'm so pleased."

"It was just like when we were first married. He couldn't keep his hands off me last night. Or this morning. Thank you." Daisy wrapped her arms around Alice and hugged her.

Alice closed her eyes and bit back her sob. If only a bath and a simple love spell could bring her and Ewan together. But their issues were far deeper than finding a forgotten love, for that implied there was any to begin with.

Ewan said the defect was his, not hers. He said he was too broken to ever be able to love. Did that likewise mean Alice, broken as well, was incapable of love? It didn't feel that way. Her entire body ached for him, and it was far deeper rooted than a physical need.

What you seek will yet be found with Ewan, just don't give up on him, a voice she had heard before whispered in her ear.

Alice dragged her attention back to the ecstatic and well-loved Daisy. At least one woman in Seabrook was deliriously happy. "I'm glad things are working for you and Jimmy. Remember to keep up with the regular baths, and I'll make you a supply of ensorcelled herbs to add to the water."

Daisy hugged her again and danced from the kitchen. Alice used the subsequent moment of quiet to pat the turnspit dog. It broke her heart to see a canine so neglected. Eilidh meant the world to her and Alice assumed everyone would love the dog that resided under their particular roof. The turnspit dog might have an ugly face, but that didn't mean he should be deprived of affection. She scratched behind his ears and wondered how her terrier would take to another dog joining their little family.

"We're both trapped, my friend, running as fast as we can to stay in one spot. Let's see if I can figure out a way for us both to break free," Alice whispered.

The dog thumped his tail and went back to sleep. Alice wiped a lone tear from her cheek, schooled her face into a pleasant smile, and pushed back into the main room.

The tavern was quieter tonight, and the fiddler played a slow tune. Jimmy took Daisy by the hand and spun her into his arms, much to the delight of his wife. Daisy giggled as they danced around the tables. Jimmy did resemble a bull let loose in the tavern, but the grin on his face was worth the occasional knocked over mug.

It gladdened Alice to see the young couple rekindle their relationship. She glanced to Ewan, who likewise watched the dancers but made no move towards her. Not that he could dance. The poultice was working and drawing the silver from his body, but the relief seemed temporary. She had hoped each day would see an improvement, until he was fully recovered and able to shift into his wolf again. An arrogant thought, given she was a diluted, fourth-generation mage blood. But what she would give for Ewan to hold her for just a few slow steps.

Distant memories formed within the mist that clouded her mind. She remembered laughing under a crystal chandelier as a young nobleman held her in his arms while she taught him the steps to the scandalous waltz. Once, she had been a carefree woman who laughed often and delighted in fripperies and parties. A sliver of that woman remained in one torn corner of soul, and she longed to dance again.

A man stopped before her and gave a courtly bow, out of place in the rough Dancing Sow. He held out his left arm. "Might I have the pleasure of this dance?"

Callum Forge. Alice's heart stopped for a beat then started again. Did she dare dance in the arms of a traitorous vampyre? But then given his standing in the tight-knit community, she couldn't refuse.

Inside her mind, the bright young woman ran and hid in her secure chamber, bolted the door, and let the fierce wolf Eilidh out to patrol. Outwardly, Alice exuded calm as she placed her hand on his forearm.

"I would be delighted—thank you, Mr Forge." She didn't dare glance at Ewan as she stepped into a clear space with Forge and the man placed a hand at her waist.

"Callum," he whispered against her ear. "I would

have you call me Callum, now you and your man are part of my family."

Memories of how Hoth lured and won her flared hot and bright in her mind. Then wolf Eilidh snapped her jaws and tore the image into pieces. With her armour in place, Alice murmured, "As you wish, Callum."

"A waltz, Freddy. Let us show the country folk what is scandalising the ton in London." Dead black eyes pierced her soul. "I will teach you the steps, it's a fairly simple dance."

"I know how to waltz," she replied.

The fiddler struck up the tune and Forge led the way. He held her hand a little too tight in his chill flesh. Alice suppressed the shiver that wanted to work down her spine.

No emotion registered on his face that the barmaid could waltz. Not even a flicker of curiosity. As he held her close, Alice realised there was no rise and fall of his chest and no breath filled his lungs. He truly was dead. Until this moment she thought such a creature impossible, even as she accepted that Ewan was a lycanthrope and that ghosts roamed the countryside trying to talk to loved ones left behind.

"How did a village lass come to learn the waltz?" he asked.

They spun as they danced and Ewan flashed in and out of her view, giving her glimpses of a scowl drawing his black eyebrows together. "I spent some time in London."

Her partner's unnerving flat eyes never wavered

from her face. He didn't need to look where he was going because everyone else got out of his way. "Well, aren't you just a mystery. Did you work as a lady's maid and glimpse your mistress practising in private? Or did you learn elsewhere?"

He didn't scare her with his softly spoken words masking the stench of death that clung to him. "The waltz was just one of many skills I learned as a courtesan."

Still nothing registered, but he tilted his head to one side as he inspected her. "A woman of the world. How refreshing. I do find country conversation dull at times."

The music flowed over her limbs as Alice danced and shook a little of her sad mood away—she could still enjoy the music even if she didn't get to dance with her choice of partner. "You are something of a mystery, yourself. You seem an educated man; what drove you to bury yourself in the countryside?"

"I am an enterprising individual, and I am here to set myself up for a very long and prosperous life. There is a fortune to be made during war, if one knows where to look." He spun her again and his hand tightened on her waist. Long nails dug through her rough wool dress.

"Particularly if one looks to the east at night," she murmured.

He barked a short laugh, but it was a cold sound like the crack of frost. "Such an intelligent and civilised woman. You are wasted on the likes of Evans, who has no prospects. You would be the perfect adornment for a wealthy man. Your conversation would relieve dreary days."

Alice smiled while inside she mentally practised her knife throws. Never again would she be a man's property, to be shattered at his whim. "Sean has prospects. He just hasn't found the right direction yet."

Forge made a noise in the back of his throat. "He has skills that add to my business, that is true. But his sort will always take orders, not give them."

"I've learned not to judge a man by his place in society, but by how he interacts with it." Her days with Ewan allowed Alice to smile at this creature and endure his hands on her. She wore a mask, while inside she plotted how to ensure this Unnatural became a resident of Hell alongside the other demon that had tortured her.

Forge's flat gaze slid to the corner and settled there for a moment. "At times, I feel there is something familiar about your husband."

Alice hid her burst of fear. He couldn't have recognised Ewan, surely? Every day she renewed the spell and even Ewan had trouble recognising himself in the mirror. "So many men have dragged themselves back to England with war injuries. I think a limp might be contagious, so many soldiers seem to have one."

A soft laugh shook his chest and then it stilled again. "Perhaps that is it."

The dance came to an end and Forge released her. Alice gave a small curtsey. "Thank you, Callum, you are a marvellous dance partner. But if you will excuse me now, I must return to my duties."

A scowl darkened Ewan' handsome face as she picked up an empty tankard and walked back to the bar. The rest of the night passed in easy conversation and Alice ignored her pretend husband sulking in the corner. He could not have things both ways; if he wouldn't touch her, perhaps she would find another man who would. Although she preferred one who had a beating heart in his chest.

Once the last patron had left and Gaffie locked the door, Ewan rose from his seat to escort her back to the cottage. They followed the same path and routine, and once inside, Alice poked the remains of the fire and then tossed in a fresh scoop of coals.

Ewan shut the door and the click of the lock seemed ominous in the quiet. "You shouldn't have danced with Forge."

Alice straightened and met his gaze. He stayed at the edge of the light, where shadows fell over his face. "He asked. How could I have refused him?"

His fingers curled into a fist and then relaxed again. "You took a huge risk."

She scoffed at him and waved her hand. "It would have been a bigger risk to say no. If he is interested in me, he will be asking fewer questions about you."

"What did he say?" Ewan walked forward to lean on the back of a chair, as though he used the piece of furniture to hold himself back from her.

Alice shrugged and sat on the bed to unlace her boots. "He thought there was something familiar about you. I pointed out that some injuries are common among the returned soldiers."

Ewan tried to pace, but only managed a few steps before his injured leg caused him to misstep. "Blast. I'm sure your spell holds, but we do not know the extent of a vampyre's abilities. At least my wolf is laid so low Forge won't be able to scent the lycanthrope within me. Let us hope that he thinks no more on the matter. But I don't want you to talk to him again."

Alice laughed. "If I ignored him, that would look decidedly odd. Besides, I will talk to whomever I please. You do not control me."

He turned, reached out a hand to her, and then paused. He closed his fist and dropped the hand back to his side. "He is a cold -blooded killer. I would rather not have you in his path."

"Your mission is almost at an end. We have found him, and now you have simply to tie the noose around his neck. Or plunge a knife into his body and remove his liver." Even as Alice said the words, a chill wind blew through her soul.

What would happen once Ewan brought the murderous traitor to justice? No doubt he would he ride off, never to glance backwards at her again. She would trek back to Ianthe alone and continue her work on the farm.

Her chest heaved as she pulled off her boots and dropped them to the floor. She wriggled her toes in her stockings. It seemed hard to imagine going back to a rural life. If she wanted to stop men like Hoth, then she needed to stalk them in their favourite hunting ground —London.

Ewan dropped into the chair and pulled off his

Hessians. "I bide my time. All I need is Forge alone, without Jimmy at his back. I only lack the right opportunity."

Taking the man on by himself sounded incredibly foolish to Alice. When Ewan was fully healed and able to shift into his wolf perhaps, but as an injured man?

She bit her lip. There must be another way, one that included her. Her gaze rested on the mortar and pestle sitting under the window. Some ways of dealing with an enemy were quieter but as effective as a direct assault. She needed a way to use the vervain.

"Give me the chance to see if I can work a spell to increase the effectiveness of the vervain. I just need to think what it would need to find or hide within him."

Ewan's full lips spread in a smile. "Are you worried about me?"

Some things she couldn't hide, like her fear for him. "Yes. I'd rather not be a pretend widow."

He huffed a short laugh. "You would look stunning in black. Men would flock to you like moths to a dark flame."

"Don't." She held up her hand to silence his words. "Don't play with me like this. You cannot pretend to care, to dictate my actions, and then push me away. You toy with me like a cat with a frightened mouse. Do not be so cruel. Please, just stop."

She drew a deep breath and willed the tears away.

Ewan moved to sit on the bed next to her, but kept a distance between them. "I'm sorry. There is no future for us, Alice. Whatever path I walk after this, I will walk it alone. But that doesn't mean I don't care for you."

Ewan's torture was worse than the agony of Hoth shaving a flake from her soul. The only difference was that Ewan whittled her away with kindness. "How can you say you care for me and in the same breath announce that you will walk away without even a backwards glance?"

Tears sprang to her eyes and she blinked them away. She didn't understand.

Ewan reached out and caressed her face. "Did I ever say that? Don't think that I do this without regrets, Alice. If I had the capacity to love, I would give it all to you. I would spend my life pleasing you, if only I could."

She shook her head and balled up her fists. "Stop it! Just stop it! Do you not see that your words are a knife blade to my heart?"

He slipped an arm around her and drew her to him. By instinct, she wrapped her arms around his torso and buried her face in his shirt. Why could he not see that they fit together? She saw the boy deep inside him who wanted to be loved. Beside the lad stood his wolf, and like the turnspit dog, it was desperate for a kind word and gentle touch. She just had to figure out how to reach them.

He kissed the top of her head. "I will treasure every moment of our time together, Alice, but I know it must come to an end."

She tried to blink the tears away, but it hurt too much. She let them fall and soak into his shirt. "Why? I don't understand."

He stroked her face. "Because monsters are real, and I am one of them."

Such a ridiculous thing to say when she knew he was a lycanthrope. She had seen Quinn's wolf and was more fascinated than scared by the creature. There was no prejudice against the Unnatural within her. Alice drew a breath, ready to sally forth with an argument, but he laid a finger on her lips.

"Let's just go to bed, please. Let me hold you, and let us both pretend that we are simply Sean and Alice Evans, a married couple who will grow old together."

Her heart splintered at his words and reformed, as when she had re-stitched her shredded soul into something new. From the ruins of the old Alice broke free the new woman. One who wouldn't be stopped when she set her mind to something.

"Very well." She lay in his arms, her head resting on his chest as she listened to the steady thump of his heart. How could he say he didn't possess one? Here was all the proof she needed. It beat within him and lulled her to sleep.

Many weeks ago, in the Christmas snow, she had stood in the waterfall glade and made a promise to a spirit that she wouldn't give up on Ewan. She vowed to find a way to heal his wolf and let both halves of him come together again.

There was only one thing that needed to be shattered now—Ewan's belief in his lack of a heart.

22

Ewan

EWAN ROSE EARLY. He took Alice's hands and pressed them to the sides of his face. As though she spoke from a trance, the half-asleep woman whispered the words to renew the hiding spell and obscure his features. Then he slipped away to spend an hour or two gazing out to sea. His thoughts swirled with the mist rising off the ocean, not that he found any solution hiding among the waves.

Alice's words had been a punch to his gut. He tortured her by playing with her affections, but that was never his intention. More than catching Forge or figuring out his future, he wanted to protect Alice. Even though his wolf whimpered that it would protect her. What could the beast bound in chains of silver do against the other monster?

Once Alice might have been broken, but not anymore. Every day revealed her new strength, and it drew him like a siren's song. He wanted her, and only having her near soothed the fractures in his soul. Now he knew how Tantalus felt. His throat was parched and Alice was the wine he would drink, but she stayed eternally beyond his reach. Frustration made him want to scream.

His desire for her was an assault on his resolve to stay away. As he watched the sun feebly battle dark clouds, he admitted his fight was doomed. With his wolf unable to fight the other demon, it would soon break free. Would he shatter Alice's body like his father had done to his mother? For that was all he knew of love, crushing a woman in your fist until the light faded from her eyes.

The damp of approaching bad weather made his broken bones ache. He needed to swallow his pride and let Alice continue to apply the poultices to draw out the poison from his blood. Except her touch was an addiction, and each time she left him wanting more. Her concentration as she lavished care upon him, purely for the sake of trying to heal his body, had become his opiate.

Since his mother died, Ewan had spent his life keeping others at a distance. He had learned independence and self-reliance. He needed no one and no one needed him, a mantra for his life. The only exceptions were his brothers-in-arms, who had become his pack.

When it came to women, he used them for physical

release and then moved on to the next one. He didn't linger and he had no regrets.

Until now.

He should have kept physical space between him and Alice. But his body was a cowardly traitor. The chill in his soul could only be alleviated by her touch, and only Alice soothed his wolf so it could snatch a few moments of peace. To hold her at night was to touch something infinitely human and precious. Things he could never be.

For the first time in his life, he desperately wanted something he couldn't have, and it confused him. The small boy who still dwelt deep inside him longed for the guidance of his mother. She would have known what to do. He pulled the slim volume of Robbie Burns from his pocket and ran a thumb over the cover.

What would his mother have advised? She would have smiled and read a poem. Although the advice a ten-year-old boy needed was quite different to what a thirty-year-old lycanthrope needed to hear.

The book fell open in his hands at "Tae a Moose." Or, "To A Mouse." The poem was about a mouse's nest in the field that the farmer ploughed up by accident, destroying its safe haven for winter. The last two verses touched him most, for he couldn't help casting his mind backwards over troubled events and dreading he would repeat them in the future.

But Mousie, thou art no thy lane,
In proving foresight may be vain:
The best-laid schemes o' mice an' men
Gang aft agley,

An' lea'e us nought but grief an' pain,
For promis'd joy!
Still thou are blest, compared wi' me!
The present only toucheth thee:
But och! I backward cast my e'e,
On prospects drear!
An' forward, tho' I canna see,
I guess an' fear!

A roll of thunder made him glance up. Offshore, a storm rolled over the ocean from France. Black clouds amassed on the horizon and set course for England. They churned and moved above as though they contained a living thing trying to break free of its constrictions. Once it hit, they would be in for a cold, wet, and miserable afternoon. Alice might have time to draw more of the silver free before she had to work in the tavern.

He growled deep in his throat. Another night of watching other men take her in their arms to dance. Another night of watching other men with lust in their eyes as they gazed at her form, wondering if one would make her an offer. Their marriage was a pretence for the purposes of his mission, and she was free to bestow her affections elsewhere. So why did the idea of another man touching her make his mouth go dry?

Because she was his mate.

Bile rose to the back of his throat and he stared at his hand curled into a fist. He was the worst sort of monster. He'd thought the process of becoming a Highland Wolf would burn all trace of his father's blood from him. Instead, that demon merged with the wolf and urged him to use violence to mark Alice as his and to ensure no other man cast glances at her.

This was why she could never be his; just as she recovered, he would break her anew.

Ewan tucked the book back into his pocket and led the gelding to a fallen tree. He used the ride back to the inn to plot. All he needed was to get Forge alone. Perhaps he would head down to the hidden cave on the pretence of doing more bookkeeping. Then he could peek at whatever hid in all those barrels.

Back in the barn, he unsaddled the horse and wiped down its damp coat. The rain arrived in fat, heavy drops. Ewan patted the gelding's neck and, seeing Alice's horse eating hay next door, he walked to the cottage to find her.

"Alice?" The fire crackled in the grate, but she wasn't there. Perhaps she was making more pies in the kitchen. He stood outside and glanced around as the rain fell heavier. A bark drew his attention from the neighbouring field. Turning his back to the warm tavern, he headed to the open paddock instead.

The rain pounded the ground and the odour of damp earth rose into the air. Sitting amid the lush grass was Alice. She rubbed her arms as her thin dress became soaked.

Ewan raised a hand to attract her attention. "Let's go inside before you catch your death of cold."

She shook her head. When she raised her face to him, he couldn't tell if rain or tears ran down her cheeks. "No. I cannot do this anymore, Ewan. I cannot move until you tell me why you can never love."

"What?" That wasn't the question he expected. Nor was it one he ever wanted to answer, let alone in the middle of a field with a storm about to burst overhead.

She still didn't move, and the terrier huddled into her mistress, either seeking or trying to give warmth. "I need to know. You are so adamant that you don't have a heart, but I think the fault resides in me. I am too broken to be loved."

"Never!" The answer flew to his lips. How could she ever assume that? Her fractures, scars and the sheer resolve she used to overcome them were what attracted him to her.

"Come inside. We can talk about it once you are warm and dry." Or preferably they'd never broach the subject. Stubborn woman. He shrugged the jacket from his shoulders and tried to wrap it around her.

Alice pushed it away as she rose. Her hair was plastered to her face and water ran down her neck. "Tell me, Ewan, or I shall stand here all day. If the fault is not mine, why can you not offer me the smallest scrap of affection?"

He wanted to reassure her, to spill the whole terrible truth, but what could he tell her that wouldn't scare her? His history was no fairy tale but a nightmare. He wouldn't burden a woman with his story of woe. "Because the men of my family are monsters, worse than Hoth or Forge."

Her eyes widened but she held her position in front of him. "You keep saying that, but I do not believe you. I know you are an Unnatural, but there is no flicker of Hoth's evil residing in you. I would know."

He shook his head. He had years of practice at hiding his foul creature from anyone's view. "Come back to the cottage, please?"

He needed to get her out of the rain before she caught a chill. He shook droplets from his eyes. The scenery blurred and distorted in the rain. Memories threatened to push in from the sides and he wiped them away.

Tell her, his mother urged.

One tiny sliver, that's what he could give her. The smallest glimpse into his black soul to make her stop asking and to lure her back to the cottage. "My family are entirely natural demons, not Unnatural ones. When I was ten years old, my father killed my mother. That violence runs through me. I would kill any woman who got too close to me. I thought the lycanthrope curse would remove it from me, but it only made it sink deeper into my soul."

Her gaze never left his face. "You're wrong. You wouldn't hurt me. There is more to your story than that. Tell me what happened."

He ground his jaw as he regarded her. He could scoff, say he had only been ten and didn't know why, but he did. The knowing sat at the bottom of his heart and weighed him down. Truth was an anchor embedded in the ocean floor, holding the ship above immobile. Until he pulled it free, he could never move on.

"My father was a brute. A true bastard who wielded power like a weapon and enjoyed beating women, children, and the servants. My mother stood between him and me, and I hated myself that she took my blows and that I could not protect her."

Alice laid a hand on his arm. "You were a child. Any mother would do the same."

No. It proved he was weak, and that weakness had cost his mother her life. If he had been a man, or a wolf, he would have defended her and she would still be alive. "One night, my mother refused him, and he chased her out to the landing. The noise roused me from sleep, and even me watching from the doorway didn't stop him. He bashed her head on the wall until she went limp, then he used her. When he had finished, she dropped to the floor. I will never forget the anguish in her eyes as she tried to crawl to me. Her hand reached for me but before our fingertips touched, Father kicked her down the stairs. The servants were told it was an accident and that she fell."

Alice swallowed, her eyes wide.

Would she turn and run? Confession didn't ease his soul, it troubled him further. His family were demons just like Hoth, men who took what they wanted without any care for those they abused. During the one visit Ewan made to his ancestral home as an adult, he had seen the bruises on his sister-in-law. Like father, like son. Why should he be any different?

Her fingers curled into the linen of his shirt. "Why does that make you incapable of love?"

"Because that is my blood, the poison that taints my soul. I possess the desire to hurt. The ability to beat the woman who loves me. It is a demon that calls to me, and I can never rid myself of it." His hands clenched into fists, his right hand now able to fully contract and stretch.

There was the horrid secret he kept well hidden. He relished taking the life of another. It thrilled him and set his blood on fire to see the life drain from an enemy's eyes. That was why he kept his wolf on a tight leash, for if the true brute inside him ever broke free, nothing and no one would ever stop his blood lust.

"I don't believe you. You are more than that. I know what Ianthe has told me of the wolves, and above all else you protect, not destroy." She laid her other hand on his arm and faced him as the heavens above opened and thunder crashed.

Part of him, the small child who loved his mother, desperately wanted to believe her. Instead, he scoffed. "I was born a natural monster, then the army made me an Unnatural one. I am the worst of both worlds combined."

She leaned closer to him and despite the cold rain, warmth radiated from her. If she swayed just a fraction, her chest would press against his.

He cradled her face in his palms. "You cannot stand close to me, Alice, because I would hurt you, and that would kill me."

Her hands ran up his arms to his shoulders. "Do you think me so feeble after all that I have endured, that I would ever let a man or Unnatural hurt me again? If you would have me, I will make you a vow, Ewan Shaw. If you ever raise a hand to me, I would deliver unto you an excruciating and prolonged death."

God, this woman made his chest swell. Could he

even dare give credence to the things his wolf muttered —that she was his mate and this was truly love?

"Would my death be by knife or witchcraft?" Something about her made him doubt she would deliver a swift death with a knife to his heart.

"You have taught me well, and I would use all my skills. With a blade, my aftermage gift, and knowledge of botany, I would craft your demise." Her gaze was the lush green of a deep forest. One filled with the darkest kind of magic and wonder.

She was either an ethereal witch sent to torment him or a gift sent by his mother. All he had to do was reach for her.

Alice pressed herself tighter to him, so that even the rain couldn't come between them. "What you fail to understand, *husband*, is that you may have sworn you will not love, but I have never made any such a vow."

"Alice," he murmured. With one hand, he stroked a damp strand of hair away from her face. "Do not do this."

She smiled. "I am not a soldier, and you cannot command my affections, Captain. I offer you all that remains of my tattered heart. I love you truly and deeply, and you cannot stop me."

The ache constricted in his chest. "I cannot dare to love, Alice. I must deny what I and my wolf want, for it is the only way to ensure I never hurt a woman."

She tapped a finger against his forehead. "You're not listening. You cannot chase me away. I am here and refuse to move from your side. I give you my love, and all I ask in return is for your company and your touch."

Her eyes flared a deeper green. Her arms slid around his neck and she looked up at him. Standing on tiptoe, she brushed her lips against his. A butterfly kiss. A soft, gentle thing, as though a newly-emerged insect tested its wings.

She whispered against his mouth. "I want your skin sliding against mine, and for your mouth to know my cries as we are joined. If you cannot give me your love, then I demand that you give me pleasure."

There was something he could give her. Pleasure. Lightning lit the clouds as though it would tear the sky apart, and he surrendered to the storm. He wrapped his arms tight around her and kissed her hard.

23

Alice

THE STORM BROKE OVERHEAD and drenched Alice to the skin, but she didn't care. The taste of Ewan on her lips made her body tingle and vibrate as though she were the sky and lightning ran through her limbs.

He broke away and rested his forehead against hers. "Promise me that if the time arrives, you will do it."

She would promise him the moon if it meant he would carry on kissing her, but she didn't think that was what he meant. Her mind was dizzy with pleasure already as she tried to concentrate on his request.

He pulled back further to meet her gaze, his hands moving from her hair to frame her face. "Promise me that if I ever raise a hand to you, you will kill me. I never want to become the vile creature that lurks inside me. Better to be put out of my misery than harm you."

Why could he not see that this was why they were meant to be together? They were beautiful together in all their brokenness. No other woman would promise to kill the man they loved. "I promise, I will end you before you ever become like your father or Hoth."

Satisfied, he kissed her again until her knees buckled and she slumped against him. Only then did he tuck her close and guide her back to the cottage. The rain didn't matter anymore. Alice barely noticed it trickling down the back of her dress, for Ewan had his arm around her waist and anticipation bubbled under her skin.

With the cottage door shut against the storm, Ewan stirred the embers of the fire and tossed on more coal. Alice unbuttoned her dress with fingers that shook as her teeth chattered. Possibly it was far colder outside than she thought, but Ewan would soon warm her from the inside out. In fact, she suspected he would make her burn.

She stepped out of the soaking dress and tossed it over a chair to dry by the fire. Ewan pulled her close and claimed her mouth again. His hands tangled in her short hair as he held her in place and took control of the kiss. He kissed her with a skill that made her whimper and fist his shirt.

Lord, the man turned her into a pyre of longing as though she burned at the stake of her love.

"You're frozen. Let's get you into bed, and I shall warm you up." He helped her peel the shift from her body and laid it over the damp dress. She was naked before him except for her stockings, and it sent a thrill through her body.

Ewan walked her backwards until she sat on the edge of the bed. With drawn out motions and one muttered curse, he managed to drop to his knees. He knelt, a penitent at her feet.

"Are you all right?" Concern wrinkled her brow when he remained still and silent for too long. Had he hurt himself in attempting to kneel?

When he looked up, a sad smile crossed his full lips. "I have not tasted a woman's pleasure since before I was injured. I don't want to disappoint you."

How could he disappoint her? But she suspected it wasn't worry about too brief a physical performance that ate at him. His pain cut through her, and Alice brushed her hands through his black hair and made his gaze meet hers. "The simple act of your touch brings more pleasure than I have ever known. You could never disappoint me, but later I will put another poultice on that leg to draw out more silver. I'll not have you suffering when I can ease your pain."

"Let's deal with one ache at a time," he whispered, then dropped a kiss on her skin.

Alice sucked in a breath at the heat hie generate within her. He slid a finger under the top of her stocking, and with agonising slowness he rolled it down her leg, over her knee, and all the way to her ankle. He caressed every inch of skin on his way down her limb. Then he pulled the first stocking off of her foot and turned her attention to the other leg.

His blue eyes blazed with cool fire as, once again, he

began by placing a kiss on her skin. Then he slid his fingers under the knitted stocking before taking a leisurely journey down her leg.

Alice closed her eyes, her attention focused on the light strokes as he dragged his knuckles down her thigh. Around and behind her knee Ewan placed caresses before his fingers fluttered along her calf to encircle her ankle.

By the time stocking number two was discarded, her chest rose and fell with sharp breaths as anticipation and longing collided inside her. Alice was glad she was sitting down, for her knees had turned to jelly. It had been so long since a man saw her as something desirable that she didn't know how she would bear the agony of waiting for him.

"Get under the blankets," he said, resting his hands on the mattress to lever himself up to his feet.

Only when she pulled the blanket over her shoulders did he begin to undress. His wet shirt joined an equally sodden pair of trousers over a chair.

Ewan was beautiful in the pale light. Shadows flickered and played over his muscles. He reminded Alice of a fine statue, carved in the image of the Gods. Old injuries and faded scars made him easier to look at, as though the artist had deliberately added an imperfection to his masterpiece. That savage touch marred his beauty and made him human as opposed to an otherworldly creature, too good for her.

Alice licked her lips and imagined how his body would feel under her tongue. Would his skin taste of salt from the ocean air and beach?

He climbed into the bed and drew her into his arms. This time, they were skin to skin, and she drank in the contact. He radiated heat even though he should have been as cold as her. He projected such icy control, and yet once naked, he burned like a furnace so that Alice craved his heat.

"You're so warm, yet you are as drenched as I am." Her hands stroked over his chest, following the lines around muscles to where an old scar ran under his ribs.

She sighed as she slid closer to him and angled her head, eager for more of his scorching kisses.

"Body heat is a wolf trait. We burn hotter, and it makes us ideal wintertime bed companions," he murmured against her skin.

Alice envied those Highland maidens who spent long, snowy winters in bed with their lycanthrope lovers. A hundred such winters wouldn't be enough to ever satisfy her hunger for him.

Ewan took his time with languid, leisurely kisses that stole her breath. With a gentle exploration of her body, he added fuel to her pyre, yet he batted away all her attempts to hurry or direct his attention. If this was a rusty, out of practice performance, then she was grateful for it. Any more and she would surely explode like a volcano, unable to contain the pressure.

He rolled her to the mattress as he began a descent of blazing kisses down her body.

"I will have you know that I take it as a matter of honour to ensure the woman always reaches completion first. And second."

Alice found coherent thoughts became impossible

under his touch. Words swirled in her mind, dancing beyond her reach as her world spun. All she could do was curl her fingers into his shoulders to anchor herself. Higher and higher, Alice circled in a night sky. Each time, she thought Ewan could throw her no farther, but then her body responded to his ministrations and she flew until she struggled for breath and her mind splintered in the most amazing burst of ecstasy.

Ewan's wolf appeared to her, running across the sky. Its ebony fur was a shimmer against the stars and its eyes glowed like sapphires. The enormous creature stopped before her. It clutched something in its jaws, and shafts of light tried to escape as though it held a star on its tongue.

Alice reached out a hand and the wolf dropped the object into her hand. When she uncurled her fingers, a tiny silvery orb lay in her palm. The last piece of her soul.

Complete at last, she cried out as pleasure exploded through her body in time with the storm that raged outside.

Ewan groaned and the two of them clung to each other as they floated in a velvet sky lit by sparkling gems. The wolf played, chasing stars just like Eilidh chased rabbits in a meadow.

Moment by quiet moment, Alice fluttered back to Earth with Ewan, and the wolf faded back into the velvet night sky.

They dozed for a little while, both sated and content to let their minds drift in and out of slumber.

Alice lay in the arms of the man she loved and wondered how to shatter the last barriers around his heart.

At least now she understood his reluctance to let a woman close. How it must have scarred the young boy to see his mother die at the hands of his father. Abuse had broken both their minds, but like the blade, they were forged in fire and emerged on the other side stronger.

"You're wrong," she whispered in the pale afternoon light. The storm had exhausted itself outside the window. The rain lightened to a steady patter and dusk was not far away.

Ewan pulled her atop him. "About what?"

Alice straddled his hips and laid her hands on his shoulders. "Love."

She moved her body above him. Ewan might not be able to shift forms to heal his physical injuries, but other parts of him exhibited remarkable recovery powers.

"Oh? Enlighten me. I will admit it is a topic that I know little about." His hands made lazy circles up and down her back.

She trod carefully, wanting to reach him but not scare him away. He seemed so adamant that love meant destruction for any woman who he let close. He just couldn't see that Alice was already under his skin, and part of her had been protected by his wolf.

"Your father and brother never loved. What you described was possession. If you truly love someone, you cannot harm them. Look inside yourself and look to your pack brothers. Wolves protect as fiercely as they love. You would lay down your life for the one you love." She would. If anyone threatened Ewan, she would use whatever arcane knowledge and power she possessed to keep him safe.

His hands stopped their movement as he considered her words. "How can you be so sure?"

"I have been possessed, but I have never been loved." There was another sad truth that had fractured her soul. Hoth had possessed her, but no man had ever loved her. Knowing one allowed her an insight into the other. Obsession wasn't love; it was a disguise for controlling someone. Like a child who guards a favourite toy they don't want someone else to touch.

"Well, I confess to knowing nothing about love, but I know enough to fill volumes about pleasure. Let me show you."

He rolled her under him and claimed her mouth in a slow, breath-stealing kiss.

Alice had given Ewan something to ponder. Now she plotted how to use her gift to keep her promise given by the waterfall. Only when Ewan truly embraced the darkest parts of himself and trusted his creature could man and wolf be free.

24

Ewan

THE BANGING that awoke Ewan was not unlike the unwelcome intrusion of a hangover, except he was sober. As he roused, he identified the source of the noise as someone hammering on the cottage door. The worst of the storm had passed and late afternoon edged into dusk. He untangled himself from Alice's warm body and slipped from the bed. His clothing was hung over a chair and, thankfully, looked dry.

The pounding continued.

"Coming," he yelled as he pulled on his trousers. Not an easy thing to do when one leg wouldn't hold his weight and he had to balance his buttocks on the table to get his foot in the right leg hole.

Alice stirred. "Who is it?"

He cast a glance in her direction and motioned for

her to stay in bed. The sooner he told whoever it was to sod off, the sooner he could climb back into bed and pull her on top of him. "Some inconsiderate buffoon who is lucky I don't put a knife in him for disturbing us."

He lit the lantern on the table and then pulled the door open to see two figures standing in the rain. Jimmy and Crufts. They didn't wait to be invited but pushed inside and shut the door behind them before the gust of wind blew the candle out. Crufts chortled on seeing Alice. Ewan moved to stand between the men and the naked woman.

"What do you want?" He eyed the intruders as they dripped water on the floor.

"Nice way to pass the afternoon," Crufts said, peering around Ewan to leer at Alice.

Ewan shrugged. "I have a beautiful wife and it's raining—what would you do, play cards?"

Jimmy scowled at Crufts and then pointed out the window. "Boat's coming in and weather's rough. We need all hands to help."

Ewan swore under his breath. There went his plans for the rest of the evening. "Very well, but I need to finish dressing."

Alice rolled over to her side and the sheet barely covered half her body. It slid down to her hip and revealed the swell and dip of her form. Ewan sucked in a breath. The woman could play the temptress. Next to him Crufts was drawing in shallow breaths like a panting dog.

"Wouldn't you rather come back to bed, husband?"

she asked, running a finger along her swollen bottom lip.

What he would give to shove the men out the door and return to her. He wanted to spend hours, or preferably days, learning every inch of her skin and finding the hidden spots that drove her wild. His wolf wanted to inhale her scent and rub against her, but this was his chance to have at Forge. "I need to go, love. Work calls."

"Hurry up—five minutes and we leave. We'll have your horse saddled and waiting." Jimmy grabbed Crufts by the collar of his jacket and hauled him out the door.

Ewan walked back to Alice, cradled her head, and took a long kiss.

"I am going to need to call out Crufts after that," he whispered.

Alice laughed as he grabbed the rest of his clothing and dressed as fast as his body allowed. With a final look at her, he hurried out into the rain.

Outside, the horses were already saddled and waiting, rain running down their coats. Ewan patted his gelding and silently thanked Quinn for finding a placid horse. The others were spooked by the weather, but his bay was too dense to be worried by a bit of cold water. He walked the horse to the well and balanced on the stone edge to climb on.

As he awkwardly landed in the saddle, he remembered a summer day two years before, when he and the other Highland Wolves had played at tent pegging. He used to be able to hang off the side of the saddle to spear a token or bounce from one side to the other. But no more. Not until he rid his body of the blasted French magic. At least Alice had reminded him that he still possessed mastery of other skills, judging by the soft cries she had made all afternoon.

The rain eased to a persistent drizzle as they rode down to the cove. Due to the storm, dusk had dropped straight into night. Luckily, the men all knew the way as darkness wrapped around them. Ewan wiped rain from his eyes and squinted out to sea. He couldn't see a vessel approaching, but rough waves might conceal her, and they often ran with no light showing to avoid detection by the excise men.

The sheltered cove had conveniently close trees that shadowed the path to the beach. On the other side of the semi-circle of sand was a trail up the bank that could only be traversed by men. That path led to a small opening half way up, invisible from above due to the angle of the rock.

Half way down the path, the men pulled their horses to a halt. Ewan slid from his mount, hanging on to its mane to keep his legs under him, and then looped the reins over a tree branch.

"Where's the boat?" he asked Jimmy.

The big man shrugged. "Must be running late due to the weather."

Highly possible the storm would delay its progress. But they had sought him out saying the boat was coming in, which implied a lookout had spotted it. Perhaps the swell and waves kept it farther off shore.

A cold feeling slithered down Ewan's back along

with the rain, and deep inside his wolf growled a warning.

Ewan paused on the beach. His gaze flicked from the narrow track cut through the rock and then back out to the rough ocean. "Should we not wait here for the boat to approach?"

"The other lads were going to meet us in the cave, they'll know where it is." Jimmy led off towards the tunnels. Crufts dropped behind Ewan, and the ice that ran along his spine turned to a lump of dread in his gut. There should have been at least five other men ready to man the dinghies and cart barrels and crates from the main vessel. If they were in the cavern, then where were their horses?

The tunnel gave one last twist and then a flicker of light revealed their destination. Lanterns were set on barrels at the back, and flames within an iron brazier created a small bubble of warmth in the chill cavern. Around the edges of the space were the rows of tightly stacked barrels. Ewan let out a sigh that Forge had not yet begun distributing the contents.

A single figure sat in the shadows, using a box as a chair and a barrel as a table. He played with a deck of cards, laying them one at a time on the circular top. The rest of the crew were absent. Crufts shuffled to a halt behind Ewan, and Jimmy side stepped out of his way.

Ewan had been collected for a private meeting with the vampyre. Somehow he doubted it was to discuss a promotion.

"Do take a seat, Lieutenant Shaw." Forge gestured to the tea chest on the opposite side of his table.

"Captain, actually; I was promoted a year ago when Hamish became major." Ewan considered his options as he walked over and sat down. Jimmy alone could overpower him, even if he weren't still nursing a broken body. Three to one was foul odds, and he had to admit the situation was dire.

"I do apologise—*Captain* Shaw." Forge tapped the remaining cards in his hand and then set them down. "You very nearly fooled me with your extra flesh and muddy hair and eyes. A simple disguising spell, I assume. Recently one of the lads said you helped him tie an impeccable knot in a cravat. That triggered my memory—such a strange detail for an average soldier. Then when I danced with your lovely wife, I couldn't help but notice the necklace she wears—a wolf."

Done in by a piece of jewellery, and it wasn't even a thing Ewan had given Alice.

Forge held up a small compass, but instead of pointing north the needle swung around to point at Ewan. "A French mage gave me this. There's wolfsbane inside the case, and with a simple spell, the needle now points to the nearest lupine. I never thought to need it here, but imagine my surprise when it revealed that a wolf sat across from me in the Dancing Sow. I heard the French shot one of you with a silver bullet, and I am delighted to learn it was you. I do hope the pain is excruciating."

Ewan glared at the compass. There was a piece of intelligence he needed to pass on to his regiment. It would be handy if the British mages created a similar device to locate vampyres.

"Speaking of bullets, as I recollect last time we met in London you took a shot in the chest from Alick's wife. Made quite the hole in your chest. I'm curious, if you take off your shirt could we see right through you?" Ewan asked.

"Unlike a mangy cur such as yourself, I cannot be killed. All I required was a little time to heal and a fortifying . . . wine." He grinned and exposed sharp canines.

"Did you invite me down here for a catch up, or do you wish to surrender in private?" Ewan glanced to the other men. If he could reach the knife in his boot, it would even the odds and he might yet escape the situation.

"Oh, we have much more to discuss yet. Tie him up, Jimmy. I have a few questions I would like the captain to answer." Forge leaned back against the cavern wall and watched from under hooded eyes.

Jimmy grinned as he and Crufts stepped forward with a length of rope.

Ewan rose to his feet while instinct told him events were not going to unfold in his favour.

"Dirty traitor." Jimmy spat on the floor and then struck out, punching Ewan hard in the gut.

Ewan doubled over as the breath left his body with a whoosh. While he tried to regain his composure, Crufts seized his arms and Jimmy looped the rope tight around his torso and wrists, locking his arms behind him. Then they shoved him back down on the tea chest.

"You do realise I fight for England, Jimmy. The only *traitor* in this cavern is that creature who does the bidding of French masters." Ewan gestured to Forge with a shrug of his shoulder. He figured Jimmy wasn't very bright, but even he should have realised that Ewan was not the traitor.

Jimmy frowned and glanced to his boss. The cogs were slow to turn in his thick skull, and Ewan hoped he realised he was backing the wrong man. With Jimmy on his side, he could capture the vampyre.

"Hit him again, Jimmy," Forge said as he rose and came to stand in front of Ewan.

Jimmy lashed out again, punching Ewan hard in the face, and his head snapped back. His vision turned black as pain burst over his cheek and eye. His wolf tried to rise to the surface, but the silver yanked it back down.

"Where are the others?" Forge asked.

Ewan blinked to clear the stars dancing in front of his eyes and then frowned. "Others?"

Forge moved with lightning speed, his fingers wrapping around Ewan's throat. Then he squeezed hard enough to make the blood pound in Ewan's ears and his vision narrow. Inside him the wolf was frantic, trying to free itself. Now both of them were bound and helpless.

"You never work alone—where is Logan? He must be close by, but I cannot smell him, nor does my compass reveal any other dogs but you." Forge leaned closer.

Blood washed over Ewan's tongue and he did a

quick count of his teeth. "If by close you mean across the Channel, then certainly, he is close to hand."

Forge squeezed tighter. Air was cut off to Ewan's lungs, and his body burned with the need to draw a breath. His only consolation was that Forge wouldn't kill him like this. It was too clean.

"What do you mean?" Forge asked with the same tone you might ask someone to pass the salt. He never raised his voice, and neither frustration nor anger coloured his words.

Ewan huffed a brief laugh. "In case you have forgotten, the war is not yet over. While I am of no use to my regiment, they continue to fight the French. Sorry to disappoint you, but I am alone."

"No, you're not." For the briefest second, interest flared in Forge's dead eyes and then it was gone.

Dread plummeted through Ewan so fast his stomach nearly turned. He swallowed down bile and forced his features to remain impassive. "Leave her out of this. Alice knows nothing."

Inside Ewan, a storm was unleashed while his exterior remained as still as the glass surface of a millpond. The bonds that kept his darkest demon under control shattered as Forge whispered the words of danger aimed at Alice. In that instant, Ewan understood the truth of her words. His father and brother had never loved.

The demon flowed over his prone wolf and enveloped it. All the parts of Ewan merged and became one monstrous creature that bayed for Forge's blood for daring to bring Alice into this. The creature flexed and strained against the silver chains, and link by link, they cracked and gave way.

He would either tear these men apart or lay down his life to protect Alice, such was his love for her. Never could he harm her; every bone in his body ached to ensure her safety.

"You can torture me all you want, I have nothing to tell." Ewan tried to bring Forge's focus back to him. Alice was a smart woman and would know something was afoot when he didn't return.

"You and I are too similar, Shaw. Pain is something we embrace, but I see your weakness." He pulled the knife free of Ewan's boot and used it to pick at his claw-like nails as he spoke.

Ewan swallowed the rage. He needed to keep a clear mind, to think his way out of this. Anger burned through his veins in such quantities that it battled the silver leached by the bullet. A little longer, and he would be able to release his beast.

"You've been drinking too much of your brandy. Alice is part of my cover and nothing more," Ewan said.

Forge laughed, a chill sound that conjured images of a crypt. He pointed the dagger at Jimmy and Crufts. "Fetch the woman."

25

Alice

AFTER EWAN LEFT, Alice stretched and rolled her shoulders. Deep within her, the last piece settled into its place within the mosaic of her soul. One sliver of her shredded soul had lodged within a handsome cavalry officer with a cool demeanour and, as other women whispered behind their fans, impenetrable armour around his heart.

Alice had, unknowingly, used her aftermage gift to conceal a shard within Ewan. His wolf had curled itself around the fragment as though it were a dragon hiding a gem. As they joined their bodies, the wolf had returned the piece to her.

Peace drifted through her as she relished being complete after so long being fractured. Her hand stretched out to where Ewan had lain and the sheets were still warm from his body. Alice rolled over and hugged the pillow to her. Being with Ewan was far different than her limited previous experience. His entire focus had been on her as though she were the only woman in the entire world.

While she had enjoyed the physical act before, society taught a woman that the man's pleasure was paramount and a woman's incidental. Ewan turned society's expectations upside down as he threw her to levels of ecstasy she never dreamed were possible.

He raised her to the sky where all her broken pieces became glittering jewels to be celebrated, not broken pottery to be discarded. She knew with certainly that she loved Ewan and that he had an equal capacity to love her. He just didn't know it yet.

Long ago, as they sat by the waterfall they had talked of transformations. Ewan had said she could never be fixed, but she could become something new. She had hidden away for long enough. The time had come to tear away the silken cloth binding her and reveal the new Alice—the stronger version, the one who would confront the world head on. Starting with helping the man she loved bring a traitor to justice and freeing his wolf.

Ideas formed in her mind as she pondered how to kill an undead creature. She let her mind wander and explore how to merge herbs and magic. When something finally coalesced that might work, she left the bed and dressed.

Alice gathered up what she needed in a basket and then she told Eilidh to stay put. Better the terrier was safe and warm in the cottage than a participant of what Alice had planned. The dog sighed, stared at her from under bushy eyebrows, and went back to sleep in front of the fire.

She ran through the rain to the tavern. With her gift, she reached out to find Ewan. The air around her rippled and stroked her skin. Like throwing a rock into water, all she had to do was follow the ripples back to their point of origin to find him.

Inside the tavern, she found the women in the kitchen, keeping watch on the evening's supper.

"The men came and got Sean—they said a boat is coming in. His leg has been bothering him something terrible lately, and I thought I would brew up a special potion to help ease some of his pain." She grabbed a small pot and dropped it onto a free grate. What she planned to brew shouldn't be ingested, and saying it was medicinal should stop anyone sticking a finger in to sample it.

Alice added a glug of ale to the pot before measuring out her herbs. "I was hoping to take it down to him tonight, if you could do without me for an hour or so?"

"With the lads busy and the tail of the storm out there, tonight will be a quiet one. Why don't both you girls have the evening to yourselves? I'll cope on my own. Daisy can hitch up the cart and take you out." Gaffie continued stirring her pots.

"Of course I could, it would be lovely to surprise Jimmy." Daisy winked. The woman was in a fine mood since her relationship had begun to heal.

Alice needed to go alone, and she'd rather her new friend didn't get hurt. "No point in two of us getting wet. Why don't you stay here and draw a bath for yourself? I can find Sean with my gift."

Gaffie laughed. "That would have been a handy skill when my man was still alive. He was forever sneaking off, that one."

"Are you sure?" Daisy had a dreamy look in her eyes.

Alice found a long spoon to stir her brew. "Of course. I'll tell Jimmy to hurry home because you are waiting for him with a free evening."

Daisy hugged Alice from behind. "You are a grand friend. I'll go drag the bath to our room."

"I'll give you a hand once this is boiling. It needs to reduce down to a syrup." Alice waited until her concoction was bubbling away, and then she helped Daisy carry the tin bath up the stairs to the large room she shared with Jimmy.

The couple's room was the direct opposite of Alice's bare room in Ianthe's house. Here every surface was crammed with ornaments and knickknacks. Quite apart from the sheer volume of items, Daisy seemed inordinately fond of pink. Alice had difficulty imaging the great lumbering Jimmy sleeping surrounded by pink porcelain figurines and pillows.

Alice picked up a pink poodle from the mantel and stroked a finger down its smooth back. "You have so many pretty things."

Daisy beamed like a proud mother. "I do adore shopping in Hythe for things to make our room pretty.

Next time we have a day off, we should go together. We could find something to cheer up the cottage for you and Sean."

"I'd like that." Alice managed a smile but wondered if she and Ewan would be in the area much longer. "I better get back to my brew, I don't want it to burn."

When Alice returned to the kitchen, the mixture had simmered down to a thick syrup. She found a metal flask and spooned the concoction in, being careful not to splash any on her skin.

"I'll go give this to Ewan to ease his troubles and make sure Jimmy comes straight home to you, Daisy." Alice wrapped her woollen shawl around her body and tied the ends tight. Then she dropped the flask into her apron pocket.

"Thank you," Daisy called out as she poured water into the large pots on the stove.

Alice ran across to the stables and saddled her horse. Thankfully, the heavy rain had diminished to a steady drizzle by the time she climbed into the saddle and gave the horse a kick. They trotted along the dirt track, through the murky gloom.

As she rode, Alice touched her gift and the air rippled around her. She knew the men would be somewhere along the stretch of coast, she just needed to pinpoint which cove was used by the smugglers.

At a spot where the land rose to make a cliff overshadowing the beach, the ripples became closer together until they almost merged into a solid wave.

"Found you," Alice whispered as she pulled the horse to a halt.

As she dropped to the ground and scanned the area, she heard a soft nicker. Horses were tied to trees just out of sight. She walked her horse over to the others and tied the reins to a branch.

A chill washed over Alice's skin. There were no lights out at sea and no movement on the beach below. The men had either already met the boat or there was no boat at all. The prickle at the back of her neck told her it was the latter.

She walked the worn path slowly in the gathering dark. Down on the beach, sand shifted under her feet, but still there was no sign of men, boat, or contraband. Dragged up where the high tide couldn't reach, the upturned hulls of two boats were just visible in the lee of an outcrop.

Alice paused and heeded the warning whispered in her mind. She unlaced the knife and sheath from her calf and tied it around her waist. Then she tucked the weapon under the ends of her shawl in the small of her back. There it was hidden from sight but easily within reach.

She carried on across the beach and up the narrow path on the other side. A dark, open mouth turned into a tunnel. Light flickered at the end and long shadows were cast along the rocky roof. The pound of surf against the beach became the pound of feet, as two shapes appeared holding aloft lanterns.

"Jimmy," Alice said on recognising the men. "I have come to fetch you."

His brow furrowed. "Fetch me? No, I am to fetch you."

Alice glanced to Crufts, who narrowed his eyes at her and wet his lips. That one was dangerous. Jimmy was simpler to handle for all his greater size. "I have saved you a trip then. Gaffie gave Daisy and me the evening off. Your lovely wife is even now having a bath and eagerly awaiting your return."

"But—" Jimmy screwed up his face, the dilemma clearly written on his face. Stay or go?

Crufts nudged his friend. "Why don't you head home, Jimmy? I'll escort Alice to the boss."

Alice kept the smile on her face. Crufts' words confirmed her worst fears. She laid a hand on Jimmy's arm. "Go home, Jimmy and spend some time with Daisy. Crufts will take me to my husband."

The big man swallowed. "Reckon I will then." He nodded at her and then took off down the tunnel and towards the beach.

Alice took a step further into the dark when Crufts reached out and grabbed her arm. "There's no need for us to hurry. The boss thinks we are riding to the Sow to fetch you. We can linger here awhile."

"There is no need to keep my husband waiting, thank you." She turned and tried to tug herself free.

Crufts dropped his lantern to the ground and shoved her to the side of the tunnel, where cold stone dug into Alice's back. The tall man caged her with his arms by her head as he leaned his body against her, using his larger size to hold her captive. "You put on a fine display earlier. You liked showing me your body, didn't you? Now I want a feel."

Alice drew a slow breath as he ground his pelvis

against her stomach. "Let me go, or Mr Forge will hear of this."

He dropped one hand and squeezed her breast. His breath came faster as he mauled her flesh. "Mr Forge doesn't care. We know your husband is a filthy traitor who will turn us over to the excise men."

Alice wrenched her body to one side and knocked away his hand. She struggled but he leaned more weight on her and wedged his knee between her legs. "Let me go or you will regret it. You have been warned."

He laughed, but not too loud in case it echoed down the tunnel to Forge. "I'll let you go once you've taken care of me. Flashing yourself made me hard, and now I'm going to give it to you, just like you want."

Crufts reached down, fisted her skirt, and yanked it up. Chill air swirled around Alice's knees as he dragged her skirts higher. She placed her hands on his chest and tried to push him away, but he didn't budge.

"Give us a kiss." Wet lips pressed against hers and a tongue tried to gain access to her mouth as Alice gritted her teeth. His hand continued to raise her skirts until they were bunched up between them.

She edged one hand behind her back and her fingers grasped the hilt of the knife. There wasn't room to move with him grinding her into the rock, and the first blow was important. Alice slowed her breathing to calm her thoughts and ignored his hands on her body.

When she decided where to strike, she held it in her mind and mentally traced the line. She only had one chance and needed to get it right. Then in one fluid move she drew the knife from the sheath and her arm made an arc, driving the knife up and under his left armpit. A large artery ran under the arm to the heart, and she touched her gift to allow the blade to find the right spot.

Crufts staggered backwards, swearing, and nearly tripped over the lantern. Alice had another decision to make. Run down the tunnel towards Ewan, or make sure Crufts didn't try to rape another woman. She chose the latter.

"Stupid bitch!" He roared and lifted his left arm.

Alice ducked under his arm, pulled the knife free, and then plunged it into his chest.

Crufts staggered backwards into the opposite wall. His eyes widened as a dark patch bloomed over the front of his jacket. His fingers grabbed at the hilt and tugged it free of his flesh.

Alice didn't wait to see what he did next. She snatched up the lantern and took off down the tunnel. The light shook back and forth as she ran. Up ahead, a soft yellow orb enlarged until it turned into the end of the tunnel. She slowed her pace and entered a large cavern.

Ewan sat on a crate, his arms lashed to his torso. His head dropped on his chest as blood ruined his shirt.

"Ewan!" she called his name and ran towards him. Alice set the lantern on a barrel and took Ewan's face in her hands.

A large bruise spread over one cheek, the eye on the same side was bloody and swelling shut, and his lip was cut. His blue eyes focused on her and a sad smile touched his lips. "You should have stayed away."

Forge coughed into his hand. "I sent my men to fetch you, Alice. What exactly have you done with them?"

Alice wiped blood from the corner of Ewan's mouth and then turned to face the vampyre. "Jimmy has returned to the Dancing Sow. Crufts thought he would rape me in the tunnel."

A low growl came from behind her that sounded distinctly lupine.

"I assume he was unsuccessful since you are here and he is not." Forge took a step closer towards her. He sniffed the air around her, like a hyena scenting its prey. "I smell blood, but it's not yours."

"No. I left him bleeding in the tunnel." Alice wished she had paused long enough to retrieve her knife. All she had now was the flask and its poisonous contents.

Forge advanced another step. Cold black eyes fixed her to the spot as he reached out and wrapped his hand around her throat. "Oh, you are intriguing. Such a strong pulse you have."

Alice kept her panic locked away in the room in her mind. She had a plan. All she needed was the chance to implement it.

"Let her go, Forge. Alice knows nothing." Ewan looked up. He seemed stronger, as though raw energy pulsed around him. His shoulders flexed against the ropes, but they held him in place.

Forge leaned close to Alice, but not a whisper of breath escaped from between his dead lips. "Captain Shaw is playing coy, but I'm sure with your help we can make him very talkative."

Ewan's head raised and he squinted at Alice. "Really Forge, use your brain. She knows nothing. Alice was a convenient cover and a pleasurable distraction at night."

"Oh, she's far more than that, and we both know it. I can smell your wolf all over her." The hand around her throat moved and his thumb stroked her jaw. "Besides, what she knows is irrelevant. What matters is what you will tell me to end her agony."

Ewan growled as he rocked and twisted in his seat. "You'll not harm her."

Alice might have imagined it, but Ewan's features seem to blur and shift as he spoke, as though his wolf tried to emerge. She scanned the cavern as her mind whirled. The brazier held a fire too small to be of any use against the creature holding her. Embedded in a barrel was a familiar knife belonging to Ewan. Would she be strong enough to summon the weapon to her hand?

"I don't think so." The vampyre saw what caught her attention and dragged her two strides further away from it.

"You must realise this is futile. Too many people will ask questions if Ewan and I disappear. You cannot drain the entire village to cover your crimes." Alice stood taller and twisted in his grasp to meet his dead eyes.

Forge huffed a soft laugh. "Only one person will disappear tonight, and we'll tell the others he drowned bringing the shipment ashore."

Inside her safe room she screamed *NO!* and

slammed her fists into the walls. She and Ewan would escape and thwart this creature; there had to be a way.

"I will not be complicit in your evil plans." She would keep him talking while waiting for her moment to snatch the flask from her pocket.

Forge placed his hands on her shoulders and turned her to face the rows of neatly stacked barrels. "Look here and imagine each keg full of gold. My mission will make me a wealthy man for all of my long life. But I have realised I might grow bored. As much as I dislike people, I find the idea appealing of a fine form to listen to me narrate my victories. Once I have you in my thrall, you will be complicit in whatever I ask of you."

"I would rather die than spend a moment alone with you," she said between clenched teeth.

Ewan fell silent and still. He didn't rage or scream, but it washed off him as though he bathed the air around him in cold fury.

"You might yet get your wish." Forge circled behind Alice. He placed one hand under her chin and tilted her head to one side, exposing her neck. Then he addressed Ewan. "Do you know how to make a new vampyre? First you drain your victim to the point of death. You need to stop just before their heart gives the final beat. I've tried a few times, but I'm rather greedy and always end up killing them."

"Let Alice go, and I will say no more of your operation here. You can do what you please with me, just let her walk away," Ewan said.

"Oh I will do what I please with you. Once I have

pleased myself with her." Forge rubbed his thumb over the vein in Alice's neck. "Once they are almost dead, you open a vein and feed them your blood. With no pulse, our blood is thick and sluggish, and they have to suck quite hard to draw enough to effect the change. I was fed from the wrist, but with a creature like this, I think I'd rather have her hungry mouth fastened somewhere else."

"I will erase you from this earth for touching her." Ewan's blue eyes blazed.

"Why don't you say goodbye to the captain, and then we'll start. All this talking is making me quite parched, and you don't want me drinking too deeply of you." Forge pushed her towards Ewan.

Alice stumbled forward and placed both hands on his thighs. She looked up into his battered face and whispered, "I love you, and I'm sorry."

A frown pulled at his brow. "None of this is your fault, only mine."

"No, I'm sorry for this. It's going to hurt." Her fingers curled into his flesh.

Her time with Hoth taught Alice one valuable lesson. In moments of the greatest need, desperation and necessity can combine to give a person strength they never knew they possessed. Alice needed to find those resources within her now. She couldn't try and fail because that simply wasn't an option. She let her gift find the silver bullet buried deep in Ewan's femur.

Then she summoned it to her hand.

26

Ewan

RAGE ALREADY BURNED through Ewan like cold fire, but now he became a pyre as the bullet reversed its long ago journey. He gritted his teeth as pain scorched his flesh and nerves. Then, as rain soothes dry summer earth, behind the wash of agony came cool relief as Alice drew the ensorcelled bullet from his body.

In the last few hours, Ewan hadn't physically moved, but he had come a long way. He acknowledged how deeply he loved Alice and saw that his wolf had been right all along. She was his mate, the one woman who understood and loved him as no other ever could. The one person who made his life infinitely better and for whom he would risk everything, even death.

For years he thought he had locked away a demon, but he had instead shut away a pivotal piece of himself.

He thought he became a cold statue to protect others, but he was deceived. He did it to protect himself.

It had torn his young heart to shreds to lose the mother he had loved so dearly. To shield himself from ever experiencing such pain again, he locked away his heart, his passion, and all those emotions that added colour and texture to life.

Finally, he embraced his wolf and absorbed it as part of him instead of viewing it as a weapon to wield and control. Just as Alice stitched back her soul, so Ewan pulled together all his pieces and become one. He drew a deep breath as the wolf flowed through every part of him and made him something better. Fiercer. A creature that would love and protect its mate without limits.

And now it was free.

Alice curled her hand around the bloody bullet as Forge hauled her backwards. The vampyre exposed his sharp canines as he fisted his hand in Alice's short hair and pulled her head back to bare her throat.

I love you, Ewan mouthed to Alice. Then he surrendered to the beast.

Ewan the man shimmered and dissolved as the other creature emerged. The ropes binding him were cut with the swipe of a claw as bones broke and reformed. Skin erupted with silken ebony fur and fangs dropped into his mouth. His body morphed into a different shape in a matter of just a few seconds.

As Forge's prepared to plunge his teeth into Alice's skin, Ewan's wolf burst free. It didn't want to hurt Alice, and protecting her was the creature's overriding instinct. As it jumped, the wolf angled its body so that its shoulder hit Forge's with the brunt of its attack. The vampyre spun backwards as Alice was knocked clear and to the ground.

The wolf hit the dirt, spun, and leapt again, this time with a clear path to its enemy. Paws hit the vampyre direct in the chest, and the force carried both Unnaturals to the ground. The wolf had the advantage of bulk, but Forge was strong and the two predators were equally matched.

They rolled in the dirt, first one and then the other on top as they fought for dominance. Forge roared and wrapped his hands around the wolf's neck, squeezing so hard that his eyes bulged with the exertion. But the wolf was free after such a long time. It revelled in having a solid form and finally being able to exact revenge.

For nearly a year, French magic had tortured its every breath, and it would repay pain with pain. Massive jaws snapped at the vampyre. It used all four paws to scrabble at clothing and rake Forge's cold flesh underneath.

"Hold him down!" Alice yelled as she rushed forward with a flask in her hands.

The wolf snarled and bit into Forge's neck. Canines sank into stringy flesh either side of the vampyre's neck as the beast closed its jaws. It ignored the nails raking its muzzle and trying to gouge its eyes from the sockets. It would endure and hold the foul tasting demon still for its mate.

Alice poured the contents of the flask into Forge's

open mouth as he tried to thrash his head from side to side. Thick golden syrup trickled over his tongue and down his throat as he gurgled and spat.

"That will slow him down." She disappeared from the wolf's line of sight as it growled and increased the pressure on the demon under its paws.

The traitor laughed and his voice rasped from a constricted throat. "Stupid woman. You cannot kill me, and the beast will tire eventually. Then all I need do is drain you and I will be restored."

Then Forge began to cough. His chest heaved as spasms racked his frame. A thin trickle of golden syrup dribbled from the corner of his mouth. The pungent odour made the wolf wrinkle its nose and try to turn away. The hands clawing at the wolf's body slowed and long fingers twitched.

The vampyre coughed and wheezed, even though no breath was within him. "What did you pour into me?"

"My own brew. The most potent poisons I could acquire, yew and nightshade, mixed with vervain and distilled to increase the effect. Then I cast a simple spell telling it to find your muscles. I thought that would be the quickest way to incapacitate you." Alice scanned the cavern and then pointed to the wall. "Ewan, the boat hook."

A long pole with a hook on one end was wedged into a fissure in the stone. The men used it to hang a lantern, but Crufts had taken the lantern earlier when he went in search of Alice.

The wolf rolled off Forge, grabbed a mouthful of jacket, and hauled him up.

The vampyre stood on unsteady legs. He sneered down at the lupine and lashed out with sharpened nails. "I will shake this off. Already I feel the vervain diminishing within me."

Forge lunged to one side towards Alice, but the wolf blocked him with its large body. Then it saw its opportunity and shifted its weight to its large hind legs before leaping. It hit Forge in the chest and thrust him backwards to the cavern wall and the waiting boat hook.

The dead creature omitted a soft *oomph* as the hook pierced his torso, but it wasn't enough. The wolf jumped again, this time channelling its weight to its front paws as it shoved Forge deeper onto the hook.

The end popped through the vampyre's chest. He frowned down at it and tried to shift his weight forward, but couldn't because of the upward angle of the pole and the curved end of the hook. When that didn't work, he threw his body sideways, trying to dislodge the hook from the crack. It held, but for how long?

The wolf couldn't finish Forge, but the man could. Ewan shifted forms, folding the wolf back inside him as he emerged, naked, from the fur that dissolved into nothing around him.

"The knife," he said to Alice and held out his hand.

Alice slipped the hilt into his palm and his fingers curled around it.

"No. No." Forge squirmed, trying to lever himself free, but his toes barely touched the dirt and he couldn't lift his weight high enough to wrench free of the hook. "I'll let her go free and we can finish this like men."

"But we aren't men, we're Unnaturals." Ewan tore away the shredded fabric of the jacket. Underneath, long gashes ran across the vampyre's torso from the wolf's claws. Without hesitation, he thrust the blade into Forge's right side and made a large gash. Thick, dark blood that resembled tar oozed from the wound. Ewan shoved his hand in the slit and prodded up under the rib cage.

"I will give you a cut of what I have earned. You will be the wealthiest dog in all of England." The traitor tried to buy his freedom. His pleas became more frantic as Ewan's hand reached further into his body. "I will give you anything, just name your price. "

Ewan told himself it was no different than gutting a rabbit, just on a larger scale. His fingers found what he sought and he tugged the organ down towards the hole.

"No. Don't do this. We are brothers, you and I. Unnaturals should inherit this Earth from lesser mortals." For the first time in their long association, Forge displayed emotion as panic laced his words.

Ewan didn't even look up as he severed the arteries holding the liver in place. As it was cut free, the vampyre sighed and slumped against the pole. Ewan walked over to the brazier and tossed the heavy, meaty organ on the flames. Alice added a shovel of extra coals to fuel the fire.

Forge screamed as flames licked the liver, tasting it, and then the outer surface turned black as it charred.

The liver was soaked with the same thick tar-like substance that clotted Forge's veins, and as it transpired, the stuff was combustible. Fizzing and pops jumped within the flames as the fire slowly consumed the large organ.

The vampyre's body danced and shook on the spike, as though a giant hand rattled the piece of metal. Forge reached out with one hand, like he intended to retrieve his missing liver, then it made a fist and dropped. The fingers splayed, limp, at his side.

"Is he dead?" Alice asked.

Ewan slipped his arm around her waist, needing to have her close to him. "He died a long time ago. The bigger question is whether we stopped him once and for all. Aster said the only way to destroy him was to destroy his liver."

"The liver, the organ of regeneration," Alice whispered.

Of course his clever mate would know that. "It was what allowed him to heal any injury and how his kind use the blood of their victims to keep their dead bodies looking fresh and animated."

He turned her in his arms and gazed into her forest green eyes. "I love you, Alice, and I shall spend the rest of my life making sure you know it."

She smiled and it warmed him to his core. "I already told you that I wasn't going anywhere. I love you."

She arched her neck and he kissed her, gentle and aware of the cut to his lip and the slow trickle of blood down his face.

"You are hurt, though. These need to be dressed."
She touched the scratches on his face and torso made
by Forge's nails.

He captured her hand and kissed her fingers.
"They'll heal fast now I can shift forms. There is still
much to be done here. Let us see what these barrels
contain."

He picked one barrel from the row and carried it to
an open space, away from the brazier. Then he found a
metal bar to lever apart the planks. "Stay away—we
don't know what these hold."

Alice stood by the entrance to the tunnel as Ewan
levered the top of the barrel open. He sniffed as the
planks popped and gave way. Nothing jumped out at
him or blew up, which was reassuring. That meant
there was no booby trap within the barrels.

He stared into the container, trying to make sense of
what he saw. The brandy barrel was packed tight with
numerous parcels. He reached in and pulled out a
wrapped bundle the size of a book.

"What is it?" Alice asked, venturing closer.

Unrolling the oilskin revealed five small jars. Three
were porcelain with gold edging and scenes in vibrant
colours painted in miniature on their sides. Two others
were cut crystal that revealed pale pink contents. Ewan
flicked the lid open to reveal creamy powder and a soft
face puff.

"Face powder? That doesn't make any sense." Alice
reached for the container.

"No!" Ewan shouted and knocked her hand out of
the way. "Don't touch it. I've smelt this before."

He leaned a little closer and inhaled. The aroma coming off the powder triggered a memory. Long ago on the battlefield, he encountered a French officer who stank of death and fired a magic bullet at him. The powder had the same aroma of decay.

Alice glanced from him to the innocent looking container. "Poison?"

He closed the lid with one finger. "Yes, of some sort. If this was concocted by the French mages, there is no knowing what it might do. It could kill or turn the user into another type of Unnatural."

There was a horrifying thought. What if the contents turned the user into a vampyre? They would have an English epidemic of nocturnal creatures who fed on blood. Tens of thousands of innocents would die in such an outbreak.

Alice turned to stare at all the wooden barrels. "Do you think they all hold the same thing?"

He shrugged. "We won't know until we look. Let's try another."

The next one held the same book-sized, oilskin-wrapped packages. When Ewan peeled back the wrapping they found an assortment of silver snuff boxes. The stink of death clung to the white powder within.

"Snuff and powder. Two items people from all walks of life use on a regular basis," he muttered.

"How many people would have been infected with whatever these contain?" Alice stared at the rows of barrels.

Thousands, Ewan estimated. "Whatever this does, Forge was stockpiling it. He planned to release his entire supply at once. Thankfully we have foiled their plot against England."

Alice leaned against his side and reminded him that he was naked and she was not. "What now? Do you fetch the authorities from Hythe?"

"No. I cannot risk this falling into anyone's hands. I will take care of things here. Take the horses back to the tavern and pack up our belongings. I want to get as far away from Seabrook as we can tonight." Ewan stroked her face and marvelled at how much love his once-cold heart contained for this woman.

Alice frowned. "Won't you need a horse?"

"No. My wolf needs to run after so long trapped within me. When I am done here, I will meet you on the road between Hythe and London, at the first marker."

He kissed her again, and then Alice grabbed her shawl and disappeared down the tunnel.

There was much for Ewan to do, and fortunately the smugglers kept the supplies he needed. But there was one task he needed to do first.

While Aster had written that destroying the vampyre's liver would likewise end the creature, Ewan wanted to make doubly sure. The traitor had a habit of turning up over and over like a bad penny. He picked up the knife and approached the dangling body. If the creature was going to piece itself back together, Ewan was going to make the job as difficult as possible for him.

His task was not an easy one. What he would have given for a cavalry sabre, but he made do with the weapon at hand. Thick black tar seeped from each cut he made. The fluid was slow and viscous like sap on a cut tree. Eventually he prised apart the vertebra and Forge's head dropped to the ground.

Ewan picked the head up by the hair and stuffed it into a barrel. Then he moved to the next phase of his plan, how to get rid of the hoarded French weapon. Luckily, the last load of smuggled goods was still in the cavern, and those barrels actually contained brandy.

The smugglers kept all sorts of things in case they ran into trouble, including a quantity of gun powder, and Ewan poured a measure into Forge's mouth. The rest he mounded between barrels. When he was satisfied with his preparations, Ewan tapped a barrel and splashed the contents all over the others.

He kept opening barrels of brandy and spilling their contents, careful to stay away from the brazier that still devoured the vampyre's liver. At length he had emptied all the containers but one and had saturated the rows of kegs with their powder and snuff.

Then Ewan picked up the last barrel and carried it back down the tunnel, leaving a glistening trail as he walked. At one point he stumbled over debris in the dark. He set the brandy on the ground and swung the lantern around to reveal the body of Crufts slumped across the path.

The man's eyes were open and his hands clutched at a stain on his chest. Ewan kicked the man's foot, but there was no response. He got what he deserved for laying his hands on Alice. Within him, the wolf swelled with pride. Its mate was a lethal beauty.

Ewan picked up barrel and lantern and carried on out into the cool air. On the sand by the entrance, he emptied the last dregs and then dropped the lantern into the puddle. It flickered for a moment, as though unsure of a course of action, then it raced along the liquor.

Time for him to leave. He turned and shifted, dropping to all fours within the space of a heartbeat. Silently the large wolf padded back up the track. When it was some distance away from the cavern, it sat and waited. A few minutes later, the earth under its feet shook as a *whump* boomed through the night. Flames shot out from the cliff and reached for the ocean, before they were sucked back in again. The tremble grew stronger as a rumble raced along the ground.

A roar followed as part of the cliff crumbled and fell in upon itself.

Satisfied, the wolf took off at a lope.

27

Alice

ALICE COULD HAVE FLOWN BACK to the tavern; her heart was so light she had no need of a horse. Ewan loved her. Those were words she would never tire of hearing from his lips. It didn't matter what the future held from this point forward, because they would be together. Once you grasped the moon in your hand, anything seemed possible.

As she rode back to the cottage, she sorted out the order of her actions in her head. Their saddlebags were stashed under the bed and she was grateful it wouldn't be too difficult to pack their few belongings. Daisy and Jimmy should be occupied with each other up in their room. She only hoped she didn't meet Gaffie in the dark.

At the cottage, she hitched the horses to the rail out front and unlocked their door. Eilidh rushed to greet her and she fussed over the dog. "We're off on a new adventure, Eilidh. Let me pack first, and there is something else I must do before we leave."

She worked by the light of one candle and soon had all their belongings in the battered leather bags. Then she called the terrier to heel and closed the cottage door one final time. With the saddlebags fastened behind each saddle, they were ready to depart; there was just one last thing she needed to do.

There was someone else at the Dancing Sow in dire need of rescue.

Alice told Eilidh to stay with the horses. Her heart raced as she approached the back door to the kitchen. She lifted the handle, pushed it open a fraction, and stole a glance inside. The room beyond seemed empty. Gaffie must be in the main room since she was running the bar on her own this evening. Now was her chance.

Alice crept across the floor to the large fire. The turnspit dog was asleep, its ugly head resting on stout paws as he took a brief respite from his hours of running. Alice laid a hand on his head and ruffled his ears.

"Wake up, sleepy—time to leave. No more running, I promise, not unless you want to."

He opened one eye and blinked as she wrapped her arms under his body and picked him up. Then Alice carried him to the door. She refused to leave without him. Every dog, no matter how ugly, deserved the chance to be loved. As though he sensed freedom, the grateful little dog licked her face.

"Toby," she whispered to him. "I shall call you Toby."

Alice placed the dog in front on her saddle and climbed up behind him. She hoped Eilidh would forgive the infraction, but she couldn't make the other dog run behind the horses after his life spent running in a wheel. Eilidh yipped and ran on ahead, happy to bound through the dark after being shut in the cottage.

With the reins to the other horse in one hand, Alice guided her mount out the courtyard and left Seabrook behind. Through the night she rode, grateful for the company of the two small dogs. There was something about the soft snuffles from Toby and Eilidh's excited yips that made the dirt road less lonely.

Toby leaned into her and occasionally looked up, as though he had never seen the countryside before. He reminded her of herself when Aunt Maggie had taken her to Scotland. It had been hard for her mind to grasp that she could run in any direction without hitting the stone walls of her prison.

As she headed southwest towards London, she soon spotted the marker stone. Waist high, it had the number sixty-three carved into the old stone and denoted the distance to London. She slid to the ground and placed the turnspit dog on the soft grass. Her heart beat loud in the silence as she waited. The horses dropped their heads and appeared to doze.

Toby and Eilidh sniffed noses and gave cautious

wags of respective tails. Alice hoped they would become friends; at least Toby would no longer labour all day without so much as a thank-you pat. He had a pack now, who would share whatever they had with him. Alice sat on the damp grass, lost in her own thoughts.

Eilidh gave a soft yip and stared off into the night. Alice rose and placed a hand on the marker stone. She glanced at the dog, who seemed to gaze at something as yet unseen. It could be anyone, but given the dog's reaction, it was someone they knew.

Two blue stars punctuated the dark and approached along the tree-lined road. Eyes turned into a muzzle and midnight fur of the enormous wolf. It sat on the road, several feet away from Alice and the small dogs.

Alice felt no fear, for this was Ewan in a different form. Her protector who had guarded a tiny piece of her through her long nightmare and kept that spark safe until recently. She approached with a hand extended.

The wolf nuzzled her palm and then nudged her hand along its face. Her fingers caressed over its sides and through its silky fur. Alice knelt next to the animal and leaned into its warm sides. She buried her face into ebony fur.

"Thank you for protecting the fragment of my soul," she whispered.

Eilidh bounded over and then slid to a stop before the wolf. She lowered her head and eyes as she edged closer to her mistress.

"Be nice to Eilidh," Alice murmured.

The wolf blew a sigh, then leaned down and licked the terrier's face.

Toby, emboldened by the family bonding occurring, crept forward to sit by Alice's heels. The wolf cocked its head to one side and glanced from ugly Turnspit dog to Alice.

The night shimmered as fur broke apart and reformed into a naked Ewan.

"You stole the kitchen dog?" he said as he stood and held out a hand to Alice.

"I prefer to think of it as liberating the prisoner." She rose and kissed him. She tried to keep the kiss gentle, for while his face seemed improved, he still bore the scratches and bruises from his encounter with Forge.

Ewan chuckled but didn't break contact with her lips. "I love you, Alice. Whatever spell you have cast, you have bewitched me completely."

Alice's heart soared as he repeated his declaration. She could abandon herself to this man; he would protect her if she needed it or stand beside her.

Then other thoughts crowded into her mind and she broke the kiss. As much as she wanted all of him pressed against her, the most dominant thought was getting their family to safety and tending to his wounds. "We had better keep moving. The rest of Forge's gang might come looking for us."

Ewan stroked her cheek. For once, he didn't hide the play of emotion on his face and worry was written between his brows. "I found Crufts. If he harmed you—"

She kissed his palm and silenced him. "He didn't. I doubt I was the first woman he tried to rape, but I made sure I was the last."

He placed a kiss on her forehead. "You are a remarkable woman. I could not have succeeded tonight without you removing the bullet from my leg."

"Will you ride or run back to London? If you plan to ride, you might want to consider clothes to stop any chafing," she murmured as her fingers ran along his naked shoulders.

He laughed. "I will ride, so that we can talk."

Ewan gathered his clothes from the saddlebags and dressed.

Alice picked up Eilidh and placed her in front of her saddle. Then she picked up Toby and handed him to Ewan. "Ewan, this is Toby. Toby, this is Ewan. I think Toby has done quite enough running for a lifetime, so he gets to ride."

Ewan climbed into the saddle and tucked the ugly dog next to him. "I see we have our own pack already. You are an extraordinary woman, and my mother would have loved you."

Alice nudged her heel against the horse's warm sides. "It was your mother who asked me to help you."

Ewan frowned as they headed along the road towards London. "You are mistaken. My mother is dead."

"While my gift is not the ability to converse with shades, if a spirit is seeking something strongly enough, I can sense them." She patted Eilidh. So much had changed since the puppy was thrust into her arms.

Ewan fell silent for a moment, the night only broken by the steady clop of their horses' hooves. When he spoke, his words were cautious and thick with held-back emotion.

"How do you know it was my mother who came to you?" He kept his gaze on the centre of the road and his hands tightened on the reins.

"Because you look much like her, with the same raven black hair and bright blue eyes. She wanted you to find love and asked me to help." She could never tell him that his mother suffered because her death planted ice deep in her son. The tragic woman had traversed the realms, seeking a way to warm Ewan's frozen heart. She had whispered to Alice that only a shattered woman could piece together her broken son.

He reached across the distance between them, took her right hand, and then kissed her knuckles. "Thank you."

It was over sixty miles from the marker to London, far more than they could travel in one night. Ewan and Alice rode until they nearly dropped from the saddle and then found an inn to shelter them. They were both too tired to make love; it took all their energy to undress and fall into bed. Ewan muttered about a promise to let Alice shave him once they reached London, then they slumbered until dawn lit the room. They dressed, ate a quiet meal shared with both dogs, and set out for their final destination.

It was late afternoon when they reached Aunt

Maggie's Kensington terrace house. Alice glanced up at
the cannon peeking over the roof edge. She had
expected more. Aunt Maggie's castle in Scotland posi-
tively bristled with armaments from the turrets. The
old woman was sure that there would either be a Scottish revolution, or an English initiative to round up
troublesome Scots.

The door opened as they walked up the steps and a
butler stepped to one side. A sense of home washed
over Alice as she stood on the tile entranceway. Aunt
Maggie's large personality imbued the house and Alice
wrapped it around her.

"Who is it?" a voice demanded from a side parlour.

"Mr Shaw, madam, and a guest," the butler
responded in a much lower tone. His gaze dropped to
the two dogs that raced in, skidded on the tiles, and
spun to a stop by Alice.

The door shut as a shriek erupted from within, and
then a diminutive woman dressed all in black barrelled
from the parlour.

"Ewan!" She screeched to a halt, her eyes wide and
sparkling. "And Alice, my dear." She promptly diverted
her course from Ewan and held her arms open. Alice
stooped down to hug the much older woman.

She owed this woman so much. Ianthe had freed
her from Bedlam, but Aunt Maggie had set her on the
path that ultimately allowed her to free herself.

After a hug that could crack ribs, Aunt Maggie held
Alice at arm's length. "Let me look at you, my girl." Her
piercing gaze searched Alice's face for several long

moments, then she made a noise in the back of her throat. "Good. The shadows are gone. I do so look forward to getting to know the new you; I suspect you are quite remarkable."

"I know she is remarkable," Ewan said from her side, and he raised Alice's hand to kiss her knuckles.

"Well, there is an unexpected development—but you always did have an eye for the best in life, my boy." Aunt Maggie grinned. Then her hands went to her hips and she arched a white eyebrow. "Ewan, you look a complete fright. I heard you had been injured, but when did you become a vagabond?"

Ewan chuckled and scratched his jaw. "All in the course of duty, Aunt Maggie. Alice and I have been on an assignment, and I must report to the War Office tomorrow."

"Not without a bath, a change of clothes, and a shave." She narrowed her eyes at Ewan. "In fact, we might just throw those clothes on a bonfire. Whatever were you thinking?"

"I was thinking of trying to secure my future," he said.

Aunt Maggie snorted. "You can go upstairs and make yourself presentable. Then I want to hear everything, including your intentions towards Alice."

Alice smiled. Aunt Maggie was a force of nature similar to any storm and should be treated the same— one should hunker down and let it pass over. The older woman shooed them towards the stairs as a maid appeared.

"This way, miss." She gestured for Alice to follow.

Ewan walked close behind Alice on the stairs. His breath feathered over her skin as he whispered in her ear, "I do believe I am in need of a shave."

Alice shivered. She would give him the closest shave he had ever experienced.

28

Ewan

EWAN WAS TRANSPORTED TO HEAVEN. The woman he loved straddled his lap, giving him a shave so close he was almost scared to breathe. A hot bath awaited his naked body, and a fine suit of clothes was laid out on the bed—and did he mention the glorious, naked woman shaving him?

Lord, how she tested his control. His hands rested on her hips, his thumbs making circles on her skin as he drew each slow breath in through his nose with his eyes shut.

Their bodies were joined, but he couldn't move with the razor at his throat. With each stoke, Alice tensed and released her internal muscles, and it was the most exquisite torture he had ever endured. Ewan couldn't wait to do it all again tomorrow night. In fact, he would request a shave twice a day if he could convince his beard to co-operate.

At last, Alice laid down the blade and wiped his face with a warm cloth. "All done," she murmured before kissing him.

His fingers tightened on her waist as he gave in to the pressure inside him and broke his rule of honour. Alice was a close second, but honour would demand he remedy the situation next time. After the bath, or perhaps during, with her trapped against his chest.

Ewan's wounds healed far quicker than a normal man's, now that his wolf was free. Time spent in his wolf form encouraged each cut, gash, and bruise to fade away. Not that he minded Alice fussing over him, but he'd much rather explore her body and listen to her soft cries as he pleasured her.

He also couldn't put off the inevitable. He had to report to the War Office and hand over what he had found. He wanted to plan his future with Alice, but now he was healed, he would probably be sent back to his regiment.

The next morning, he took a hansom cab to the War Office and sat on a hard chair, awaiting his interview with the Earl of Bathurst, the Secretary of War.

"Ah, Captain Shaw." Bathurst gestured for him to come into his office. "What news?"

"A success, my lord; the vampyre Forge will bother England no longer." Ewan stood at ease, hands clasped behind his back as the other man leaned his hip on the window ledge.

The office looked much like the interior of a gentleman's club, with dark wood panelled walls and buttoned, brown leather sofas. Hard to imagine that the future of nations was often decided while men sipped brandy in front of the ornately-tiled fireplace. But then, true politics was less about paperwork and more about secret negotiations.

Bathurst crossed his arms. "Good. Any sign of the French weapon?"

Ewan withdrew a small, oilskin-wrapped package from his pocket and set it gently on the desk. He pulled back the wrapping to reveal the porcelain container within. A bright design of fat pink cupids on the side aimed their bows at the lid.

"What is it?" Bathurst reached out a hand and then stopped inches above the item.

The container looked so innocent and would sit, unremarked upon, on any lady's dressing table. But what would happen when she dabbed the powder to her skin? "Some sort of poison, I believe. It smells of death to my wolf."

The war secretary made a noise deep in his throat and then with thumb and forefinger, picked up the edge of the oilskin and draped it back over the pot. "I will have this sent to our mages and see if they can learn more. How much did he have?"

"There were five of these in each package. Based on how many packages fitted into a barrel and how many barrels he had, possibly two thousand small containers of facepowder and snuff." Ewan had blown the whole lot up and the cliff had collapsed on the cavern. He had alerted the Hythe agent to what was buried, to ensure no one tried picking among the rocks.

The war secretary stepped away from his desk and waved a hand at Ewan. "I had heard you were wounded by French magic. You seemed remarkably recovered."

Ewan pulled the bullet from his pocket and laid it on top of the oilskin. "A gifted woman was able to summon the bullet from my bone. There is a layer of ensorcellment to it beyond the silver that may also be of interest to our mages. If the French are going to fire these at the Highland Wolves, it would be helpful to know how to counteract them."

"Tell me, Shaw, have you given much thought to your future?"

"A little, my lord." In fact, Ewan thought of nothing else. He assumed in the first instance he would be sent to re-join the Highland Wolves. While it lightened his heart to have Alice's love, he had to figure out how to support them once the war ended. He wanted to shower her with the small luxuries she had never experienced. Like a roof over her head and regular meals. From the bigger issues, he would work his way down to silk gowns, parasols, and reticules. And perhaps a ribbon for Eilidh and a bow for Toby.

"While you are a valuable addition to the Highland Wolves, I'd like you to consider another option." The earl walked to his enormous desk and shuffled some papers around, staying well clear of the ensorcelled face powder.

He pulled a sheet free and held it up and scanned the contents, as though reminding himself of what it held. "I believe you would be of more use here. To that end, I am offering you Sir Harry Wilkes' old position. The job will include his house in Berkley Street, a modest shipping portfolio to give you a reason for snooping in various corners of the Empire, and we can wrangle a knighthood to make sure certain doors are open to you."

"Sir Wilkes' old position?" Ewan frowned. He wasn't a stupid man, but what Bathurst offered him seemed too fortuitous to be true. Harry Wilkes had been spy master for England, until Forge had killed him. Such a position would keep Ewan in London with Alice and not fighting on foreign soil and trying to dodge magic bullets.

The secretary of war regarded him from under bushy eyebrows. "Yes. At this juncture in the war, it is vital we find a suitable candidate to manage our intelligence network. It takes a certain delicate touch when dealing with secrets at the highest level—a knack you have. Your Unnatural status is handy in dealing with creatures like these French vampyres and who knows what else they are concocting to use against us. What do you say?"

Quite apart from sending him an extraordinary woman to love, life now offered a house, a title, and a regular income. Ewan pinched the back of his hand, needing the brief stab of pain to ensure he hadn't died on the battlefield and this was all a dream.

He seemed to be alive, so how could he refuse? Then he thought of Alice. Could he trap her in London and make her play the role of society lady? He swallowed. "I need to consult with someone else before deciding, my lord. Not that it isn't an exceedingly generous offer, but I am no longer a single man. I have made a commitment to someone."

"Ah." Bathurst frowned. "Completely understand if you don't want to expose a woman to this sort of danger. They can be delicate things that need protecting."

"Not an issue with my intended. She is the one who removed the bullet and weakened Forge so I could destroy him," Ewan murmured.

Lord Bathurst stared at Ewan and then laughed. "Well. Hang on to that one, and we always have room in our family for a capable female agent, if she is willing."

Ewan smiled and his wolf stretched, basking in the praise of its mate. "I fully intend to keep hold of her. And if she is willing, she would be the most excellent partner in this venture."

"Get back to me tomorrow. I can't give you any longer, I want to win this war and see Bonaparte defeated." Bathurst waved his hand and Ewan was dismissed.

All the way back to Kensington, he struggled to contain his growing excitement. Bathurst offered him an extraordinary opportunity, but he would pass it up if Alice wanted to retreat to the country. Perhaps they could breed dogs to pass the time?

At the terrace house, two women awaited him in the front parlour.

Alice lifted her face for his kiss, her gaze searching his face for any hint of what had happened. If anyone could peer beneath his mask, it was her. Ewan handed over his top hat and gloves and dropped to the seat next to Alice.

There was no point in beating around the bush. He laid out the full proposal. "The secretary of war has given me two options. I can either return to the Highland Wolves and active service or he has offered me the vacant position of spymaster. It comes with a London townhouse, a shipping portfolio, and a knighthood."

Alice laid her hands over his. "Both options are dangerous."

Ewan didn't hide the emotion on his face, he had promised no subterfuge with this woman. The offer gladdened his heart and neatly solved so many problems and presented many opportunities. "As much as I do not want to abandon my regiment and my brothers, spymaster does fit my abilities. But I have your desires to consider also. What do you think, Alice? Could you survive life in London as a minor noble's wife or would you prefer to seek the solitude of the countryside after the war?"

She glanced down at their laced fingers as she pondered his proposal. Then she raised her face to his. "I have my own goals now, and slipping amongst the ton would help me find and free women who have no voice of their own."

He kissed her cheek. "I am afraid it will involve some frightfully boring events we shall be forced to endure."

She played with the wolf's head necklace as she pondered his offer. "I'm sure I could think of some way to enliven dull dinner parties. Drinks to loosen tongues perhaps."

Ewan laughed. Alice's aftermage gift complimented his wolf and when they worked together, there was nothing beyond their reach. They were both predators, and he would watch his divine witch stalk monsters in the parlours of London. No demon, whether natural or Unnatural, would escape them.

"Then it is settled. I shall accept the position." He grinned, and it felt good to let hope for the future flow through his body.

"Excellent." Aunt Maggie rose and yanked on the bell pull. "Let's have champagne to celebrate. Then we have a quiet wedding to plan if Alice is to be your partner in this venture. Society will not have it any other way, so you two will just have to bear it."

"He has not asked yet, Aunt Maggie." Alice smiled at him, mischief dancing in her eyes.

"Oh, I will. I promise you that." He knew her answer would be yes, but first, he wanted to plan the most outrageously romantic marriage proposal that would keep the ton talking all season. He had an idea forming already....

ONE MONTH LATER

A small theatre in Kent

The woman stared into the mirror. A tired white painted face with bright pink cheeks stared back. A confection of silver curls bounced as she tugged the ornate silver wig from her head and tossed it to a chair. Then she ran her fingers through short dark hair and scratched her scalp.

The door opened, and a young lad placed a bowl of hot water on the dressing table and then disappeared back through the door.

With a sigh, she wrung out the cloth in the water and wiped her face. Lines of paint came off with each stoke, revealing the woman underneath. Soon the water had a pink tinge, as though a cloud bled.

The door opened again and a middle aged gent walked in. His greying hair was trimmed short. His jacket had once been of fine quality but now the edges were frayed and a button was missing. The garment hung loosely on his shoulders, as though it had been made for someone larger.

"When are you going to take me to London like you promised?" she asked the image in the mirror.

"Soon, my turtle dove, soon." He held the door open as two men carried in large wooden kegs and placed them on the floor. He tossed one a coin and then shut the door on their retreating figures.

"What have you wasted our money on now?" she waved the cloth at the two barrels.

"I have wasted nothing! I won these in a game of cards. Each contains the finest brandy from France. We can make some extra money selling a small tipple to the patrons before the show." The man rapped his knuckles on the wood.

She dropped the cloth into the bowl and turned around on her stool. "Give us a taste, then. My throat is parched after all that singing tonight."

He pulled open a draw in a cabinet and rummaged through the contents. He made a satisfied noise as he found the device he required. The knocked the tap into the side of a barrel and held a glass underneath. With a flourish as though it were a magic trick, he turned the tap.

Nothing happened.

His face screwed up in a scowl and he rocked the barrel with one hand then tipped it towards the tap.

"Come on," he muttered.

Still nothing flowed from the container.

The woman rolled her eyes. "You've been had. Those are empty."

"No they're not. You can feel it." He knocked on the wood and it gave a solid response and not a hollow echo.

"They're probably full of sand." What would she do with him? He promised the moon and couldn't even deliver a tin plate. His foolish dreams wouldn't be food in her belly.

With the edge of a large knife, he levered off the lid and peered inside. "Not sand my love. But I'm not sure what I have acquired."

He reached in and pulled out a package wrapped in oilskin. The contents shifted and clanked against each other. He laid the parcel on the table and unwrapped it to reveal five small porcelain containers.

The woman picked one up and flicked open the lid. "It's face powder." She leaned in and sniffed. "Why would someone stuff face powder into a brandy barrel?"

The man levered the top from the other barrel and extracted an identical parcel. "Both barrels appear to be packed tight with them. There could easily be two hundred or more such small delights in each. I bet someone was smuggling them out of France and they got confused with the actual brandy shipment."

She dipped a fingertip in the powder and rubbed it between her fingers. It was smooth as silk, not gritty like the cheap stuff at the market. "What good is a load of face powder?"

The man tapped his chin as he thought. He picked up one of the containers and held it to the light. "Look at these, this is delicate porcelain. That's why they are all wrapped to keep them from breaking. I bet that is real gold around the edge, and those paintings are quality. This isn't your cheap penny-a-pottle face stuff that's half sand. This is quality."

She rolled her eyes and finished washing her face. "Still doesn't do us any good, does it? We run a theatre, not a shop."

He set down the container with the others and placed a kiss on the back of her neck. "Oh my turtle dove, don't you realise the fates have finally smiled upon us? This is far more valuable than a barrel of brandy."

"How do you figure that?" She rubbed the spot on her neck. He was still a fool.

"You and I are going to London. Then we're going to buy you a pretty dress, you're going to put on that fancy Russian accent you do, and we're going to sell this to the toffs. We'll say it's the same face powder used by the tsarina smuggled out of Europe."

His idea was mad enough to work. They could charge as much as a guinea a container. The more expensive and exclusive they made the powder sound, the more the wives of wealthy men would clamour to own a pottle.

She let out a sigh and held a hand to her breast. London. At last. And she'd get to perform for the finest ladies and gents in England. She could say she was an exiled Russian noble. "Tatiana, I want to be called Tatiana. It sounds Russian and noble."

He took her hand and kissed her knuckles. "This is finally our moment in the sun. Soon, all of society will know the name Tatiana!"

THE END

History. Magic. Family.

I do hope you enjoyed this adventure with for the Highland Wolves. If you would like to dive deeper into the world, or learn more about the odd assortment of characters that populate it, you can join the community by signing up at:

www.tillywallace.com/newsletter

While this concludes the Highland Wolves series, the journey continues. Find out more in:

MANNERS and MONSTERS

A lady never reveals the true extent of her decay...

Hannah Miles lives a quiet existence helping her parents conduct research into a most terrible affliction —until a gruesome murder during her best friend's engagement party pulls her from the shadows. With her specialist knowledge and demur disposition, Hannah is requested to aid the investigation.

Except Hannah discovers her role is to apologise in the wake of the rude and disgraced man tasked with finding the murderer. The obnoxious Viscount Wycliff thinks to employ Hannah purely as a front to satisfy Whitehall, but she'll have none of that. The viscount is about to meet his greatest challenge, and it's not a member of the ton with a hankering for brains.

Can the two work together to find the murderer before the season is ruined?

Buy book 1: MANNERS and MONSTERS
http://tillywallace.com/books/manners-and-monsters/manners-and-monsters/

ABOUT THE AUTHOR

Tilly writes whimsical historical fantasy books, set in a bygone time where magic is real. Her books combine vintage magic and gentle humour with an oddball cast. Through fierce friendships her characters discover that in an uncertain world, the most loyal family is the one you create.

To be the first to hear about new releases and special offers, sign up at:
www.tillywallace.com/newsletter

Tilly would love to hear from you:
www.tillywallace.com
tilly@tillywallace.com

f facebook.com/tillywallaceauthor
BB bookbub.com/authors/tilly-wallace

ALSO BY TILLY WALLACE

A complete list of books by Tilly can be found HERE

Highland Wolves

Secrets to Reveal

Kisses to Steal

Layers to Peel

Souls to Heal

Manner and Monsters

Manners and Monsters

Galvanism and Ghouls

Gossip and Gorgons

Vanity and Vampyres

Sixpence and Selkies

Printed in Great Britain
by Amazon

40373411R00199